CRY HAVOC

CRY HAVOC

METAL LEGION™ BOOK SIX

CH GIDEON   CALEB WACHTER   CRAIG MARTELLE

DISRUPTIVE IMAGINATION

LMBPN Publishing
PMB 196, 2540 South Maryland Pkwy
Las Vegas, NV 89109

First US edition, May 2019
eBook ISBN: 978-1-64202-311-4

DEDICATION

We can't write without those who support us. On the home front, we thank you for being there for us.

We wouldn't be able to do this for a living if it weren't for our readers. We thank you for reading our books.

CRY HAVOC TEAM

Thanks to our Beta Readers

Micky Cocker, James Caplan, Kelly O'Donnell, and John Ashmore

Thanks to the JIT Readers

John Ashmore
Misty Roa
Peter Manis
Kelly O'Donnell
Jeff Eaton
Paul Westman
James Caplan
Micky Cocker
Jeff Goode

If I've missed anyone, please let me know!

Editor
Lynne Stiegler

ACRONYMS

- AP = Armor Piercing
- APC = Advanced Personnel Carrier or Armored Personnel Carrier
- CAC = Command And Control center
- CIG = Commander Intercept Group
- CIP = Combat Interceptor Patrol
- DIE = Durgan Industrial Enterprises
- ER = Extended Range
- FGF = Fleet Ground Force
- HE = High Explosive
- HQ = Headquarters
- HUD = Heads Up Display
- HPC = Heavy Plasma Cannon
- HVM = hyper-velocity missile
- HWP = Heavy Weapons Platform
- ILPF = Illumination League Peacekeeping Force
- KPH = kilometers per hour
- LRM = Long-Range Missile
- LZ = Landing Zone

- MIRV = Multiple Independently-targetable Reentry Vehicles
- MRM = Mid-Range Missile
- P2P = Point to Point
- PD = Point Defense
- PDF = Planetary Defense Force
- POI = Point of Interest
- RAP = Rocket Assisted Projectile
- SAM = Surface-to-Air Missile
- SOP = Standard Operating Procedure
- SRM = Short-Range Missile
- TAC = Terran Armor Corps
- TFMC = Terran Fleet Marine Corps
- THCG = Terra Han Colonial Guard
- TRMC = Terran Republic Marine Corps
- ZOC = Zone of Control

THE MARTIAN MATTER

Striding briskly onto the *William Wallace*'s bridge, Lieutenant Andrew "Podsy" Podsednik wiped grease from his fingers on a rag he'd snatched from the drop deck and prepared to make his latest report to the ship's Commanding Officer.

"Lieutenant." Brigadier General Moon greeted him without looking up from the command chair's virtual interface. Ever since the private meeting between Moon and him a few days earlier, palpable tension had overshadowed their interactions. "How are the railguns?"

Podsy drew himself to attention. "One and Two are ready for test fires. Four's still got a problem with its targeting system. There's a thirty-two-millisecond delay between input and response, which appears to be an issue with the targeting processor's hardware. But RG Three," he grimaced, looking down at what remained of his left middle finger's nail, "needs a complete rebuild of its Y-axis servos. Chief Rimmer says it's a four-day job, and it can't be done underway. Whoever stowed it in the yard didn't backflush the bushings before grit-blasting it clean, so silica's worked its way through the whole mechanism. On the outside, the system looks perfect, but I don't think it'll withstand more than twenty or thirty cycles before bricking, which breaks down to five or six target engagements."

"And the drop deck?" Moon asked disinterestedly while tapping out commands on his chair's interface.

"Chief Rimmer's people corrected the issue with the inner airlocks an hour ago," Podsy reported, "and they've gotten the rolling stock and overhead cranes into working order...barely. We don't want to shuffle the deck during combat maneuvers, but the gear will hold up for a few missions before we have to start replacing nuts and bolts. This ship was ridden hard and put away wet, General. There's metal fatigue in just about every load-bearing member and serious degradation in most of the high-impact moving parts, but Admiral Zhao was right. It's combat-ready, if only by the skin of its teeth."

"All three of them," Moon grunted, sighing as he finished working on whatever had the other half of his attention. "Well, three and a half."

"Don't forget the Vipers, General," Podsy chided, expecting and receiving a withering look from the Legion's ranking officer aboard the ship.

"I dusted rock-biters on sortie when you were still learning to walk, Lieutenant," Moon quipped. "And even sixteen Vipers aren't enough to make this ship a match for the *Bonhoeffer* in combat. It's just as slow as the *Bonhoeffer* was, but it has the added 'merit' of having armor that's less than half as thick and only a quarter the throw weight of a proper assault cruiser. There are many reasons, some good and some not, why the old man kept his flag exclusively aboard the *Dietrich Bonhoeffer*, but the more I see how the options stack up, the more I come around to his way of thinking. On ship selection, if nothing else," he added with a trace of the same tension that had pervaded every interaction between them since the conclusion of Watery Grave.

Podsy couldn't blame the general too much. He had made several questionable decisions during his time in the Legion, including landing in the brig for violating the *Bonhoeffer's* computer core. His doing so had been instrumental in achieving victory over the Jemmin, who had infected the assault carrier's mainframe with a virus that effectively hid them from the ship's sensors.

But he knew the ends couldn't justify the means, especially not when the means included multiple actions that directly violated the chain of command. His virtual infection of the Bonhoeffer's computer core had been an excellent example of "bad process, good result," and he was man enough to admit he probably could have handled it better.

Probably.

The doors to the bridge swished open, revealing the square-jawed CIP leader, Lieutenant Commander Teresa Knighton.

"General." She saluted, drawing its counterpart from Moon before she commenced her report. "The birds are prepped and locked into their cradles."

"Good work, Commander." The general's tone was cordial, unlike how he spoke to Podsy. "I'm glad you took up my offer to taxi in your shipboard couches instead of your cockpits."

"We're happy to defer to your judgment on that front, General," she replied with a curt nod, and Podsy fought to hide a smile at her obvious brown-nosing.

Moon chuckled. "That's the spirit, Commander. You'll fit into the Legion just fine with that attitude."

She nodded wordlessly before turning to Podsednik. "Can my people be of assistance with pre-launch operations?"

The offer took him by surprise, but he wasn't about to look a gift gun up the barrel. "Chief Rimmer's having some issues with the ship's virtual architecture, mostly dealing with the railguns and point defense targeting systems. It's probably hardware-related, but extra eyes would be appreciated."

"Understood," she acknowledged. "We'll report our progress every quarter-hour."

"Excellent." Moon returned to his interface, prompting Knighton to leave the bridge with her characteristically purposeful strides. "We're fortunate to have her," the general said after she'd gone. "With ninety-one combat flights on her wings, the only thing holding her back from promotion is Fleet politics."

Podsy reflexively bristled. "I still can't believe Fleet has held her back because of Willow Bark."

"The stain of mutiny doesn't wash off," Moon said grimly. "It doesn't matter that she wasn't the one who pulled the trigger on your CO. TAF can't afford to let that kind of example be seen as anything but a detriment."

Podsy smirked. "Do you think she would have had a better chance at promotion if she had done for me like I did for Aquino?"

"Definitely," the general agreed.

Podsy shook his head. "Begging the general's pardon, but that's all kinds of fucked up."

"It is what it is." Moon shrugged indifferently. "Politics are rarely if ever concerned with supporting what's right. Expediency to power is their primary, secondary, and tertiary concerns. The bureaucrats, of which I admit the Terran Armed Forces has more than its share, would rather deal with the fallout of a dead messenger than whatever message he might have carried. It's simpler, cleaner, and—"

"More expedient?" Podsy finished in disgust.

"Exactly." Moon nodded. "That doesn't make it right, and it doesn't make it wrong. It's just the way things work."

An update chimed on Podsy's wrist-link, and he reported

the details. "Both of the Tripoli-class dropships have been secured to the forward hull by the modular cradles provided by Fleet. Major Trapper is en route to the bridge now."

"They're ten minutes ahead of schedule." Moon pursed his lips as he mentally reviewed the next steps before the ship departed. "Colonel Jenkins originally founded his test program to help augment Marine deployments in Arh'Kel engagement zones. It's ironic that they'll be providing us with support on our first official joint venture."

Podsy grinned. "I hear General Pushkin had his work cut out for him thwarting Fleet's attempted mission takeover."

"Can you blame them?" Moon gave the barest hint of a smile. "The Legion is the only fighting force to successfully invade Solar space. *Ever.*"

His grin turned to a faint sneer before he continued, "When Fleet heard we'd been *invited* back for round two, they couldn't stand by while we went and got all the press. They want to get their oar in the water and, given the operation's scale, the general was right to accept whatever help they offered. Even if the price tag was higher than we'd have liked."

Podsy didn't know precisely what the general meant by that last bit, but most of him was glad to be ignorant of the upper-level politics involved in inter-branch operations.

"Despite his early blustering to the contrary," Moon continued, "Admiral Zhao is every bit as committed to Colonel Jenkins' proposal of joint TAC-Marine operations. He's more pragmatic than most of the Admiralty in that regard, but I'm afraid his pull in Fleet has weakened of late."

Podsy nodded grimly. "I've heard rumors about New Ukraine and Admiral Fitzgerald, but nothing more."

"Fleet's got intel under wraps. We'll learn what we need to know, hopefully before it's too late," Moon grumbled. "We might not learn the details for months...or even years." The pause in the exchange was broken by a chime at the general's command chair signaling an inbound communique, which he accepted. *"Wallace* Actual, go ahead."

"General," greeted the newly-minted Captain Stravinsky, whose official transfer from Fleet had unexpectedly gone through and who was now a captain in both rank and title as the *Vercingetorix's* CO. "The *Vercingetorix* has completed pre-op preparations. Captain Koch's Fixers are ready to deploy on your order, sir."

"Very good, Captain." General Moon pursed his lips again while he contemplated something without giving away his thoughts. Podsy made a subtle show of checking the bridge's clock, which showed the ambitious CO of the *Vercingetorix* was fully three hours ahead of schedule. "Stand by while the rest of us play catch-up to the *Vercingetorix* and her crew."

"Yes, sir," she acknowledged before the general closed the link.

Podsy checked the *Vercingetorix's* readiness reports and couldn't help but admire the ambitious captain's results. "I'm not sure how she did it, General, but it looks like she's not kidding."

"There are things we can learn from career-minded Fleeters like Stravinsky, Lieutenant," Moon chided, making brief but meaningful eye contact with Podsy. "Especially those of us who maintain overwatch for our grounded Metalheads. Nobody battens down the hatches like Fleet."

"Not yet, sir," Podsy retorted, drawing a soft snicker from his CO and the Legion's second most senior officer.

"That's the spirit, Lieutenant." Moon straightened in his chair. "Now let's see that spirit turn into action."

"Yes, sir," Podsy replied as the blast doors to the *William Wallace's* bridge opened, revealing the shaven-headed Major Tim Trapper Jr.

Wearing the green and gray fatigues of the Fleet Ground Forces, he strode across the bridge as General Moon rose from his chair to greet him.

"Major, it's good to have you aboard." The general proffered a hand. "I haven't had the opportunity to relay my condolences."

Trapper accepted the general's hand and nodded, his bushy mustache concealing whatever emotion his lips might have shown. "It's good to be here, General. And I appreciate the sentiment."

"Your father left a huge void in the Legion's leadership, Major," Moon said pointedly. "It's one we're still trying to fill. Know anyone who might want the job?"

Even Trapper Jr.'s mustache couldn't conceal his smirk. "You Metalheads don't give up, do you?"

Moon grinned. "Metal never dies, Major."

"So I hear. But before you try to stamp your brand on my hide, let's see if we can put a good spin on Colonel Jenkins' Combined Arms project for the Admiralty to review. The way things are breaking lately, strengthening TAC-Fleet relations might be more valuable than solidifying the Legion's chain of command over your Pounders." Trapper turned to Podsy. "I understand you were there with my old man at the end."

Podsednik steeled his features. "I was." Major Trapper had missed his father's funeral due to his deployment schedule and had opted to immediately sign on with Operation War God after returning from his mission there. Due to the still-classified status of Operation Antivenom's details, he had probably not heard anything more than that his father was dead.

"How'd he go, Lieutenant?" Trapper asked bluntly.

Without missing a beat, having considered how to answer this question for several weeks, Podsy replied, "With an RPG tube on his shoulder, Solar Marines in his sights, and my butterfingers fumbling a reload, Major."

Trapper snorted. "Did he get any of 'em beforehand?"

Podsy nodded. "He did. A shitload of 'em."

"Good," the younger Trapper said approvingly before scowling. "He wouldn't have had you as his feeder if you weren't up to it. Self-pity and a guilty conscience have no place in my old man's pounders."

Podsy flushed, while also feeling a strange sense of relief as he said, "Understood, Major."

Trapper nodded curtly before returning his attention to General Moon, who had watched the exchange with more than passing interest. "The Marines are under the command of Lieutenants Briggs and Worthington, so my involvement is officially that of a technical advisor. They're good men who want to see this thing work, so ego won't be a problem. Frankly, they're perfect for a job like this. We're lucky to have them, but we only get one shot at impressing their superiors."

"We were just saying as much before you arrived," Moon agreed, glancing toward Podsednik. "It's time to take our place, because we sure as hell aren't going to step aside when no one is better."

Podsy knew that last bit was purely for his benefit. He also knew the general was prodding him in the hope of pushing him up (or off) the Legion's chain of command. Moon wanted him to succeed, or he wouldn't have kept him around. But unlike Captain Stravinsky, whose tireless efforts were driven in no small part by her desire to reach her career goals, Podsy had no interest in climbing the ladder. He wasn't here in search of pips or ribbons; he hadn't stayed on with the Legion after losing his legs because he loved the competition or even the thrill of victory.

He was here to do his part to safeguard humanity. He knew

better than most the cost of failure and had decided to spend his life preventing tragedies like New Australia.

Thoughts of his devastated home never strayed far from his mind. With that focus, he turned to the monumental task of getting the *William Wallace* ready for its first active-duty deployment in thirty-eight years.

2

PLANNING THE INVASION

"Links secure, Colonel," Styles reported as Colonel Lee Jenkins' grav couch filled with gel in preparation for the voyage ahead.

"All right," Jenkins acknowledged, seeing the operation's officers were in virtual attendance. "This will be the first virtual war room for some of you, and while we're confident of the integrity of our encrypted P2P comm lines, we'll nonetheless be operating on local data stores and observing open-air comm protocols."

"Understood, Colonel," Major Xi Bao, the war room's youngest attendee by a full decade, acknowledged in a tone that made clear she knew his message was primarily intended for her.

"Ordinarily, I'd convene a physical war room prior to deployment," Jenkins continued, "but the situation on Mars is so dire that we can't afford even a two-hour delay unless we run into serious snags in the planning phase. So unless we encounter unforeseen difficulty getting and staying on the same page, we'll be remaining aboard our respective ships until we drop. Let's begin with mission parameters." He forwarded a series of alphanumerics corresponding to coded file names for maps of

Mars and technical specifications for the points of interest they would be securing. "The way I see it, we have two options: we scatter our deployment and secure the objectives simultaneously in a single push, or we establish a forward base of operations with proximity to the primary targets and use that base to launch a series of assaults on those targets. Due to the length of our transit, we're in no rush to finalize the plan, so I'm inviting all opinions. Bring me your ideas, people."

Lieutenant Commander Knighton, *William Wallace*'s CIG, was predictably first to speak. "We've only got sixteen Vipers and two Tripoli-class dropships. Even spreading them out into pairs, we can't achieve aerial superiority over all the POIs, Colonel."

"Not to mention," Captain Stravinsky interjected, "that coordinating the simultaneous combat drop of two full Armor battalions across an area that large would require at least twenty minutes from first to last. That's more than enough time for whatever interceptive ordnance they've got to be brought online."

"Commodore Kline." Jenkins invited the Solar flag officer's opinion. "What are we looking at on that front?"

"We neutralized the majority of the Martian surface-based orbit-capable systems." The commodore's voice was strong and confident. "But at last count, there were still eight hundred rocket-driven platforms and forty mobile railguns unaccounted for. We anticipate at least half of those have fallen into rebel hands and are in position to repel any landing efforts."

Lieutenant Podsednik piped in, "Why haven't they already destroyed Hansel & Gretel, Commodore?" "Hansel" and "Gretel" were the codenames for the two tethered space elevators which, according to the latest intelligence, remained functional on Mars. "With that much firepower at the rebels' disposal, they should have been able to destroy them by now."

"Hansel & Gretel are considered Solar property, not Martian, unlike the other beanstalks," Kline explained. "As such, 5th Fleet is allowed to defend them against aerial or orbital attacks. We are also permitted to aggressively deter surface-based encroachments, but Solar law is ambiguous on how far that permission extends. Combined with political uncertainty regarding the Martian Matter, we cannot in good conscience put boots on the ground while the issue is collectively agreed, in technical terms, to be one of rebellion against Solar authority."

"That's surprising, Commodore," Major Xi said with an unexpected degree of tact, "given Sol's history in dealing with past rebellions across the Solar System. 'Unity over sovereignty' was something of a rallying cry during Sol's interplanetary expansion phase, wasn't it? How many Martians died during the Tharsis Crisis of 2095? And what about the inhabitants of Ganymede, who were unceremoniously bombarded rather than negotiated with in 2102?"

"We frequently revise our policies, Major, in light of superior alternatives. Which is why we requested Terran assistance in this matter." Kline kept his voice even. He didn't take the question as an affront. "And it was President Abraham Lincoln who so frequently said that the preservation of the Union was his primary objective, not the moral argument over slavery which he is so often credited as championing. Sometimes, unity does indeed trump sovereignty. I would furthermore urge you to never let perfect be the enemy of good. There are times when no available course of action is ideal but action is nonetheless required."

"You're invoking Voltaire now?" Xi smirked. "Ok, I'm impressed."

"Back on track, Major," Jenkins said firmly, and Xi's silence suggested she had taken his rebuke to heart. "So 5th Fleet has secured Hansel & Gretel from aerial attacks, but engaging ground forces is beyond their authority?"

"Correct," Commodore Kline agreed before highlighting a network of tunnels on the interactive Martian map they were using as a common reference during the virtual meeting. "There are multiple approaches that can be used to get demo teams in position to destroy Hansel & Gretel, and my people are incapable of interdicting those approaches."

"Those approaches look like they provide direct access," Captain Koch mused. "Why haven't they already snuck in and done the job?"

"The approaches are secured with automated defenses," Kline explained, pulling up a series of defensive systems' specifications, "and they are also largely undocumented to ensure security in the event of a rebellion like this."

"Sounds about right." Xi snorted, drawing a glare from Jenkins, which she could unfortunately not see due to the nature of the conference. Thankfully, and before Jenkins had to mute her for a disciplinary sidebar, she highlighted the northern quadrant nestled between the beanstalks. "It looks to me like our best bet is going to be a dual insertion into these quadrants, where we take control of targets 'Scooter' and 'Echo.'"

She highlighted two POIs, including the huge Schiaparelli Compound code-named "Scooter" and an Alhambra-class fortress designated "Echo Base."

In fact, that fortress was the very facility Jenkins had identified as the best candidate to serve as the op's forward base. Without any consultation, Major Xi had arrived at precisely the same conclusion as Jenkins, once again demonstrating why she was the youngest field-grade officer in Terran Armed Forces history.

"We land, simultaneously secure these points," she continued, "and then advance on Hansel, Gretel, and the other POIs in a geographical line, forcing the dominos to fall, as it were. The interceptors should be able to clear out this LZ for us," a point began to flash in an empty plain between the initial targets, "since these first POIs are within a three-hundred-kilometer area. This lets us tighten our drop window down to fifty seconds and secure these facilities before the rebels can respond."

"Forty-five seconds, assuming the *Vercingetorix* will be dropping in the first wave," Captain Stravinsky said confidently. "The *Vercingetorix* was the slowest launch platform prior to recent upgrades being made to our drop deck, but we can now clear our tubes in forty-five seconds, Colonel," she reported with pride bordering on arrogance as the *Red Hare* began to accelerate away from its orbit en route to the New America 1-New America 2 wormhole gate.

A quick check of his HUD showed that *William Wallace* and *Vercingetorix* had left their moorings and were assuming formation behind the *Red Hare*.

"Captain Stravinsky's enthusiasm notwithstanding," General Moon interjected, "forty-five seconds is at the upper limit of our ability to coordinate, considering this will be the Legion's first multi-ship combat drop in over a decade. We need to be mindful of that fact."

"Agreed, General." Xi resumed her tactical walkthrough. "Every second we shave off the drop window decreases our exposure during descent. We need to keep tight LZs, no larger than five kilometers in diameter, in order to ensure overlapping fire support during a flank speed advance on three separate targets."

"We have to hit the ground running," Captain Chao agreed. "It cuts their ability to react to our presence. Your thoughts, Colonel?" he asked, demonstrating the professionalism Jenkins had come to expect of Admiral Zhao's once-estranged son.

"I'm interested in hearing the rest of the major's plan," Jenkins replied before urging, "Continue."

"Yes, sir," Xi acknowledged. "Once we secure both Echo and Scooter, along with whatever secondary objectives are still viable upon arrival, we consolidate there and drop pop-up SRMs and point-defense turrets from orbit to secure the site, while simultaneously advancing on Hansel, Gretel, and these other seven POIs," she explained, highlighting the second wave of priority targets which included a pair of extremely important subterranean access junctions serving as the lifeline between Mars' surface and subsurface infrastructure.

"Who takes which targets, Major?" There was more than a hint of a challenge in Jenkins' query. She had done well to this point. He always tested her, push her to the edge to see how far she would bend.

"Clover's Razorbacks are the fastest on the roster," Xi began, "and Echo is both farthest from the LZ and the most fortified, so Echo belongs to Clover. Dragon 1st Company will advance on Scooter with support from Lieutenant Worthington and his Marines, while Dragon 2nd Company moves on the cluster of secondary targets designated 'Delta Package' with Lieutenant Briggs' Marines. Dragon 2nd will serve as support for either Scooter or Echo teams if the need arises, and the Marines' dropships will provide tactical support during the push."

"When do you propose we drop, Major?" Lieutenant Worthington asked.

"Same time as the rest of us, Lieutenant," Xi replied confidently. "During our descent, your Tripolis will provide the last line of defense against any enemy ordnance that might slip through the cracks."

"What about Dragon 3rd Company, Major?" Captain Winters, who had been training at TAC HQ since Watery Grave and was now serving as company's CO.

"3rd Company stays in orbit until we secure the first round of targets, Captain. After we've consolidated at Echo, 3rd will drop, with the full support of our Vipers, to secure these sites." The pair of subterranean access points began to flash as she spoke. "For most of 3rd Company's crews, this will be their first drop. This assignment will minimize their inexperience and also keep our best people on the ground the longest."

"Enjoy the training wheels while you can, Captain. Class time's over." Koch snickered, drawing similar sounds from the rest of the virtual meeting's attendees.

"We've all been there," Jenkins chided, "but the major's right. 3rd Company will benefit most from Lieutenant Commander Knighton's support, and the best way to get them to their assigned targets is via direct drop. So it looks like you'll be sitting out the first leg of the op, Captain Winters."

"Understood, Colonel." Winters sounded disappointed, but he knew it was right. "We'll do our part, whatever it is."

"What's your plan for after we take Hansel, Gretel, and the rest of the second-wave targets?" Jenkins pressed.

"Assuming our force strength remains sufficient," Xi said, professionally phrasing the harshest truth of military life while highlighting forty subterranean foundries, manufactories, and other pieces of critical Martian infrastructure buried up to fifty kilometers beneath Mars' surface, "we secure these facilities in a priority to be determined on the ground."

"What's your timetable here, Major?" General Moon asked.

"From touchdown to securing the final POI," Xi replied with her first moment of hesitation, "no longer than two hundred standard hours, with a target of one hundred."

"Either timetable is ambitious," Commodore Kline replied skeptically. "Even a force of Solar Marines equivalent in size to this force would be hard-pressed to secure these facilities in four Earth days."

"Terran Marines would also be hard-pressed to accomplish it so quickly," TRMC Lieutenant Briggs agreed.

"Which is precisely why," Major Trapper drawled, "Colonel Jenkins has been trying to establish a Combined Arms program that puts Marines and mechs in support of each other. There are missions where the sum of both is greater than its constituent parts, and this is one of them."

"Major Trapper's right." Jenkins nodded although no one could see. "As is Commodore Kline. This is an *extremely* ambitious timetable. But it *has* to be," he added pointedly. "Because every second we delay increases the rebels' chances of spiking those factories. Humanity, both Solar and Terran, *needs* that infrastructure operational."

"We'll be exposing ourselves to potential overextension if we hit any snags," Captain Koch mused. "Even with lifelong professionals at every post, war is rarely like a ballet. Someone *always* gets tripped up when the other guys are even half-serious. It's almost like their job is to mess up our plans."

Lieutenant Worthington grunted. "And down those tunnels, things become unpredictable. Some of these assets are a thousand kilometers from each other. How do you intend to advance without exposing our flanks?"

Xi jumped back into the conversation. "That predominantly depends on our tactical strength when we commence with the third leg of the op. But I'm confident we'll have multiple options available, including a methodical, branching advance, or possibly even another simultaneous 'Prairie Fire' attack carried out at key points of the network and spreading out from there."

"Colonel Jenkins," Moon cut in, "what's your opinion of the major's proposal?"

Jenkins couldn't help but smile with equal measures of pride and eagerness. Despite being just twenty years of age, Major Xi Bao had near-perfectly duplicated his own invasion strategy. Some of the details, like those regarding how to deploy Captain Winters' people and how to deploy Commander Knighton's Vipers, were subtly different from his version. But she'd gotten the broad strokes precisely as he had hoped she would, so it was without a moment's hesitation that he replied, "We'll clean up the details and coordination. The op plan is not just sound, General, but executable."

"I agree." Moon didn't mince words. His agreement was final. "Though I think it prudent to remind everyone that while we can provide low-orbit support with the *Wallace's* guns, both the *William Wallace* and *Vercingetorix* are in various states of repair and the *Red Hare's* Starburst missiles are depleted, so she's been re-armed with Blue Boys and MIRV cluster bombs. In short, we're nominally combat-ready but far from the biggest fish in the ocean. When factoring direct support from the warships into our plan, we need to be conscious that we're not anywhere near full strength."

"Understood, General," Xi and Jenkins acknowledged simultaneously.

"5th Fleet will provide support to your ships in orbit, General," Commodore Kline assured the assemblage. "I feel it prudent to reiterate that the reason we have requested your assistance in this matter is due to the nature of this conflict. We cannot deploy ground forces or engage surface targets as long as this is fundamentally a rebellion. Sol has yet to reach consensus on how to proceed, because frankly, we had not thought this situation possible."

"Understood, Commodore," General Moon replied agreeably, "and thank you. I think I speak for the room when I say I hope we have no need of your support, but we're glad to know it's there if we do. We'll be hard-pressed to support our good people on the ground while also trying to defend ourselves in space."

"I'm still unclear on something, Major," said Lieutenant Commander Knighton. "If we're covering 3rd Company's insertion, which requires the *William Wallace* to move off overwatch during the drop, who's providing overwatch of Echo?"

"No one," Xi replied with a healthy trace of arrogance that made Jenkins' grin broaden as she explained, "We go 'Empty Fort' at Echo, both to confuse the enemy and to maximize our mobile assets during the three-pronged push. After securing Echo, Clover moves on Hansel, 1st and 2nd Companies move on Gretel, and you assist 3rd Company with their advance. The only mechs at Echo will be Captain Koch's support team, who will manage the pop-ups and other fixed assets while we expand our zone of control. Koch will also be in a position to respond to any problems with our mechs to bring them back to combat effectiveness as quickly as possible."

"'Empty Fort?'" Knighton repeated, her words dripping with wry approval. "It would never work against a proper commander, but here? It might be just what the doctor ordered."

General Moon had already agreed with the premise but reiterated his position. "I agree. We hit them hard and fast, and keep them off-balance long enough to seize control over the POIs on the surface. After that, we re-evaluate based on our force strength and enemy disposition and decide how to proceed. But let's be clear: we're talking about upwards of seventy hours on the move, in combat, without sleep or rotation for every Terran in the op."

"We've already had Doc Fellows review the neurochemical profiles of all attached personnel," Major Xi Bao said, yet again surprising Jenkins with her initiative. "Every Metalhead putting tracks down is medically cleared for stim usage as outlined in the rules of engagement."

"Good. I'll make one last pass at the ROE," Moon confirmed. "Is this how you plan to proceed, Colonel?"

"Yes, General," Jenkins replied. "I endorse the major's proposal as outlined. We'll issue detailed supporting instructions to all hands."

"Excellent," the general replied. "I've got some wireless conferences to conduct before we depart New American space. I'll check back on your progress in four hours."

"Very good, sir," Jenkins acknowledged before Moon disconnected from the virtual conference. "All right, people," he declared purposefully, "it's time to make sure Mr. Murphy knows he's not on the guest list for this one. If anyone sees anything they think is a flaw or failure point, don't hesitate to call it out. We've got six days before we make orbit, and I intend to make the most of them. Understood?"

"Yes, sir!" came the chorus of confirmations.

"Good." He quirked a grin. "Now let's start again at the top."

3

TRANSIT

"Are things really that bad?" Jenkins asked during the second two-hour break in the virtual meeting. Alice had pinged him with a request for a sidebar, and he had decided everyone could use a brief respite after twelve hours of ironing out War God's details. It was tough enough being stuck inside the grav couches during transit from wormhole gate to wormhole gate, and the contentious nature of the planning meeting was enough to wear on even the most hardened officer's nerves.

But Jenkins learned he would be getting no such reprieve after hearing what Alice had just said.

"I'm afraid so, Lee." She sighed in frustration. "Venus' latest population figures, as of four days ago, are down to three-point-four billion and still falling. We had anticipated the situation to have largely stabilized by now, but Jemmin interference appears to run deeper than we originally estimated."

"What do the latest projections suggest the final tally will be?" Jenkins asked, knowing that every single death was directly traceable to Operation Antivenom.

His operation.

"Confidence is extremely high that the population will

remain above three billion," she replied, "but the vast majority of Venusian infrastructure was destroyed. Venus was a completely self-sustaining world, capable of contributing to the rest of Sol with the resource surpluses generated by their automated industry. But now? They will be a serious drain on Solar resources, one which I suspect my people have yet to fully quantify."

"Are we talking food? Energy? Medical supplies?"

"All that and more," she agreed grimly. "Of the sky cities which remain at stable altitudes, over half suffered serious sabotage to their primary buoyancy systems following Antivenom. They are therefore relying on emergency attitude-control systems, which have limited fuel stores. Even if we manage to get them enough fuel, which is a dubious proposition, those systems were not designed for continuous use. Normally, they would manufacture the necessary components locally, but with their infrastructure depleted and with Martian infrastructure equally unavailable to Sol..."

"That leaves Earth as the only source of supplies." Jenkins nodded in comprehension.

"With a decided lack of available logistical capacity to transfer those supplies," she said ominously. "We have more than enough freighters and slow-drive haulers in the outer Solar System, ferrying supplies to and from our various automated and semi-automated facilities there, but recalling them will take time I fear Venus might not have."

"I'm sorry, Alice," he said with feeling. "I'm not seeking your absolution, but I—"

"You did the right thing, Lee," she interrupted with conviction. "Our latest estimates show a greater than ninety-eight percent probability that had you not executed Antivenom, there would not be a single living human within Venus' atmosphere at this moment. And whatever we hope to rescue on Mars would likewise be destroyed, to say nothing of Earth's population, which comprises ninety percent of all living humans in the universe."

"That's...you know, I've never really thought about it that way." He had been told that before, but with each re-telling it still surprised him because he couldn't believe it was the whole truth. Humans had a way of surviving. Look at the Metal Legion, and how they'd come through when they had no chance to survive. "But that's insane. We can't have that many of us on one rock. It's irresponsible. Too much centralization of *anything* creates unnecessary and potentially catastrophic failure points. We Terrans learned that lesson the hard way, and, honestly, we'd prefer for you to learn from our experience rather than repeating our mistakes."

"It is easy to advocate for something when doing so serves your needs," Alice warned. "Decentralized authority has many advantages, but also many disadvantages. It is difficult but necessary to set bias aside and seek the truth rather than simply fight for a position you currently hold. Otherwise, we descend into the political deadlocks and violence of the early twenty-first century West. When it comes to learning from history, one would think that lesson would be front and center for a man like yourself."

"I'm not advocating anything except what I see as superior, or at worst, functional." Jenkins shook his head. "I understand the difference between advocacy and truth-seeking, and in my mind, the only cause worth advocating is truth. Little 't,' because I don't want to be sacrilegious."

He chuckled at his own joke, but the immensity of War God was weighing on his shoulders. He wasn't sure discussing political philosophy at that moment in time was in his best interests.

"You're willingly supporting an obvious paradox as a central tenet?" she mused. "However, on this issue, Solar sentiment is presently moving toward alignment with your own. I sometimes wonder how much of us and our history was truly our own from these past two centuries, and how much was merely the result of Jemmin influence." She paused for a moment before finishing in an uncertain tone, "I am not prone to the melodramatic, but I find myself asking a decidedly juvenile question of late: who are we *really*?"

"There's nothing juvenile about that question, Alice."

"Perhaps not, but in a way, being juvenile is not entirely without merit. It means that leaps and bounds of growth, development, and learning still lie ahead of us. Of *me*. That our potential has not yet been defined, and that if we are careful and self-aware enough, we might just be able to steer the course of our destiny more than we previously believed possible."

He smiled. "You're more of a philosopher than I thought."

"Then I was right about you." Alice laughed. "You *still* have much to learn."

<hr />

"I am sorry for placing you in a difficult situation during our last deployment, Lieutenant Podsednik," Jem said a few minutes after Podsy had awoken from his first in-flight slumber of the six-day voyage.

"Don't worry about it, Jem. I knew the possible risks. All you did was give me the option."

"I did more than that." Jem sounded like he wasn't going to bend on the issue.

"Not really." Podsy shrugged indifferently. "But if I know you, this is just a preamble. And since we've only got an hour before the next strategy session, you should probably get on with whatever it is."

"Very well. Long ago, the Jem'un were divided into two disparate camps. The first believed that reason and logic were the final arbiters of reality and their perceptions of it. The second, much smaller in number though many would say far more passionate in their cause, believed the universe was merely a reflection of what was within each sentient being. That to project upon the universe what was within each of us was the purpose of intelligence, sentience, and limited perspective. This second group argued, with surprising success, that objectivity was less important than subjectivity. That the disprovable was more important than the possible."

"We've had similar schisms in philosophy throughout human history," Podsy agreed. "Some of them gave us concepts like 'logos,' which we used to expand our understanding of the world around us."

"For the Jem'un, personality and individual agency played a far greater role in shaping society. This was one of the formative factors behind the division of Jem and Un."

"Interesting..." Podsy mused.

"In retrospect, many of the issues which were then considered sacrosanct were uniquely responsible for much of the discord in Jem'un society during that time. Had they treated those issues as the scientifically quantifiable phenomena they had always been, they could have avoided much of the chaos that nearly stopped them from reaching the stars. However, after regrettable strife and bloodshed, Jem and Un came to accept fundamental truths about their existences, and as a result, healed the growing divide which threatened to devour them all. Jem and Un agreed that Jem, or 'reason,' should be given directive primacy while Un, or 'conscience,' should be granted what was essentially veto power over any decisions to make fundamental changes. It was an imperfect solution for an imperfect species, but it was the best they could conceive and execute."

"I feel like there's a point in here somewhere," Podsy quipped. "Get to it, Jem. I have a lot of other things I need to focus on."

"Asymmetry was what Jem'un saw when they gazed out on the universe, or when they looked within themselves. This is because even an individual Jem'un could not fully comprehend, or condone, many of their own actions or thoughts when they occupied the opposite sex."

"You're saying that Sol and Terra, no matter how different they might appear to each other, are inextricably linked. We have something to offer each other precisely *because* we're so different, and we shouldn't be too quick to dismiss the value of those differences, even if they seem incomprehensible. Next time, just start with that, and it's not anything I don't already know. Is beating around the bush an inherent trait of the Un?"

"That encapsulates the bulk of my intended message. In the future, I shall endeavor to be more concise," Jem appeared to agree before continuing, "It was only by engaging one another on extremely difficult subjects, about which to that point engagement had previously been restricted for various reasons, that Jem and Un were able to come together in an optimal fashion. Difficult compromises were reached, unsavory concessions made by both sides, and in the end, they became stronger than ever. From my perspective, Sol and Terra appear to be in a strikingly similar situation. That you are already striding between the stars should not distract from the precariousness of humanity's position in its own line of history."

"Compromise." Podsy scowled. "That's going to be a tall order for both sides, Jem. I don't think Sol is going to give up claim to human supremacy, and I seriously can't envision Terra surrendering her autonomy." Another thought occurred to him, which he hesitated before voicing. "And let's be frank: Jem'un's path led them to Jemmin."

"A perfectly valid retort. But as the last vestige of the unmolested Jem'un legacy, I must warn against ignoring the lessons of the past...especially those bought with the blood of a civilization which, as yet, humanity can only dream of matching."

4

THE HOUSE JACK BUILT

With the trudging, depressing opening riff of Metallica's *The House Jack Built* playing over each vehicle's cabin speakers, forty-eight mechs prepared to drop through the thin Martian atmosphere to kick off Operation War God.

"I still can't believe you authorized this track, Major," 2nd Lieutenant Quinn muttered disdainfully. "It's not even proper metal!"

"My order stands, Lieutenant," Xi quipped as she went through the last items on her pre-drop checklist. "Besides, he won the rights fair and square."

"I'm not even dropping in the first wave and I call shenanigans." Captain Koch scoffed. "Not with the song, but with the integrity of the system that awarded its choice to Lieutenant Staubach."

"It's not my fault none of you thought Blinky could win a staring contest." Xi grinned.

"It was probably the meds," Quinn grumbled good-naturedly. "The suppression of extrapyramidal symptoms is a well-known side effect of the cocktails they give people with his condition."

"Hey," Blinky objected. "Just because Metallica sold out to make the Black Album doesn't invalidate everything that came afterward. And besides, we *are* going down there to secure some beanstalks. What better anthem than this one?"

"I'm not sure that's how I'd have pled my case, Lieutenant," Lieutenant Benjamin, *Sargon*'s Jock, chided.

"Jesus." Blinky boggled. "The last time I heard this much bitching was when I visited Captain Winters' relatives at the canine recreational facilities."

"Think that's funny, do you, Lieutenant? Calling my family a bunch of dogs?" Winters asked, barely able to keep up the false indignation.

"Nothing funny about it, sir," Blinky replied without hesitation. "To my mind, it's a genuine tragedy worthy of its own animal rights organization. I think I'd go with the 'Fraternal Egalitarian Canine Equality Society,' or FECES for short."

"Laugh while you can, Lieutenant," Captain Winters retorted, sounding like he might have begun to take offense at being the butt of this particular joke. "What goes around, comes around."

"With all due respect, Captain," a phrase used right before the disrespect was uttered, "that's the precise line of thinking that leads one to chase his own tail."

"And Blinky wins this round by TKO," Xi declared with gusto after finishing her pre-drop checklist and seeing the rest of the mechs do likewise. Their drop window was fast approaching, only thirty seconds remaining, so she piped into the *William Wallace*'s Ground Control Officer and declared, "Ground Control, this is Dragon Actual. We are green across the board and ready to drop."

"Roger, Dragon Actual," Lieutenant Greenburg, the *Wallace*'s Ground Control Officer, acknowledged with crisp professionalism. "Drop doors open, all launch systems are five-by-five. We are T-minus fifteen seconds. Prepare for insertion."

"Acknowledged, Ground Control." Major Xi Bao, Dragon Actual, watched the seconds tick down. Although she had no real-time tactical feed to confirm it, she knew that a minute earlier, Lieutenant Commander Knighton's sixteen Vipers had engaged the first of their ground targets. The bulk of those targets were concealed fortifications, primarily remote-controlled missile launchers.

The locations of the concealed turrets and launchers had been provided by Commodore Kline in order to facilitate the Legion's successful insertion. Without that intel, it was probable that over half the drop cans and their crews would have been destroyed before they reached the Martian surface.

It might not have seemed like much help to provide a simple map, but it would save lives and mechanical assets.

"Dragon Battalion, this is *William Wallace* Ground Control," came Lieutenant Greenburg's voice. "Initiating drop at one-second offsets following my mark. Commencing drop in five...four...three...two...one...mark."

Xi's drop can lurched forward, propelled by powerful hydraulic rams, which began to pump a steady stream of her fellow Metalheads from the *William Wallace*'s quartet of launch tubes. Xi's can was in the first wave, and as soon as she was clear of the launch tube, her instruments started to register the distance to landfall on the Martian surface.

Xi Bao was not commonly afflicted with crippling sentimentality, but when she first saw the brownish-red orb of Mars through her can's external video feeds, she could not help a single thought from briefly dominating her consciousness.

We're baaack.

Her tactical feed was still dormant, as expected. One of the last changes to the op was to cut all wireless communication until the Metalheads put tracks down. The Martian segment of the One Mind comm network had been deactivated by Sol to prevent potentially toxic data streams originating from Mars, but some of the virtual infrastructure might have been hacked by the Martian rebels, and that infrastructure was more advanced than anything the Metalheads had access to.

In fact, Commodore Kline had revealed that the One Mind network was capable of executing a total virtual takeover of any system that attempted to interface with it. This was a defensive measure, generally used to neutralize hostile takeovers of the system by shutting down the unauthorized hardware attempting to interface with the One Mind. But to everyone's surprise, the commodore had gone even further to say that the system could, in theory, be used to infiltrate any system within its effective zone of control and feed misinformation into that system.

As a result, the first phase of Operation War God would take place under total radio blackout. P2P comm linkage was still authorized, but not all drop cans were equipped with secure P2P gear, so they would need to put tracks on crimson sand before the Metal Legion's crews could regain comm with one another.

As Xi's can fell toward Mars, she thought she spotted a flash of light thirty kilometers to the north of the LZ. Her eyes fixed on that spot until another flash strobed to the north of the first, followed by another several kilometers north of the second. She grinned, knowing the flashes were light reports of Knighton's Vipers scrubbing the ground clean of hardware designed with a single purpose—kill vehicles exactly like the one she was riding in.

Using enviable precision, and flying in pairs, the Metal Legion's recently transferred interceptor pilots methodically uprooted dozens of concealed bunkers and pop-ups, clearing the way for the falling drop-cans.

A warning indicator flashed on her HUD, prompting her to call, "Penny, I've got a red light on the port stabilizer fuel supply."

"On it, Major," Penny acknowledged, and a few tense seconds later the other woman reported, "The primary had a stuck valve. I've manually opened it, and prepared the bypass line just in case."

"Good work," Xi said as the cans fell toward the surface. To her amazement, the descent went off without so much as a single inbound rocket. The Vipers, using Solarian intelligence, had wiped the board clean of Martian defenses and cleared the Legion's LZ.

The can's braking thrusters engaged, snapping the can and its contents downward with ten gees of decelerative force. The feeling of weighing eight hundred kilos was now so familiar it was almost comforting.

But the sudden shock of touchdown was unpleasant as ever, and the drop-can's various systems reported minor damage due to landing on a less-than-ideal patch of rocky ground instead of the softer dust of the planet's surface.

"Popping the top," she declared, blowing the explosive bolts that held the can together and sending the delivery container's walls outward, where they fell to the ground. The Martian atmosphere didn't transfer sound well, but if it had, the heavy clang of the walls hitting would have echoed through the mech. One by one, the mechs of Dragon 1st and Dragon 2nd Companies popped their own cans, with each registering on her seismic sensors.

She opened the neural link and extended her consciousness into the mech, raising the Scorpion-class war machine from the metal floor of the open can and sidestepping off the platform. The mech's armored legs crushed human-sized boulders before digging a quarter meter into the Martian soil. Once she'd emerged from the can, Xi felt the familiar thrill of anticipation.

"1st Company, this is Dragon Actual," she intoned. "Sound off."

"*Sargon* here," replied Lieutenant Benjamin, aboard the Trebuchet-class missile mech. "The blacker, the better."

"*Cyclops*," followed Lieutenant Staubach from his heavy plasma cannon-equipped walker, "winking at you."

"*Black Widow*, mourning sans tears," continued Lieutenant Quinn from her Tactical arachnoid mech.

"*Murasame*, slicing and dicing," offered Lieutenant Nakamura aboard the mech-killing walker, equipped with a quartet of hunter-killer drones purpose-built to destroy enemy vehicles.

"*Devil's Due*, ready to pay," Corporal Haggerty reported, one of the Flakes Captain Winters had whipped into shape quickly enough to roll into an established unit like Dragon 1st Company. *Devil's Due* was a fearsome-looking humanoid walker with assorted artillery and truly devastating short-range RPGs mounted on booms that protruded from the monstrous mech's neck region. As a result, the mech's class had been named "Baphomet," and all vehicles produced under the name traditionally held demonic or Satanic names. They were so popular with Metalheads during their earliest deployments eighty years earlier that, after they stopped being produced, they continued being thrown into the front lines against Arh'Kel. Attrition had dwindled their numbers, just five of the original two hundred thirty Baphomets having escaped destruction.

"*Plague Maiden*, spreading far and wide." Second Lieutenant Wilder came next from one of two identical track-based cruisers of the Vector class, which each featured a quad of eight-tube SRM pods. Fearsome at short- and mid-ranges, Vectors were specifically designed for environments like those of the Martian surface.

"*Ebola May*, what she said," drawled 1st Company's other Second Lieutenant Wilder, whose mech was virtually identical to *Plague Maiden*, just like the Jock herself. They were Identical twins whose black senses of humor had immediately ingratiated them with their fellow Metalheads and had played no small part in the naming of their respective mechs.

"*Culture Knight*," Corporal Giles followed, "open to reason." *Culture Knight* was a Tactical-grade humanoid walker mech with dual arm-mounted eight-kilo guns. But its biggest weapons were the sixty-four mortars hidden behind its torso's armored panels. Those mortars had open-field ranges of up to eight kilometers and were theoretically capable of leveling a modestly-developed city block with a single salvo. Giles had proven his nerve and enthusiasm during Watery Grave, and Xi had given him his own command as a result.

"*Cam Frog*," Corporal Lassiter continued, "keeping it real." *Cam Frog* was, in many respects, similar to the capital-grade railgun mech *Sam Kolt*, but unlike that humanoid variant, this one was a broad, low quadruped with a central cam directly beneath the gun which served as an anchor and recoil-damper when firing the mech's main weapon. Like her nominally-former boyfriend Giles, Lassiter had proven herself more than capable during Watery Grave and had been rewarded with her own command, too.

"*Elvira III*," Xi finished, "clickin' my heels." She switched to the P2P link with *Warcrafter* as soon as it went live. "Clover, this is Dragon. 1st Company stands ready to roll."

"Copy that, Dragon Actual," Colonel Jenkins acknowledged as local tactical data fed through the P2P line populated Xi's HUD. She watched with rising envy as the state-of-the-art Razorback Mk 2-Vs of Clover sped off across the blasted

Martian plains, en route to their primary target. "Proceed according to plan, Major."

"Roger, out," she replied enthusiastically before switching to the company channel. "1st Company, roll out on target Scooter. Advance at flank speed. If anyone falls behind, they'll be scrubbing my latrine with their tongue."

"How is that a disincentive, ma'am?" *Sargon* asked, drawing a half-disgusted snort from Xi as the column assumed formation and proceeded toward the Schiaparelli Crater at ninety kilometers per hour.

"You're a sick bastard, *Sargon*." She grinned. "But on a serious note, if I find any of you mooks sniffing around my toilet, I'll subject you to forty-eight hours' mandatory cultural sensitivity training with a *heavy* emphasis on early-twenty-first-century hip hop music."

"That is cruel and unusual punishment." *Sargon* sighed wistfully.

"Aren't there war crimes statues covering abuses like that, Major?" Blinky asked with patently false disdain. "Seems like the mere threat of it might constitute a capital offense."

"Probably," she allowed, "but those statutes only protect beings with higher intelligence. Metalheads are many things, but 'intelligent' is notably absent from the list."

"Hear, hear," grumbled Quinn. "'Join Armor Corps,' they said. 'Travel the galaxy,' they said. 'Make a difference,' they said. If I'd known the job would be ninety percent trash talk, nine percent wrench-turning, and one percent sheer terror... Oh, who am I kidding? It's not like my career in underwater finger painting was going anywhere."

The column proceeded apace, never faltering in its stride as it bore down on the Schiaparelli Compound—objective Scooter. Located across the second-largest crater on Mars, the compound was the largest and most important collection of infrastructure on the planet's surface. Centered around a zone where mineral-rich asteroids were dropped by slow-drive ships that towed them from the asteroid belt back to Mars, the Schiaparelli Compound had at one time been the most important industrial compound in all of Sol.

It had taken several decades to get the system up to speed, but once it was, the site had averaged more than one asteroid deposit every ten days. At its height, the system of refineries and manufactories had processed tens of thousands of tons of raw ore each day. Platinum, gold, and other rare minerals were prioritized, with the material being converted into micro components used in all manner of human technology.

But as the decades stretched on and human technology continued to improve, micro-foundries and mini-factories became the standard and on-site processing of free-orbiting asteroids became the norm because moving big rocks through space and to a planet surface was a lot of work.

The occasional rock was still brought to Mars for breakdown, but this was generally to service local Martian needs rather than to supply the rest of the Solar System. Despite the system working at less than two percent of its peak capacity, the Schiaparelli Compound had been impressively well-maintained and therefore presented a high-value target for both the rebels and the Solar government.

So as the mechs of 1st Company came to the edge of the massive Schiaparelli Crater, the awe-inspiring scale of humanity's largest surface-based industrial complex became apparent. With a median diameter of over four hundred and sixty kilometers, the Schiaparelli Compound formed a band of burnished metal structures fifty kilometers thick at the crater's edge. It was the greatest forge ever built by humans, a testament to not only human industry, but to the human spirit as it made the species' mark on a planet they had no natural business occupying.

Looking out on it was as close to a religious experience as Xi had ever had.

Her poignant moment of reflection ended when a brilliant flash of light stabbed into *Elvira's* forward armor, setting off warning alarms all across her HUD.

"Evasive action!" she called over the local P2P net, crouching *Elvira* down and sighting in on the beam's point of origin. The mechs of 1st Company scattered, some sprinting ahead while others flattened out like *Elvira*, and still others coming about and flanking out wide in response to the fireworks of inbound beams. Her mechs' forward armor was damaged but holding as she sighted in on the source of the attacking weapon. A pair of her fellow mechs had not been as fortunate.

The wedge-shaped Cruiser *Overdrive's* left roller-treads had been blown apart in a glittering shower of molten metal by a pair of direct hits, knocking its drive train offline but doing nothing to stop the mech from launching a volley of SRMs at the targets highlighted by Xi as she bracketed them one after another.

The battlewagon, *Witch Doctor,* had been skewered bow-to-stern by a beam that vented the breathable atmosphere from the mech, although the mech's crew survived thanks to their pressurized combat suits. *Witch Doctor* returned fire, sending a pair of tungsten bolts into a bunker two hundred kilometers from 1st Company's position.

"1st Company," Xi barked as she loaded a pair of extended-range HE shells into *Elvira's* mains, "return fire on assigned targets. Burn 'em!"

Elvira's mains roared, driving the mech's rear legs into the ruddy soil while sending fifteen-kilo shells soaring into the thin air. A volley of concerted artillery and missile fire followed, with each projectile screaming through the twilight sky en route to its designated target. The missiles blasted through the air on a flat arc, while the shells took parabolic trajectories high above.

The first shell to strike its target was one of *Elvira's*, scrapping the previously-concealed pop-up with a picture-perfect bullseye. The second hit was also from Xi's guns, and it left a smoking crater where its target had been.

And then, like a line of dominoes, a ripple of explosions marked a near-perfect salvo that destroyed forty-six likely targets, most of which had already fired on them. A single SRM missed its target, being struck by interceptor rockets half a kilometer from impact and splashing down two hundred meters from the mark.

"Ground Control, this is Dragon Actual." Xi grimaced after reviewing the tactical data surrounding the beams that had struck her mechs. "We've got Jemmin-tech beam emitters down here. Forwarding local sensor data now. Requesting fire support, over."

"Dragon Actual, this is Ground Control," acknowledged Lieutenant Greenburg in an enviably calm, professional tone. "Yellowhammer is rerouting from sortie, ETA forty seconds. *William Wallace* is in position and requesting confirmation of priority targets, over."

"Confirmed, GC." She grunted after reviewing her probable targets. She had identified twelve more locations, based on energy signatures and position, of more Jemmin-tech pop-ups. She knew it was unlikely more than half of them held enemy weapons, but it was better to ask forgiveness than permission.

"Roger, Dragon Actual. Targets confirmed. Be advised," Greenburg intoned, "you have sixteen, make that 'one-six,' raindrops inbound. *Wallace* Actual suggests you cover your ears."

Xi smirked. "Copy that, GC. Bring the rain."

Moments later, *Elvira's* seismic alarms went off as a perfectly synchronized quartet of capital-grade railgun bolts fell upon the suspected pop-ups. A few seconds later, another quartet. Followed by another, and another, with each impact delivered at metronome-precise intervals. The *William Wallace*'s railguns might not have been as powerful as the *Dietrich Bonhoeffer*'s, but they were more than capable of eradicating heavily-fortified ground targets.

"Dragon Actual, this is Yellowhammer," came the voice of Lieutenant Commander Knighton after a secure P2P connection went active. "Advise you to keep your heads down. We're kissing the deck."

"Acknowledged, Yellowhammer," Xi agreed, but no sooner had she done so than eight Viper-class aerospace interceptors tore across the sky less than fifty meters above *Elvira's* mains.

Xi's enhanced senses were barely capable of processing the fact that Knighton's Vipers had unleashed a storm of ordnance less than two hundred meters past *Elvira's* position. That ordnance stabbed into another series of targets, likely identified by the *William Wallace*'s robust active sensors, and a ripple of explosions coursed across the Schiaparelli Crater. Dozens of fresh targets were scrapped, with accompanying explosions proving the merit of the *Wallace*'s targeting priority.

"Dragon Actual," Knighton declared, "this is Yellowhammer. We are bingo fuel and scratch ammo. Returning for refuel and rearm, expected turnaround thirty-five minutes. Don't have too much fun without us."

"Yellowhammer, Dragon Actual." Xi smirked. "Thank you for the assist. You guys are the bomb. On a side note, we'll have however much fun we damn well please."

"Copy that, Dragon Actual." Knighton laughed. "Yellowhammer out."

Xi switched to the Marine channel. "Lieutenant Worthington."

"Go ahead, Major."

"Looks like this place will need a little more TLC than we thought." She forwarded a set of coordinates to a nearby ore-smelting compound that measured nearly thirty kilometers across. "I'm moving *Cyclops* and *Sargon* to cover this position, but those structures are too small for my metal."

"Copy that, ma'am," Worthington acknowledged. "My people know how to deal with tight openings."

Xi grinned approvingly at receiving a relative battlefield banter softball. "I'm going to extend you the same courtesy I just requested of Commander Knighton: let's stay out of what your people do on their own time."

"Begging the major's pardon," he quipped as the Tripoli-class dropship sped across the crater, hugging the deck so close she legitimately thought they might scrape the odd boulder near the rim, "this *is* our time."

The heavily-armored dropship, once the pride of the Terran Marine Corps but now replaced by faster craft, hurtled across the Schiaparelli Crater, throwing a trail of dusty debris up in its wake. Xi scanned the horizon for any kind of movement, her fifteen-kilo mains freshly loaded with ER-AP shells. She saw a flicker of motion twelve kilometers away and spotted what looked like a small fire team of pressure-suited humans positioning a crew-served SRM launcher for a shot on the incoming dropship.

But before Xi could unleash her shells on the would-be ambushers, the Marine dropship unleashed a storm of coil gun fire. Three hundred depleted uranium shells per second slammed into the makeshift nest, annihilating its occupants and smothering their remains in a choking cloud of brown dust with precisely two-tenths of a second of fire.

Without adjusting course or speed, the Tripoli-class dropship drove on toward the target facility while Xi moved *Elvira* to the edge of the crater. Looking out at the enormous bowl-shaped depression in the Martian surface, she saw no immediate signs of danger and decided to proceed.

The major forwarded new orders to each of the mechs under her command, including those damaged by the unexpected beam fire. "1st Company, let's secure this hole."

5

THE DUELISTS

"Copy that, Ground Control," Colonel Jenkins acknowledged after receiving an update showing Jemmin weapons had been fired at Xi's people at Schiaparelli. They had anticipated direct Jemmin assistance, but confirmation that they would contend with more than just Martian rebels was nonetheless unwelcome news. "Clover Battalion, be advised," he called over the command channel as his twenty-four Razorback Mk 2-V's raced toward their objective, "Dragon 1st has encountered Jemmin beam weaponry at Schiaparelli. Anticipate the same at Echo."

A chorus of flickering acknowledgments came over his console as Clover reached the ten-kilometer mark from the military facility designated Echo Base for the duration of the op. They were already well inside Echo's defenses, which included a spiderweb-like network of three dozen narrow, deep trenches large enough to conceal enemy vehicles and pop-ups. Those trenches, which were covered by foot-thick armor panels capable of withstanding multiple direct hits from most of his weapons, extended outward from the central facility, and Jenkins suspected it was in those trenches that the rebels awaited him.

Commodore Kline had suggested it was unlikely in the extreme that the rebels would be able to operate the facility's primary systems, but that whatever vehicles had survived their takeover of the facility would be at their disposal. It made the probability of a trap so obvious that Jenkins had a rare moment of doubt that the rebels would be so predictable.

Still, trap or no, they were on the clock. They couldn't pussyfoot around the perimeter, poking and prodding before every nervous step. Since they had landed, two surface facilities had been scrapped by local demo charges, including a massive fusion power plant which was capable of furnishing fifteen percent of Martian industry with energy. Every second they wasted represented crippling industrial losses, and those losses were obviously accelerating now that the Legion had arrived.

He knew they were already well past the point of safety, and decided it was time to initiate his final ultimatum. He switched over to the broad hailing frequencies. "This is Colonel Lee Jenkins, repeating my order to acknowledge my duly-issued Solar authority to inspect Chi Bi fortress on behalf of Solar 5th Fleet. Acknowledge my transmission, or I will have no choice but to consider Chi Bi under rebel control."

He considered the heavily-fortified facility before them, with its tall, gleaming ramparts and even taller parapets surrounding a huge, centrally-located pressure dome. Fittingly, as with so much on Mars, it was not what stood above the surface but what lay beneath that represented the facility's true value.

With that thought in mind, Jenkins authorized fire packages and sent the orders to Clover's mechs. "This is Clover Actual. We are weapons hot. I say again, we are weapons hot. Engage assigned targets and fire on the run. I say again, fire!"

The fleet of speeding Razorbacks deployed their previously-concealed railguns in near-perfect unison and sent a storm of tungsten bolts into the metal walls of the fortress. The bolts slammed into key points of the above-surface fortifications, with multiple bolts converging on each of those points and gouging three- and four-meter-deep gashes in the solid wall of hardened armor. No sooner had the tungsten bolts hit home than the Razorbacks followed the opening salvo with a barrage of fifteen-kilo artillery shells and SRMs.

The devastating wave of ordnance crashed into the fortress, hammering into the already-weakened points in the fifteen-meter-high ramparts. Shell after shell slammed home, tearing multi-meter-wide chunks of solid armor from the robust surface. While the shells battered the facility's outer shell, Terran missiles streaked into the facility's interior, where they collided with pressure domes, comm towers, and every other feature of note. As those towers and domes collapsed, a pair of outer wall segments also fell to Terran fury, exploding in glittery plumes of shrapnel that would have instantly killed any human within fifty meters.

Clover was four kilometers from the battered ramparts, driving forward at a dead sprint, when the rebels made their presence known with a wave of missiles from the southern trenches. Armored panels covering fully half of the trenches receded, and a crossfire of rockets, artillery, mortars, and missiles erupted from the exposed trenches, all of which were large enough to comfortably fit the largest Legion mechs.

A pair of Razorbacks were wrecked, with one flying apart in fulminant fury as its reactor lost containment, scattering metal and meat in a cloud of plasma and shrapnel. Another eight mechs took direct hits, but their robust armor protected them, and the twenty-two remaining Razorbacks continued their charge toward the stronghold.

"Counterfire," Jenkins commanded. Without breaking stride, the Clover Razorbacks sent a hail of artillery back at their ambushers. The armored panels above the trenches slid shut, protecting the vehicles and weapons beneath, but not before a handful were struck by high-explosive shells that sent plumes of dusty debris skyward over their impact points.

Despite taking and returning fire, the Razorbacks never faltered in their sprint for the battered fortress. Twenty-two of the most powerful land vehicles ever built for human warfare, carrying sufficient combined firepower to subdue a small colony, continued pouring bolt after bolt and missile after missile into the slowly-growing breaches in the heavily-armored ramparts. Only the Razorbacks' artillery returned fire on the rebels in the trenches. The rest of the column's firepower would open the makeshift portals through to the fortress's outer walls.

Terran missiles and railgun bolts slammed into those walls, ripping meter after meter of protective metal from the smoking bulwark. All fire converged on the two breaches opened during the initial assault, and it soon became clear that the southern-most breach was opening fastest. Jenkins forwarded revised fire orders to his Jocks, who immediately re-targeted the southern breach with all ordnance.

Fifteen seconds after the first ambush, half of the remaining panels receded and another storm of mixed mortar, rocket, and artillery fire burst from the trenches. Clover was quicker to retaliate this time, with the first counterfire erupting even before the rebels' weapons struck. Again, a pair of Clover mechs were lost with all hands to the surprisingly adept ambush, but the improved reaction time by Jenkins' people saw fifteen new plumes burst skyward before the trench's protective roofs retracted once again.

"Two kilometers to the breach, Colonel," Corporal Krauthammer reported as *Warcrafter* sprinted over the top of an armored trench. It was soon followed by three of the surviving twenty Razorbacks.

Despite the constant fire pouring into the battered fortress bulwark, the gap was still too narrow for the Razorbacks to fit through. If they failed to open it in time, they would be pinned, however briefly, against the walls of the fortress. Their speed and maneuverability had thus far limited the damage done by the rebel ambushes, but without those advantages, there was little hope they could survive for long against the well-dug-in enemy.

Jenkins knew what he had to do and wasted little time making the necessary call. "Dragon Actual, this is Clover Actual requesting a Doorknocker at attached coordinates."

Without delay, Major Xi Bao acknowledged, "Doorknocker inbound. Impact in fifty-six seconds."

"Roger." Jenkins grimaced, knowing that even if the Doorknocker landed precisely where and when she had indicated, it only left four seconds before *Warcrafter*, at the tip of Clover's formation, would arrive at the same spot. At their current speed of one hundred twenty kph, and considering the scrabble terrain, it was effectively impossible for *Warcrafter* to come to a stop that quickly.

Which meant he had a choice: continue at flank speed toward the breach, trusting that the Doorknocker would do its job, or slow the column to prevent self-destruction against the solid metal ramparts of Echo Base.

To Lee Jenkins or any other Metalhead worthy of the moniker, there was no choice at all.

"Continue at flank," he called as another ambush popped up from the field surrounding the fortress. His people answered with expert precision. No Clovers were lost to this particular volley, but two were badly damaged and faltered out of formation while their fellows charged ahead.

The countdown timer for the inbound Doorknocker wound down to zero, and when it did, the ground shook with the force of its arrival. The narrow gap in Echo Base's southern wall exploded in a conical shower of debris propelled by the high-explosive warhead delivered to it by the 'Doorknocker' LRM, sent by the Legion's foremost missile platform, *Sargon*. Dropping a bunker-busting shaped charge into the solid metal wall, the Doorknocker transformed a five-meter-wide gap in the defensive barricade into a fifteen-meter gap that was more than adequate to permit the Razorbacks' passage.

At the head of the column, *Warcrafter* leapt up with a thrust of its forward legs, easily clearing the ruined wall's curved lower margin. The Doorknocker had utterly annihilated a small structure previously nestled against the wall's inner face, leaving nothing but a fan-shaped debris field of gravel and metallic shards beneath the Razorback's feet as it entered the fort's interior.

Corporal Krauthammer deftly banked the mighty war machine to port as soon as it breached the wall, and a steady stream of Clover Razorbacks soon followed.

When the dust settled, nineteen of Jenkins' original twenty-four Razorbacks had reached the safety of the fort's interior, where they quickly spread out to inspect and secure the facility.

"Status report," Jenkins called over the command channel, finding that despite some serious drive train damage to four of his mechs, none of their weapons were offline and they remained mobile under their own power. "Let's secure those ditches. Captain Chao, prepare recon drones so we can paint and eliminate targets with orbital strikes. Take Clover 2nd..." His voice trailed off when an alert flashed across his screen, prompting him to pause the order. "Stand by."

He re-scanned the information coming to him via the *Red Hare*'s priority P2P line. A sneer creased his lips as he confirmed what he had initially thought the message said: Jemmin warships detected and engaged. Neither the *Red Hare* nor the *William Wallace* would be providing orbital support for the immediate future.

"New orders. 2nd Company, send your recon drones down the trenches and prepare to paint targets for LRM bombardment." They had avoided carpet-bombing the area because the subterranean infrastructure of Echo Base was of vital importance to Operation War God's mid and late stages, but it now appeared that they had little choice. "Let's dig these ticks out one by one."

"Confirmed, General," the ship's Tactical Officer, Lieutenant Jacobsen declared. "Two Jemmin cruisers have appeared in the area of Phobos. Getting a visual now, sir."

The *Wallace's* main holodisplay sprang to life, showing a pair of identical Jemmin warships that appeared to be bursting forth from the soft rock of Mars' larger moon. Without taking his eyes off the display, which was accompanied by a stream of tactically-relevant data, Podsy commanded, "Set Condition One throughout the ship. Helm, come about to intercept vector. Gunnery, prepare fire solutions on the northern warship. All nonessential hands, report to your couches."

The acknowledgments came back while Podsy poured over the tactical data, which seemed to paint the picture of two warships not yet operating at full power. For some reason, they had opted to abandon the security of their spider holes and were making no attempt to disguise their intention to engage the Terran warships.

"Comm," Brigadier General Moon barked, "have the *Red Hare* fall in on our port flank."

The *William Wallace* and the *Red Hare* rose up from their low orbit positions in overwatch, swinging their bows around to face the new threat just fifteen thousand kilometers away. Phobos was not far from Schiaparelli Crater in its seven-and-a-half-hour orbit of Mars, and as a result, was positioned almost ideally to conceal an ambush of the Terran warships.

"Gunnery is ready to fire on hostiles, Lieutenant," reported Jacobsen at Tactical.

He flitted a glance at General Moon, who nodded in support before Podsy commanded, "Fire!"

The *William Wallace*'s railguns spat tungsten bolts at the target warship, but the Jemmin cruisers were nimble and evaded all four of the inbound projectiles by an average distance of six hundred meters. "Oh for four, Lieutenant," Jacobsen reported with a scowl.

"Recalculate solutions," Podsy snapped as the Jemmin warships scampered behind Phobos, using the twenty-two-kilometer hunk of rock as a shield while the *Wallace*'s gunners made ready for a second salvo. He accessed Lieutenant Commander Knighton's direct channel, "Commander, are you ready to scramble?"

"Negative, Lieutenant," she replied tersely. "We need another fifty seconds before we're refueled, and forty seconds more to swap out the ammo cans."

"We're too far anyway," General Moon observed calmly, his projected confidence refocusing the bridge personnel. "They wouldn't reach firing angles for at least four minutes. This won't last that long."

"Enemy ships slowing on Phobos' far side," Sensors declared. "Estimate they'll clear the horizon in thirty seconds."

"Railguns reloaded and new solutions plotted," Tactical reported. "Hit probability calculated at thirty-six percent, sir."

Podsy glanced at the tactical plotter, which showed a Solar 5th Fleet contingent of ten warships located forty-six thousand kilometers from the Jemmin warships. "They're too far for effective engagement with railguns," he muttered before turning to Commodore Kline, who had remained aboard the *William Wallace* as a liaison while Kline conducted Solar 5th Fleet's activities aboard his flagship. "When will your ships fire their missiles, Commodore?"

Kline seemed disinclined to answer but visibly overrode his reluctance by replying, "I would anticipate repeated salvos fired at intervals varying between six and nine seconds, consisting of thirty to fifty missiles apiece. Acceleration profiles will range between two hundred and three hundred fifty gees."

Podsy turned to Tactical. "Recalculate your solutions to include predicted evasive actions based on those inbound weapons."

"Yes, sir," Tactical replied. "Recalculating."

Podsy shared a knowing look with General Moon, who seemed to approve of his broaching the subject with the commodore as he had. Kline and his people had insisted they not reveal any more Solar tactical data than absolutely necessary during the op's planning phase, and it seemed Podsy had correctly surmised that this was such a situation.

Podsy knew the tasks before them were riddled with both tactical and political landmines and was glad he had navigated successfully at the outset.

The first wave of missiles leapt from the Solar warships' launchers, with time-to-impact at just under three minutes for the fastest missiles in the flight.

Staggering missile launch speeds and points of origin were basic naval tactics. Twelve-year-olds playing tactical simulators or war games knew that you didn't want all of your missiles to arrive at the same time since that made them easier to avoid or intercept, and the Solarians were executing a textbook barrage by staggering both launch times and acceleration profiles of the missiles within each flight.

"Enemy ships emerging," Tactical called. "*Red Hare* is moving to interdict direct fire."

"They don't have any capital-grade missiles left after Watery Grave." Tactical scowled. "What are they thinking?"

"It's true that Captain Guan is a maniac." Moon grunted approvingly. "But his armor's thicker than ours, and he knows the Jemmin will have all their guns aimed at the *Wallace*. Sometimes you're the shield, sometimes you're the spear."

The Jemmin Cruisers emerged from behind the irregularly-shaped Phobos, and a quartet of immensely-powerful beams hammered into the egg-shaped *Red Hare*'s forward hull. The beams crisscrossed, slashing and gouging molten rents in the *Hare*'s heavily-armored bow. Like a garden hose spraying across the lawn, outgassing propelled droplets and shards of metal from the hull out into Martian orbit. An internal explosion rocked the *Red Hare*, knocking it off-axis before the ship's maneuvering thrusters compensated and reoriented the damaged warship.

"Return fire," Moon commanded, and the *William Wallace*'s four railguns launched tungsten bolts at the increasingly agile Jemmin cruisers. The Jemmin warships juked and spun, but despite their nimble evasions, one of the *Wallace*'s bolts slammed home on the lead cruiser's port flank.

"Direct hit," Tactical declared as a storm of missiles erupted from the Jemmin cruisers. Like the Solar missiles, the Jemmin weapons featured staggered acceleration curves.

But unlike the Solar missiles, some of the Jemmin weapons were moving at constant, near-relativistic speeds.

"Hyper-velocity missiles inbound!" Sensors called urgently.

"Evasive action," Moon barked.

Podsy gripped the arms of his chair as proximity alarms went off all over the ship. "All hands, brace for impact!"

No sooner had the words left his mouth than the first HVM

struck the *William Wallace*. Moving at 0.03c, the slender fifty-gram projectile blew a two-foot-wide hole in the *Wallace*'s forward hull. The kinetic impact was so great that everyone on the *Wallace*'s bridge was whiplashed with near-lethal force.

Designed to penetrate armor significantly more robust than the *Wallace*'s, the extreme penetrative profile of the Jemmin hyper-velocity missiles actually worked to the Terran warship's advantage by permitting the bulk of its destructive energies to pass harmlessly through.

And while the *Wallace* avoided the rest of the HVMs in that initial volley, the one that did strike caused catastrophic damage to the ship's systems.

"Damage report," Podsy called as a series of alarms went off across the ship's main status board, shown to the left of the bridge's main display.

"I've got a cascade power failure on the starboard grid," Damage Control reported. "I'm re-routing to bypass and sending repair crews to the damaged areas, but starboard rail-guns are temporarily offline."

"Continue firing the port guns at will," Moon commanded, and the *William Wallace* authored a counter-salvo at the Jemmin cruisers composed of two tungsten bolts. Neither of the bolts struck home since the Jemmin warships continued to accelerate as they pulled away from the larger Martian moon.

The *Red Hare* shuddered, taking a pair of HVM strikes to its port quarter, which hit the smaller Terran Warship much harder than the *Wallace*. Being more heavily armored and generally denser than the *Wallace*, the *Red Hare* received more damage from the HVMs per strike. Its engines immediately flickered and soon cut out as critical damage was dealt to its primary systems, sending the ship into a gentle corkscrew while the *Wallace* surged past it.

Volley after volley of Solarian missiles shot out from their launchers, tearing across the void in pursuit of their Jemmin targets. But those targets were moving faster now, accelerating at fifty gees and making evasive maneuvers that would have been impossible aboard any human-built ship, Terran or Solarian.

The Jemmin cruisers lanced out with beams, slashing across the *Wallace*'s bow and violently knocking the ship off its axis. Podsy's head struck his chair's headrest with such force that he was temporarily blinded, and when his vision resumed, he saw that multiple others had sustained similarly jarring injuries, briefly robbing them of their senses.

"Explosive decompressions across the port bow, General," Damage Control reported with a mild slur. "Sealing off affected sections. Casualty reports are coming in. Starboard power grid is back online. All railguns active."

"Steady as she goes," General Moon said in a raised voice as the first of the Solar missiles approached the fleeing Jemmin warships. "Tactical, give those bastards everything we've got."

"Yes, sir," Tactical acknowledged with gusto. "Firing!"

The *William Wallace* sent four more railgun bolts into the fleeing warships, which had only increased the eccentricity of their evasive maneuvers as the lead Solar missiles approached. Point defense beams stabbed out, sniping the first missiles from the void several kilometers from the Jemmin hulls, but with each missile that was torn down, two more appeared. And when those were torn down, four more replaced them.

Like a building tsunami of ordnance, the Solarian missile storm poured into the Jemmin field of counterfire, and through that tsunami burst the four railgun bolts authored by General Moon's flagship.

Surprisingly, all four of those bolts landed, delivering utter devastation to the lead Jemmin cruiser. Its slender, curved hull was skewered by the quartet of bolts, two of which struck directly over the ship's engines, while the others hit near the warship's tapered bow. Internal explosions rocked the battered cruiser, momentarily pausing its interceptive fire.

That moment proved fatal as Solarian missiles tore through the gap in the warship's defenses and slammed one after another into the enemy ship. One of the Solar missiles, carrying a multi-megaton warhead, erupted in a miniature nova, enveloping the Jemmin cruiser. When the rad-wash had passed and visual contact was reestablished, all that remained of the first Jemmin warship was an oblong cloud of rapidly-expanding debris.

Defiant to the last, the second Jemmin cruiser continued to flee while pouring point-defense fire into the pursuing missiles. But those missiles, previously divided between two targets, began to converge on the lone remaining Jemmin. And as the weight of ordnance bearing down on it rose, even the Jemmin's advanced weapons grid was unable to stave off the inevitable.

The first missile to detonate near the Jemmin warship was another multi-megaton fusion device, which failed to destroy the ship outright. The cruiser's hull was alight with the intense wave of energy, but it unbelievably continued maneuvering under its own power for a full three seconds before the second, third and fourth missiles delivered conventional payloads into its glowing armor.

It was that fourth missile which violated the enemy's power plant, setting off a brilliant release of energy that ripped the dying warship's hull apart in a spherical cloud of fragments, most no larger than a thumbnail.

A cheer arose on the bridge as Podsy unstrapped himself from his chair and moved toward the worst-injured member of the bridge crew—Lieutenant Greenburg, the *William Wallace*'s Ground Control Officer.

Podsy saw that Greenburg was still alive but was unconscious and bleeding from his left ear while his head lay at an unnatural angle atop his neck. Podsy activated the direct line to Sickbay. "This is the XO. We need a medical team to the bridge immediately."

"We're a little busy down here, Lieutenant," Doc Fellows deadpanned as the sounds of screaming men and women came through the doctor's mic, "but I'll send a corpsman up as fast as I can. Do what you can in the meantime."

Podsy wanted to argue but suspected that things were worse in Sickbay than they were on the bridge. "Acknowledged." He cut the line and beckoned one of the sensor operators. "Help me get him down on the deck so we can stabilize his spine."

The petty officer did as bidden, and a few seconds later, they had successfully secured Greenburg to a trauma board, which was part of the bridge's first aid cupboard. Then, to his surprise, a corpsman appeared on the bridge and took over triage while Podsy returned his attention to the rest of the bridge.

The sensor officer was making a report to General Moon. "They hollowed out two of the larger craters on Phobos' surface, General," Sensors explained, pulling up new topographical images of the moon's surface, "and were hiding in there. Early indications are that they've been there for a long time, possibly years."

"Why come out now?" Tactical asked.

"Because our sensors aren't afflicted by whatever virus they might have wormed into the Solarians' systems," Podsy concluded, drawing an affirmative nod from the general. "Phobos was coming closer to our position, and the Jemmin apparently decided the risk of detection and coming under fire while stationary outweighed the risk of engagement."

"In other words," Tactical cocked his head in confusion, "they blinked? That doesn't sound like the Jemmin."

"No, it doesn't," General Moon agreed. "They had some

other motive for coming out when they did. Comm, I want a full breakdown of every transmission those ships sent out."

"You think they were sending a message to the surface," Podsy concluded, silently cursing himself for not considering the possibility.

"I do." Moon nodded as the ship's second-shift ground control officer arrived on the bridge. "Mr. Styles," the general greeted him, gesturing to the GC station, where Podsy was still working on collating the data streams that had just resumed from the Legion's mechs on the surface. "You're up."

"Yes, sir, General," Styles acknowledged, moving to the GC station and placing the bloody headset previously worn by Lieutenant Greenburg over his ears. It took him just a few seconds to make his first report. "Dragon 2nd Company has secured the fuel depot and is moving to reinforce Clover..." His voice trailed off before declaring, "Colonel Jenkins and Clover have secured Echo Base, General. Clover has eighteen fully operational mechs remaining and has already taken control of Echo's automated defenses."

"We've got our foothold," Moon said triumphantly. "Prepare Captain Koch's people for deployment as soon as we've secured overwatch territory."

"Yes, sir, General," Styles acknowledged before sending the orders down the line.

"What about Dragon 1st Company and Scooter?" Podsy pressed after Styles had finished relaying the general's orders. He saw that Dragon 2nd Company had already secured its target facility: a relatively low-value fuel depot that supplied much of the surface industry with tritium and deuterium.

Styles shook his head. "They're still encountering resistance, but have secured sixty percent of the compound, Lieutenant. They've lost two mechs, with another down-checked... and two Marines are reported KIA."

"They're behind schedule." Podsy scowled, not indifferent to the losses. The longer the op played out, the more people would die. Efficiency was critical to survival. Because he cared, it concerned him that they were behind.

"And taking greater losses than we'd hoped." Moon stroked his chin in thought. "No battle follows the plan. The major still has forty minutes to complete her assignment before we lose our op tempo, and she has my confidence she'll get the job done. Still," he allowed, "a little aerial support might expedite matters. Don't you agree, XO?"

"Yes, sir." Podsy prepared a new set of orders, which he relayed to Lieutenant Commander Knighton, whose Vipers had completed their rearmaments and were ready to launch as soon as the *William Wallace* was in position.

"Copy that, Yellowhammer," Xi acknowledged after receiving Commander Knighton's update. "We'll keep an eye out for you."

Elvira's fifteen-kilo guns fired in rapid succession, sending high-explosive shells screaming through the air toward a particularly well-fortified transfer facility near the inner edge of the Schiaparelli Compound twenty-four kilometers away. As those shells soared toward their targets, Xi drove *Elvira* straight at a recently-exposed nest containing a handful of rebels armed with shoulder-fired missiles. The rebels, two hundred meters away, fired a pair of RPGs at *Elvira*.

The first grenade struck her front left leg near the hull joint, and the second hit the armored roof just right of the mech's midline. Both impacts registered as pain through Xi's neural link, but neither was bad enough to break her focus as she destroyed them with chain-gun fire while loading four SRMs into her port launcher. Xi sent the missiles screaming through the air toward the twenty-four-kilometer-distant target, but less than a quarter second after she had done so, a pair of Marines sent railgun bolts into the same facility. She realized they had begun their leaps before she had fired the SRMs, and as their railgun bolts slammed into the facility, it exploded as something unstable was cooked off by the Marines' fire.

She gritted her teeth in annoyance. The Marines were good at what they did. *Very* good. But Colonel Jenkins' guidelines for joint operations made clear that 'fire-hopping' (the term used by Terran Marines to describe their patented jump-up-and-fire maneuver) should be treated as artillery, which required the Marines to forward their targets and anticipated fire windows to the Legion's Jocks to avoid inefficient and potentially dangerous overlap of heavy ordnance on targets, along with the waste of good missiles.

Her SRMs slammed into the rubble, further scattering the building's bones but having little effect otherwise. This wasn't the first instance of sub-optimal collaboration between the Marines and mechs, but the good news was that none of the shortcomings had cost them.

Yet.

"Tighten up, people," Xi snapped irritably as she painted a handful of remaining targets that had featured hostile move-ment in the last few minutes. "We've got vengeful angels inbound."

She forwarded the target locations to Lieutenant Commander Knighton, who acknowledged receipt of the pack-ages via the P2P link. Six Vipers flying in a pair of offset trian-gles plunged toward the Schiaparelli Crater at high speed. Rebel SAMs shot up in reply, most of which originated from the locations Xi had just painted for Knighton's people. Knighton's Vipers, hurtling toward the ground at four thousand kilometers per hour, seemed to ignore the inbound SAMs before suddenly breaking formation, splitting wide in a maneuver that seemed certain to induce fatal gee forces as the triads broke apart.

The SAMs burned skyward, passing harmlessly through the enlarged Viper formation before the aerospace fighters moved just as quickly to resume their formation as they had moved to abandon it. The entire sequence took just three seconds from start to finish, and as the Vipers resumed their dive, it was as though they had never broken apart.

Xi did not have extensive experience working alongside interceptors, but she doubted a more impressive display of combat acrobatics was possible.

Punctuating their maneuvering, the Vipers unleashed a storm of railgun bolts at the bunkers and other fortified rebel weapons positions. Plumes of dust erupted beneath each impact point, with one of the buildings exploding in an honest-to-God fireball that belched up through the thin Martian atmosphere. The fireball quickly consumed itself, leaving a black cloud climbing into the golden sky.

1st Company continued to pour artillery shells into their targets, while the Marine fire-hops added to the destruction. *Cyclops* sent a devastating ball of plasma into a nearby pile of two-cubic-meter platinum ingots, behind which another fire team of rebels had hidden in the hope of getting an up-the-skirt shot on Xi's people as they moved by. Unfortunately for them and for the platinum's former owners, the entire pile was thrown apart by the raging fireball delivered by Blinky's heavy plasma cannon.

Two minutes after the airstrike, *Elvira's* sensors finally stopped showing hostile movements across the Schiaparelli Crater.

She gritted her teeth in annoyance at seeing that her missile mech, *Sargon*, had unexpectedly been knocked out of the fight midway through the push to secure the compound. The crew had survived the ordeal, and it seemed that with a little TLC, the missile mech would be able to take the field again, but she was uncertain if she would be able to count on its contributions when it came time to secure the beanstalks.

"Thanks for the assist, Yellowhammer," Xi said gratefully as the Vipers began to climb skyward. "We'll take it from here."

"Copy that, Dragon Actual." Knighton moved her interceptors to a more secure altitude so they could assist in providing overwatch while the disparate Legion forces reconsolidated back at Echo Base.

"This is Dragon Actual to Scooter Team," she called. "Deploy seeker drones and proceed to Echo Base."

"Dragon Actual, this is Lieutenant Worthington," the Marine CO responded promptly.

"Go ahead, Lieutenant," she said, still smarting over the fire overlap and other hiccups in their joint operation.

"Our dropship can collect and return us to Echo in a sixth the time it takes your armor to roll there," he said matter-of-factly. "Recommend we perform some low-altitude sweeps and poke our noses into a few more of these buildings before pulling out."

She considered the proposal and thought she would deny his request, but after a moment's thought, she knew it was the right call. There might still be heavy weapons secreted throughout the compound, and with Commander Knighton in overwatch, the Marines would have plenty of fire support if they kicked over something too hot for them to handle alone.

"Good call, Lieutenant," she agreed. "But I want to muster at Echo no later than three hours from my mark. Mark."

"Copy that, ma'am," Worthington affirmed. "Echo muster in two-five-niner minutes and fifty-four seconds."

"Good work, Lieutenant," she said with genuine feeling.

They'd had their missteps, and they had plenty of kinks to iron out, but it was clear that the colonel was right: putting Marines and Metalheads together was going to pay big dividends. "Even with double the mechs, it would have taken us twice the time to secure this compound."

"Shields and spears, Major," he said knowingly, referring to a classic line from Terran military philosophy regarding the division of combat roles between the Republic's various Armed Forces branches. She couldn't help but chafe a little at his inference.

"I think we're a little more than just shields, Lieutenant," she chided before adding, "and I think you're a little more than just spears."

"Fair enough, ma'am." He chuckled. "We'll see you back at the barn. Worthington out."

6

BUTTING HEADS

"Keep those MK-32s vertical!" Xi barked after climbing down *Elvira's* gangplank and seeing a small team of Metalheads struggling to set up a missile-intercept rocket bank. MK-32s were just one of the many plug-and-play pop-up defensive fixtures the *Vercingetorix* had dropped from low altitude after depositing Captain Koch and his support vehicles six kilometers to the south of Echo Base. "The backup alignment gimbals are fluid-filled." She grunted, making sure her EVA suit's comm link was set to the correct channel. "If you tip them over past thirty degrees even for a few seconds, you can throw the whole system out of alignment."

"Fluid-filled?" Specialist Jackson repeated incredulously. He was a recent transfer from the New Africa Planetary Defense Force. "Were they stupid for making it that way, or were we stupid for ordering it?"

"Everyone tries to cut costs, especially when they've got guaranteed delivery clauses in their contracts." Xi smirked as she helped them slowly set the two-meter-tall, three-meter-wide rocket pod that carried thirty-two versatile missile-intercept rockets. "And besides, beggars can't be choosers. Word is we traded New Ukraine's Colonial Guard a case of eighty-year-old whisky from General Pushkin's private stock and got every single one of these babies they had in stock."

"You're not serious?" Jackson blinked in confusion, prompting Xi to snicker as the third member of the group performed a diagnostic on the MK-32's virtual systems. "Are you?"

"As a cultural revolution," Xi replied before conspiratorially adding, "But it's probably best not to tell the general. You know how he is about his whisky," she said, miming the laying of a finger to her nose even though the visor prevented any contact.

Jackson shook his head in bewilderment, drawing another laugh from Xi as the kneeling technician declared, "This one checks out, Major."

"Good." She nodded. "Bolt it down and go get another one."

"Where do you want us to secure this one, Major?" Jackson asked.

She made a show of looking up at the relatively open sky surrounding their location before gesturing to the pod. "Looks just fine where it is, Specialist."

"Yes, ma'am." He snapped a salute before resuming his work. She glanced around, seeing repair crews doing minor work to some of the damaged Razorbacks, including Colonel Jenkins' *Warcrafter*. She made her way over to the colonel's mech, finding the gangplank down and outer airlock door open.

After passing through the airlock, she found the colonel already in a conference with Major Tim Trapper Jr., Captain Chao, and Marine Lieutenant Briggs.

"Major," Jenkins greeted her as she doffed her helmet. "Good of you to join us."

"My apologies, Colonel," she said rigidly. "We ran into a few stubborn ticks buried in Scooter's fur."

"We had our own here," he sympathized before inclining his

chin toward Lieutenant Briggs, "but the lieutenant and his men made short work of them with a six-way blitz down the tunnels."

"Fast and furious, Colonel," Briggs said professionally, with just a hint of the healthy cockiness Xi had come to expect from the Marines. "We don't know any other way."

Trapper drawled, "I can vouch for that."

"Did you encounter any Jemmin weapons here, Colonel?" Xi asked.

Jenkins shook his head. "None. Everything at Echo was designed and built by Solarians."

"Which suggests," Lieutenant Briggs mused, "that either something prevented them from distributing their weapons farther than Schiaparelli, or they chose not to put any here."

"Echo Base is a key strategic point in this hemisphere." Jenkins cocked his head dubiously, gesturing to the holographic map before them. "It doesn't make sense that they'd leave it less-than-optimally protected if their goal was to secure Mars against human repossession."

Trapper rubbed his jaw thoughtfully. "Records in the base's few remaining data cores show it wasn't a full-blown military insurrection, but more an abandonment of the facility. The men and women who manned this fort up and walked away only four days after the Mars rebellion became official. There was a lot of confusion from the look of things, so much that we probably won't find much of value in the records."

"I've got technicians aboard the *Red Hare* and the *William Wallace* working to break down the data." Jenkins nodded irritably. "But their prognosis is like yours; it will probably take too long to find anything useful. What we do know is that the vehicles and platforms in the trenches weren't manned by Martian military but by enthusiastic rebels."

"They sure hit harder than most industrial colonists."

Trapper scowled. "I haven't seen that kind of discipline any lower than a high-performing PDF unit."

"The One Mind system lets people adapt quickly to new roles," Xi observed. "They must have downloaded, or installed, or whatever it is they call it," she waved dismissively, "when they add some kind of expertise to their synthetic neural hardware. But with the Martian One Mind network offline since just a few days after Antivenom, they were essentially stuck with whatever they had."

"That had to have been disorienting," Briggs mused. "If they're used to simply downloading whatever they need on demand, they probably hunkered down wherever they were, or just continued with whatever plans they'd had when the network went down."

"Commodore Kline's latest intel confirms your theory," Jenkins agreed. "Surface imagery, taken from the days before and after the One Mind went offline, shows rebel movement plummeted to less than five percent after the network crashed."

"Score another one for individualism." Trapper smirked.

"You can say that again," Xi affirmed before giving voice to rising concerns regarding the group's relative lack of urgency. "When do we roll on the beanstalks, Colonel?"

"Setting up the new defenses will take four hours at minimum," Jenkins replied. Both Trapper and Briggs nodded in agreement. Captains Chao and Hoa, on the other hand, seemed less than enthusiastic about this particular response.

"Begging pardon, Colonel," Xi said in surprise. "but with the Vipers and warships in overwatch, we could empty the fort and commence our charge now without seriously endangering our foothold."

"We stuck the landing, Major, which was no mean feat," Jenkins replied measuredly. "But it's too early for another charge. Clover's got three mechs that couldn't sprint for more than five kilometers before blowing their drive trains, and 1st has two more, according to your report."

"I understand we're diminished, Colonel." She shook her head defiantly. "But we've still got enough strength to secure the beanstalks under the original plan. Those elevators are the most valuable pieces of infrastructure on Mars, sir. We can't risk them by waiting for a couple extra mechs. Time is our friend, not the additional firepower."

Captain Chao interjected, "Colonel Jenkins, what if we pull the Vipers off overwatch, reassign them to aerial support of the charges, and immediately proceed to Hansel & Gretel with whatever metal can make the run? If we keep the down-checks here for repairs, they can provide local fire support in the event we missed rebel elements during the sweeps around Echo. This way, we don't completely empty the fort, and we maintain operational tempo while securing the space elevators. Without those elevators, the Martian industrial capacity will be functionally cut off from humanity's war effort."

"I'm aware of the strategic value of those beanstalks." Jenkins blew out a long breath. "But we put down and gained a foothold in less than three hours. For a planet the size and developmental level of Mars, that's already a record. If we pull the Vipers off overwatch and have them clear our approaches to Hansel & Gretel, we lose our ability to reinforce from the air. We've already encountered Jemmin assets on Martian soil, to say nothing of those in orbit. We need to proceed methodically, four hours to repair and resupply. It's my call, and I've made it."

"I agree," Lieutenant Briggs confirmed, drawing a nod from Major Trapper. "The rebels aren't in a position to respond quickly enough with Martian assets. I don't doubt we'll encounter more Jemmin weapons, but if they could have cut the 'stalks, they would have already done it. That leads me to think there aren't that many Jemmin assets planetside."

Xi shook her head adamantly. "I'm sorry, that doesn't track. Those warships in overwatch could have blown the beanstalks down, but instead they engaged our warships. That engagement might have bought them a few more minutes of flight, but that was all it ended up doing. They had to have known that, but they still called the play."

"What are you implying, Major?" Jenkins wasn't amused.

She bit back an angry retort. "I'm saying, Colonel, that scrapping the beanstalks wasn't Jemmin's top priority down here. There's something else going on, which makes *me* think," she sliced an annoyed look toward Lieutenant Briggs, "we need to keep 'fast and furious' as our operational pace until we have better intel. Also, if we suppose the Jemmin would have destroyed the beanstalks already if they wanted to, I have to assume they need them for some reason. I don't care why, but I think that gives us some latitude until we can deny the enemy that asset. "

"Every book written on warfare urges caution while suffering an intelligence deficit, Major," Trapper offered.

"That's true." Xi wasn't backing down. "But I doubt there's a book written on warfare that would endorse using a force the size of ours to besiege an industrial planet like Mars. Slow and steady can and does win wars, Major Trapper, but this *isn't* a war. This is a multi-zone capture-the-flag op on a planetary scale. Speed is *everything*. We already know the rebels have surface-to-air missile capability, and until we establish defensive shells around those beanstalks, they're vulner—"

"That's enough, Major," Jenkins interrupted sharply. "I've made my decision; we roll on Phase Two in three hours fifty-two minutes or when the last pop-ups are online, whichever comes first."

Xi wanted to argue further, and while it seemed that Captains Chao and Hao were in support of her position, some battles were best conceded in order to win the war. They were outranked, and the truth was that precious few decisions made at this level of a military hierarchy were better than sixty-forty propositions.

Xi saw this as a relatively extreme example of, to her mind, an obvious mistake in the big picture sense, but she also knew she didn't know everything. Colonel Jenkins and Major Trapper had each been doing this for *decades*, and even Lieutenant Briggs was a ten-year veteran of the TRMC. Despite her lofty rank, Xi had only seen active duty for a little over a year. These men had forgotten more about warfare than she had learned in her brief career.

"Understood, sir." She braced to attention, snapping a salute and doing her best to keep her frustration from showing. "Request permission to assist in erecting the defenses."

"Granted." Jenkins nodded, prompting her to turn on her heel. Before she replaced her vacuum helmet, he called, "And Major, good work at the Crater. We needed that win to be on-time, and you delivered."

"Thank you, Colonel, but we didn't do it alone," she replied smartly before replacing her helmet and making her way outside.

Once there, and after ensuring that her suit's mic was off, she screamed so loud her neural implants' noise-canceling systems activated, muffling her voice to her own ears and leaving the low-pitch reverberations in her skull as the only sounds she could consciously process.

And if she questioned the patronage and sexual proclivities of the colonel, the major, and Marine Lieutenant during that frustrated scream, she might have felt a small measure of shame at losing *that* much control, even in the heat of the moment.

She stopped in her tracks a dozen paces from *Warcrafter's* gangplank and drew a series of long, steadying breaths. She soon caught sight of Lieutenant Staubach, who was working with Lieutenant Quinn to repair *Black Widow*'s damaged right rear leg.

As she strode toward them, Blinky greeted her with, "What's the good word, Major?"

"How long until you're finished with this?" she asked, ignoring the pleasantry since she felt anything but pleasant at that particular moment.

Quinn gestured to the twenty-centimeter sleeve of metal. "We've already replaced the rotational bearing, but if we've got the time, we'd like to run a full diagnostic of the hydraulics. There's a leak somewhere we haven't been able to pin down, but it's not bad enough to hold her out of the fight."

"How long will the diagnostic take?" Xi pressed.

"Forty-one minutes, ma'am," Quinn replied promptly, and it seemed from her tone that she knew Xi wasn't pleased with something.

To forestall concern, Xi waved dismissively. "It's not you guys. I tried to convince the colonel to roll on Hansel & Gretel ASAP, but he insists we lock down Echo and patch our dings and dents first." She gestured in disgust toward *Black Widow*'s disassembled leg joint.

"He's got a point, Major," Blinky observed staidly, trying not to inflame Xi. And it was that note in his voice, the not-quite-fearful-but still-worried-for-his-own-ass tone in his words, that finally banished the last of Xi's lingering resentment at being overruled by Colonel Jenkins. She had no problem snapping people up, or even breaking them down if the situation called for it. But she absolutely did not want her subordinates and fellow Metalheads thinking she was some capricious tyrant.

She exhaled in frustration. "Of course he does, Blinky. That's not my point. My point is that we've been on this rock for four hours, and shock and awe doesn't even come close to describing how effectively we've accomplished our Phase One objectives. If I were the enemy, I'd be cowering in my foxhole right now wondering if I really wanted anything to do with the metal monsters that fell from the skies."

Quinn laughed nervously, with Blinky following suit before replying, "I was a little worried for a second there, ma'am. You can't take any of this stuff personally." He waved toward *Warcrafter*. "War's a business like any other, and the colonel's in charge. I'm sure you voiced your concerns eloquently."

She shook her head. "Maybe. Probably." Her voice trailed off before she aired any discontent to her subordinates. She shook her head in an effort to clear it of lingering doubts. "It's a good plan. It'll work," she said with a confidence she mostly felt before flashing a lopsided grin. "I guess I'm just not used to losing arguments. Get your diagnostics finished, slackers."

Again the lieutenants laughed, and this time it was Quinn who quipped, "Why do you think we ride with you, Major?"

"I thought it was for the view," Xi deadpanned, drawing another round of laughter before she made her way to *Elvira* where, much as she hated to admit it, she had a few semi-pressing maintenance issues to go over.

7

CONUNDRA

"Those missile waves are textbook," Podsy muttered after completing his review of the Solar assault on the Jemmin cruisers. "I've never seen anything so precisely coordinated. Their launch times are accurate to the microsecond, and their accelerations were so perfectly mixed that they would have overwhelmed the Jemmin warships even without our assist."

"Probably," General Moon agreed. "I guess we have to hand the One Minders this much: they know how to coordinate when they're jacked together. Just don't start advocating for it on *my* ship, Lieutenant," he added with a smirk.

"No, sir." Podsy grinned before continuing. "I'll take whatever inefficiency comes with our way of doing things because it's pretty clear that the extra performance," he waved at the frozen holographic image of the missile swarm-mid-flight, "isn't worth the cost if it means exposing an entire star system to something like the Jemmin takeover. Still," he allowed, thinking back to what Jem had said about the prospect of reuniting humanity under a single banner, much as the Jem'un had, "we could probably learn a thing or two from them."

"Maybe," Moon said, not sounding like he believed it.

Podsy examined the latest data from Echo Base and voiced a growing concern. "Why didn't Dragon and Clover immediately advance on the beanstalks after securing the Phase One objectives, General?"

"You think it's a mistake to consolidate their position before advancing?" Moon challenged.

"I think it limits our later options," Podsy explained. "If we had rolled on the beanstalks as soon as we took Echo, we could have removed a handful of high-value assets from rebel control before they had the opportunity to counterattack or sabotage them. That opens up possibilities when it comes to Phase Three of the op. By holding back, we're narrowing our future options."

"Your reasoning appears to be sound." Moon spoke evenly, not giving away his preference. "But attacking too aggressively could have also overextended our forces. This is known as a tactical pause, Lieutenant. The rebels are off-balance after us taking Echo, Scooter, and other locations. The Solarian psyche profiles suggest this will knock them on their heels. When the colonel resumes operations, you can be sure the rebels will not be in a hurry to turn their positions into impact craters. They've been almost as good as a well-trained military force so far, but they'll break down after sustaining continuous losses as Dragon rolls through their positions. The pause gives us a chance to reinforce the advance before proceeding with Phase Two. If we hadn't discovered Jemmin weapons on Martian soil and Jemmin warships in orbit, a sprint to Phase Two would have been correct, but with the added variables, I also recommend caution."

"I understand the reasoning, General, but when it comes to coin flips like this, I pick the speed option every time."

Moon chuckled. "Now, where have I heard that before?"

"Sir?"

"Never mind, Lieutenant." Moon shook his head.

Commodore Kline cleared his throat, drawing the general's attention. "Yes, Commodore?"

"In general, Solar strategies align with Lieutenant Podsednik's," Kline replied. "Considering the sole known failure points in this operation are the space elevators, securing them, even at significant cost, is of paramount importance."

"You would prefer the colonel executes a sprint to Hansel & Gretel?" Moon asked.

"That was not the purpose of my comment, General. We requested Terran aid in this matter, not only because of political complications, but also because your people have extensive experience in these operations. Sol has not executed a large-scale ground invasion in over a century. We understand the value of operational experience and institutional knowledge, both of which the Terran Armor Corps clearly possesses in sufficient quantity to execute this mission."

Moon quirked a hollow grin. "Some might suggest that what you're really trying to say is you're content to sit back and observe the results."

"We are not as callous as that, General." Kline visibly stiffened, and to Podsy, it was becoming increasingly clear that Solarians were not as adept as Terrans at concealing or moderating their emotions. The connection to the One Mind system likely played some part in this almost comical deficiency, which all Solar delegates except Alice had demonstrated on multiple occasions. "Mars is of great cultural and economic value to Sol," the commodore continued, gaining some small measure of control over his expression as he spoke. "To say nothing of its strategic importance to human affairs. There is more industrial capacity on or beneath Mars' surface than on every other human-controlled world, Solar or Terran, *combined.*"

"Even Earth?" Podsy blurted in surprise.

"Even Earth." Kline nodded gravely, again displaying more

emotion than any Terran might in the same circumstances. But despite his outward emotional displays, his words continued with the clarity and precision Podsy had come to expect of Solarians. "For a variety of reasons irrelevant to the moment, Earth's industrial architecture is based on a model of self-sustenance, not the generation of surplus. If the population of Earth was suddenly reduced to less than one-twentieth of its current level, Earth's surplus industrial capacity would equal that on Mars due to the reduction in local demand. But barring a catastrophe of that magnitude, Mars represents the single greatest industrial resource in the human sphere."

"That seems...tactically unsound," General Moon remarked. "Specializing is key to maximizing individual contributions, but too much specialization and dependence is something we Terrans learned to avoid after paying a heavy price in human lives. Maintaining an industrial surplus is, to any Terran, an obvious component of maintaining national security."

"Our species' most valuable resource is the human mind, General, not the product of our hands and physical labors." Kline shrugged. "The One Mind does not require extensive material resources to operate. The maintenance of the virtual systems is inconsequential compared with the cost of an ever-growing industrial base."

"General," Sensors called, "we've got movement near the Southern Transit Hub."

"XO," Moon commanded, and Podsy made his way to the sensor pit, where a trio of operators was dissecting new data streams from the surface.

A quick review of their data showed a handful of vehicles emerging from the Southern Transit Hub, which was to be 2nd Company's objective as soon as Captain Winters landed with his Nuggets and Flakes. "They look to be mobile SRM and LRM platforms, General," Podsednik reported urgently while double-checking the findings. "Six Hwacha-class SRM systems and four Tranquility-class LRM trucks. Radiological scans show active warheads aboard two of the Tranquilities. They've stopped moving. Estimated time to launch, twenty seconds!"

"Helm, orient the ship for surface bombardment of the Southern Transit Hub," the general barked. "Tactical, you are weapons free to engage those LRMs."

"Targeting LRMs," Tactical acknowledged as the ship spun and twisted around them, inducing mild vertigo as it aligned its railguns at the enemy missile platforms. "Firing in five...four..."

"Your orders for ground forces, General?" Styles asked as Tactical made his countdown.

"...one...firing!" Tactical declared, and the *William Wallace* sent a four-pack of tungsten bolts into the cluster of vehicles. Three scored direct hits against the mobile LRM platforms, while the fourth near-missed its target with devastating effect.

Omnidirectional showers of dust and debris burst, with the farthest bits landing a kilometer from the impact points. Almost as an afterthought, all but one of the Hwacha-class SRM launchers were destroyed by the multi-kiloton bolts, and after just two seconds, Sensors confidently reported, "Tranquility platforms neutralized, General."

"Run an active sweep of the Southern Hub," Moon commanded, referring to the planned insertion point to the subterranean industrial complex they would need to secure during the operation's Phase Three. "Those launchers could have targeted either of the beanstalks, but we could have intercepted the missiles in-flight. At that range, I doubt the rebels would have come out of concealment for a Hail Mary. They're hiding something. Find what it is. Now."

"Yes, General," Sensors acknowledged. "Deploying seismic probes and local EM pickups," he declared as the *William*

Wallace fired a pair of rockets carrying the indicated sensor gear toward the Southern Hub.

The general turned to Chief Styles. "Ground Control, inform Colonel Jenkins of our bombardment at the Southern Hub."

Styles did as commanded and quickly replied, "Colonel Jenkins acknowledges update and confirms operational timetable. Two hours, thirteen minutes before crossing the line of departure on Phase Two."

"Very good." Moon's features and tone did nothing to betray whatever emotions he might have had at receiving Jenkins' reply.

"Initial scan complete, General," Sensors reported. "No EM detected at the Southern Hub. Nothing on thermals, either. Seismic probes will reach the target area in four minutes."

"*Red Hare*'s telemetry confirms ours, General," Podsy reported after checking the forwarded sensor data. "*Vercingetorix* is still deploying Captain Koch's Jokers to Echo Base and is unable to assist in the sweep."

"Keep our guns loaded and eyes peeled until those seismics hit the ground," Moon ordered before switching over to the CIG channel. "Commander Knighton, scramble three formations to conduct ongoing sweeps of the Southern Hub and surrounding grids."

"Yes, sir," she acknowledged, and the first pair of Vipers detached from the *William Wallace*'s hull mere seconds later. The interceptors were working overtime, already at nearly double their anticipated flight time this far into the op, and surprisingly had not suffered any serious damage. Knighton was even better than he remembered, but General Moon was pushing her people past the redline.

Podsy hesitated before voicing his concerns on that front.

"General, the Vipers haven't yet undergone their mandatory post-flight inspections."

"Standard protocols are overridden during War God." Moon sliced him a final look. "The ships will be fine. What worries me more is their pilots. They all passed the redline on neuro-stims during their last missions. I've already got Doc Fellows pumping counteracting cocktails into them, but I wouldn't be surprised to see a few of these pilots never fly again after War God due to neural burnout. We've learned a lot about the human brain, but the biggest thing is just how delicate it is. And *nobody* knows that better than an interceptor pilot."

"Second Viper formation away, General," reported Commander Knighton from the cockpit of her interceptor. "Third formation to launch in twenty seconds."

"Roger, Commander," Moon acknowledged. "Good hunting."

"Your people operate efficiently, General." As the commodore spoke, the third pair of Vipers released from their cradles and sped toward the Southern Hub.

"You expected otherwise, Commodore?"

"Frankly, yes," Kline replied, seemingly oblivious to the general's souring mood. "Our briefings on Terran Armed Forces protocol painted a very different picture than the one I've observed aboard your vessel. I suspect Jemmin played a larger role in misshaping Solar sentiment than we initially suspected."

"To be equally frank," Moon replied after a moment's pause, "your people have performed precisely as we expected they would. That missile barrage on the Jemmin cruisers was exemplary."

Kline broke into an unguarded grin. "Your point, then, is that Terra has a better measure of Sol than Sol has of Terra?"

"That's not how I'd put it." Moon slowly returned the grin. "But I wouldn't argue with someone who did."

Kline chuckled, turning a pointed look in Podsy's direction. "For all our differences, we still have more in common than not."

Podsy felt as though that last bit was aimed precisely at him and Xi for supporting a continued sprint across Mars instead of the methodical approach adopted by Colonel Jenkins.

And for the briefest of moments, as he came to realize the commodore was suggesting that Podsy and Xi both thought more like Solarians than Terrans, he understood what Nietzsche had meant about looking into the abyss.

And that particular thought chilled him to the bone.

8

PLAYING TO THE SYMPHONY

With the opening guitar riff of Megadeth's *Symphony of Destruction* playing throughout the Legion's mechs, Colonel Jenkins finally gave the order. "Metalheads, we are go for Phase Two. All units execute your tactical plans. Let's rock!"

The vehicles of the Metal Legion leapt out of Echo Base, surging toward their assigned targets Major Xi Bao led 1st Company, supported by Lieutenant Worthington's Marines, to the eastern space elevator code-named "Gretel," while Colonel Jenkins led the eighteen sprint-capable Razorbacks of Clover Battalion to the western "Hansel."

"And no offense, Blinky," Jenkins chided as the vehicles sped out from the now fully-secured facility, nearing the cut-off point for cross-talk between individual mechs attached to the divergent missions, "but next time, you might opt for some *real* metal like this instead of that dreck we listened to during drop."

"Everyone's a critic." Staubach sighed, drawing a chuckle from both Jenkins and his Jock, Krauthammer. "I just don't know how you can argue that a group with 'metal' right there in the name *isn't* 'real metal,' Colonel."

"You know what they say about truth in advertising, Lieutenant," Xi piped in. "And is it just me, or is it a little weird that *we're* lecturing *you* on judging something by its appearance, Mr. I-just-won-a-staring-contest-with-sixty-nine-other-Jocks."

"Sixty-nine?" Blinky deadpanned. "Thought you'd slip that one by me, did you, Major?"

"Fifty sovereigns says he fails the post-op drug tests," Captain Chao unexpectedly put in. "Nobody can hold their eyes open that long without pharmaceutical assistance."

"Don't be a sore loser, Chao." Hammer laughed. "Second place isn't all bad."

"Second is the first loser," Chao quipped.

"Operation clocks are at two-forty-one and thirty seconds on my mark..." Jenkins called. "Mark. Local comm only from now until all objectives secured," he ordered, receiving acknowledgments from each mech before he ended the Legion-wide comm link.

As the Metal Legion advanced on the pair of beanstalks, the *William Wallace* moved into a low-orbit to deploy Captain Winters and 2nd Company on the third Phase Two target of the operation.

Despite Major Xi's objections, Jenkins saw the operation as proceeding apace. They had encountered as much resistance as anticipated at Echo and Scooter, though some of that resistance had come in the form of Jemmin hardware rather than rebel-seized Solar assets.

All told, War God was going as well as could be expected, which always left a lingering dread in Jenkins' mind. Because in his experience, *nothing* in an operation of this scale went according to plan.

"Contact!" *Sargon* declared as a series of icons appeared in 1st Company's path less than an hour into the advance on Gretel.

"Break and engage," Xi barked, prompting her Metalheads to break formation and unleash a storm of ordnance on the newly-appeared formation, sixty kilometers to the east.

In reply, the enemy sent their own hail of fire, consisting primarily of Solar railguns. The railgun bolts traveled along gently arcing trajectories before delivering their destructive energies into the midst of Xi's ten fully-functional 1st Company mechs. Elvira was spared during the initial exchange, and as damage reports came back to her HUD, she saw that while accurate and voluminous, the rebel fire had been relatively ineffective.

Solar railguns and Terran railguns differed in a key respect: Solar hardware was limited to standard railgun velocities, which generally kept their projectiles from exceeding four or five kilometers per second. Terran railguns, on the other hand, incorporated certain highly-classified elements into their design that permitted them to accelerate tungsten slivers or needles to near-relativistic speeds. As a result, while Terran railgun bolts were only tiny fractions the size of their Solar counterparts, they had far greater penetrative power and were much more likely to do major damage to internal components.

There was considerable debate regarding how Terra had managed to make this particular technological advance while their richer, better-organized Solar cousins had failed to do likewise. Some even suggested that Terra had stolen the tech, or received it in an unauthorized exchange, which would have violated Illumination League laws. Xi didn't really care how her people came by the tech but was glad to see it used to full effect when a pair of railgun-equipped mechs in 1st Company scored instant kills on their Solar counterparts with precision railgun fire.

"Scratch two," she declared while forwarding new targets to her company's mechs. As she did, she saw the first images of the enemy vehicles and was momentarily taken aback.

They were sleek, low-lying, and shaped like rounded arrowheads, with a distinctive wedge shape from bow to stern. Their armor was a bright gold color, and after accelerating for just six seconds, they were moving at two hundred ten kilometers per hour.

"Damn..." she hissed as the enemy scattered, having emerged from a pair of previously-concealed foxholes. "Those things are *fast*." She double-checked the vehicles' estimated masses and found that they were all comparable to heavy cruiser-grade mechs. Whatever they were using for motive power was a full step better than anything the Legion had available.

As the golden tanks scattered, her Metalheads rained artillery fire down on them. Shell after shell splashed into Martian soil, with the first strikes missing by several dozen meters each.

"Are those Jemmin?" *Sargon* asked while sending a flight of SRMs into the dispersing tanks. Surprisingly, the enemy vehicles sent out streams of coil gun fire and scrapped the majority of the missiles mid-flight.

"Negative," Quinn said confidently as both *Plague Maiden* and *Ebola May* prepared another storm of SRMs against the dispersing vehicles. "They're putting out standard Solar fusion core footprints."

"They're moving *that fast* with standard power cores?" Blinky asked disbelievingly as his heavy plasma cannon charged, thrumming in eager anticipation of the destruction it was about to unleash. When it reached full charge, *Cyclops'* HPC hurled a blue-white portal to hell into the enemy's midst. Predictably, the rebels used their superior speed and maneuverability to evade the roaring ball of plasma before it crashed into the ground. The wedge-shaped mechs avoided the worst of the damage as the plasma projectile threw a cloud of fiery debris two hundred meters into the air.

But Xi was far from disappointed, because none of the Metalheads had expected his plasma cannon to score a direct hit. Instead, as the plasma bolt had soared through the thin atmosphere, *Plague Maiden* and *Ebola May* fired thirty-two SRMs apiece on the predictably-scattering rebels. Sixty-four missiles streaked out, divided evenly among eight targets, and this time even the rebels' formidable counterfire was unable to shield them from Dragon's fiery breath.

Three of the rebel vehicles suffered direct hits, with one destroyed outright by a trio of center-mass strikes. Another was flipped over by a strike directly beneath it that violated a capacitor, scrapping the vehicle's starboard flank and leaving the overturned mech's innards exposed, like a turtle that swallowed a lit firecracker. The third was hit hard in the port flank by a missile, which tore a four-meter chunk of armored hull from its frame. Despite the catastrophic damage, which should have been lethal to anyone within, the battered mech sped away from the impact zone, albeit at half its previous speed.

"Artillery," Xi barked, sending a pair of HE shells downrange, "suppressing fire! Corral them into kill-chutes for the twins."

The company's artillery rained down shell after shell, with *Elvira's* dual fifteens pumping ordnance into the air as fast as they could cycle. Xi sent sixteen shells into the fleeing rebels, two of which managed near-misses, while a third somehow struck a lucky blow against the already-damaged vehicle.

Even the direct hit failed to pierce the golden mech's armor, although it did leave a two-meter gash in its topside. Smoke poured out from the mech's interior, and a few seconds later, the vehicle came to a screeching halt before exploding in a fiery ball suggestive of a liquid fuel flash.

As the remaining arrowheads fled, *Plague Maiden* and *Ebola May* unleashed another storm of missiles flying low over the Martian plain. *Sargon* added a dozen SRMs to the flock, which splashed four more enemy vehicles before a second alarm flared to life on Xi's HUD.

"We've got more hostiles," Xi declared as another dozen arrowheads appeared a hundred kilometers to the north. This second group immediately opened fire with railguns and missiles, hammering deafeningly loud bolts into *Elvira's* starboard hull and temporarily disorienting Xi. Despite her foggy senses, she returned fire with eight MRMs from *Elvira's* launchers.

This second batch of enemy vehicles was far enough away that their impressive counterfire would likely intercept them.

So Xi made a call she had been itching to make since breaking orbit at New America.

"All crews, target Bravo formation and fire for effect on my mark," she intoned before switching to the direct line with *Sargon*. "*Sargon*, give me two P-92-Zs to the following coordinates. Fire on my mark," she commanded, forwarding the target points in the middle of the new enemy formation. "Authorization Bravo Tango Foxtrot Oscar Six Niner."

"Bravo Tango Foxtrot Oscar Six Niner," *Sargon* confirmed before sending a pair of the powerful platforms streaking toward the enemy at as low a trajectory as viable. "On the way, Major."

"Mark," she enthusiastically intoned. "Fire! Fire! Fire!"

A storm of ordnance erupted from Dragon 1st Company's mechs, with a hundred and ten mixed Terran projectiles tearing across the sky. Hidden within that wave of extended-range artillery, hypervelocity railgun slivers, and rocket-propelled hellfire were two pulse missiles of identical design to the one she had called down on herself and Podsy aboard the original *Elvira* on Durgan's Folly. The pulse missiles flew at a significantly lower altitude than the rest of the missiles, which marked them as different from the others but also made them much harder to intercept with coil gun fire.

Railgun bolts stabbed into the enemy vehicles, scratching one outright and causing serious drive train issues for the other. Coil guns sprayed bright red projectiles into the gold Martian sky, sweeping back and forth as the deadly barrage drove steadily nearer.

Explosions punctuated the sky when MRMs were intercepted by precision counterfire as the Terran salvo closed on the rebels, but despite the Martian rebels' best efforts, fifteen Terran projectiles pierced their formidable defensive shell.

Including both pulse missiles.

Brilliant flashes illuminated the flaxen dome of the red planet's skies, each of which would have blinded any nearby human not wearing eye protection. The blast waves of the explosive EMP generators rippled across the Martian soil as each of the missiles struck a bullseye on Xi's targets.

After the radiant flashes had come and gone, and after the shockwaves of their explosive generators finally abated, all of the new Solar-built war machines sat motionless. The EMPs had been precisely attuned for both the Martian atmosphere and the Solar virtual architecture, maximizing their effects on both fronts. Commodore Kline had been reticent to hand over technical details regarding state-of-the-art Solar virtual hardware, but had surprised everyone by doing precisely that in the hope that it might save Solar lives.

"They're stunned," Xi declared triumphantly. "Finish 'em!"

A second wave of ordnance went up, but this one was much more precise and focused. Two MRMs targeted each of the frozen vehicles, which would reboot their systems in a matter of seconds and resume the fight if given the chance.

The Metal Legion had no intention of giving them that chance.

MRMs punched into the defenseless vehicles. When the dust settled, just two Solarian mechs, both belonging to the first group of would-be ambushers, remained mobile.

"Major, this is Lieutenant Worthington," came the Terran Marine's expected communication. "Request permission to break formation and engage those stragglers."

"Permission granted," Xi acknowledged with a fierce grin. "We saved them just for you. After all, it would be rude of us to let you boys go unsatisfied."

"Copy that, ma'am," he replied with a chuckle as his Tripoli-class dropship rocketed toward the fleeing rebel vehicles. Burning across the reddish-brown terrain, the Tripoli moved into railgun range and unleashed a pair of bolts at the fleeing vehicles. Both were hits, with one causing its target to falter, while the other continued burning for all it was worth in a vain effort to flee the engagement zone.

Lieutenant Worthington fired another pair of railgun bolts, both targeting the slower-moving vehicle, and was rewarded with a thoroughly satisfying explosion as the golden-hulled target's power core failed, sending most of its remains skittering across the Martian soil.

Unexpectedly, the last remaining rebel vehicle slowed before coming to a complete stop. "Major, I'm receiving their unconditional surrender on all open frequencies," Lieutenant Worthington said with ambivalent disappointment and satisfaction.

"Confirmed, Lieutenant," Xi acknowledged as she too received their unexpected surrender. "Seeing as you're the closest, I'd appreciate if you did the honors of having them exit their vehicle so you can take them into custody."

"Affirmative, ma'am," Worthington replied. "We're en route, and will have them secure in fifty seconds."

"And, Lieutenant?" she added pointedly. "I'm not familiar with that type of vehicle. Are you?"

"No, Major," he said firmly. "And there was nothing in the Solarian briefing on them either. As far as Terra's concerned, they're new."

"Then consider securing that vehicle a top priority," she declared. "I've never seen anything that size move that fast, and our Wrenches will have a field day examining that armor."

"Understood," Worthington agreed as Xi sent a comm relay drone skyward in preparation to link up with Captain Koch so his people could retrieve the peculiar vehicle while Dragon continued its advance on Gretel.

Impressively, none of her mechs had suffered enough damage to warrant removal from the advance. They had expended a significant amount of ordnance, depleting half of their magazines, but she suspected they had just dealt with the stiffest resistance the rebels could field. This was an ideal patch of ground to execute an ambush, and the enemy had done a decent job of doing just that.

Unfortunately for them, Xi's Metalheads were quite a bit better than "decent," and as a testament to the skill gap between the rebels and Terrans, twenty-three golden-skinned yard ornaments now decorated the Martian soil.

9

A MORTAL MAN

One moment the westward skies were clear, as day slowly gave way to night, then the golden skies turned azure as the Metalheads of Operation War God experienced their first Martian sunset. Unlike planets with thick oxygen-rich atmospheres, Martian sunsets were predominantly blue, while the daytime skies were brownish-gold. Poets had dedicated considerable effort to this dichotomy, with Earth's blue daytime skies reflected only as night falls upon Mars.

But when thirty-four rebel Interceptors appeared in those skies and unleashed a devastating volley of railgun fire on Jenkins' sprinting Razorbacks, poetry couldn't have been farther from his mind.

"Damage report!" Jenkins barked after *Warcrafter* took a pair of rapid-fire hits to its forward armor. An ominous hissing sound, punctuated by the dull buzz of short-circuited electrical current, filled the cabin as *Warcrafter's* Wrench and Monkey burst into action.

"We lost the Number Two relay," shouted Chief Stratton after a quick inspection, "and we're leaking coolant. Closing off the affected areas now."

A check of his tactical display showed that he had already lost four Clover mechs to the barrage, prompting him to declare, "Shattered skies! I say again, shattered skies!"

On his command, the mechs of Clover ceased their sprint and rhythmically unleashed a storm of rockets at the approaching Interceptors. Like the galloping beat of an Iron Maiden track, the missiles poured one after another into the air, streaking toward the inbound hostiles in a relentless wave that would be nearly impossible to avoid.

Clover railguns launched tungsten bolts into the approaching enemy, which darted and juked through the air faster than any human could survive. Lurching this way and that, they evaded all but a pair of lucky strikes from Clover's railguns, but those two hits scored kills on the relatively frail Interceptors.

"Drones..." Jenkins grimaced. It was unlikely that these flyers were fully automated, but whether they were autonomous or remotely operated from somewhere nearby made little difference. The fact that they were unmanned made them significantly harder to hit, but it also made them much easier to destroy since little, if any, consideration was given to their ability to absorb damage.

He watched with grim anticipation as the steady stream of Terran missiles abated, with the mechs having emptied their pre-loaded tubes. And as the first missiles approached the swarm, it dispersed with impressive alacrity. Missiles exploded mid-air rather than sailing past their targets completely, and a trio of the Interceptors was scratched by shrapnel—but that still left twenty-nine inbound hostiles, each armed with a railgun.

And according to the specs provided by Commodore Kline on this particular platform, they would be ready to fire again in twelve seconds.

"Load air-bursters and fire for effect in Blue Nebula pattern," he called as the swarm of interceptors reached the twenty-kilometer mark while rocketing forward at seven hundred kph. "Fire! Fire! Fire!"

The Razorbacks' fifteen-kilo mains roared, sending explosive shells into the approaching swarm. The Interceptor drones scattered, but the Blue Nebula pattern was one designed to funnel enemy aircraft into a handful of kill-zones with staggered shots placed in precise, seemingly unpredictable patterns. Blue Nebula would help determine whether these were automated or remote-operated; if automated, they would see through the seemingly random pattern and evade the entire barrage, but if they were remote-controlled, he would score at least a few kills with this first airburst salvo.

The shells erupted mid-air, and he nodded in approval as his people tore down two more of the drones. It was increasingly likely that these were remote-operated, and that fact would play heavily into the Legion's tactics in neutralizing them. As he formulated those tactics and prepared to send them to the rest of Clover Battalion, the surviving rebel aircraft hurtled toward his position, seemingly heedless of their losses.

And then the second salvo hit.

Warcrafter was rocked port-to-starboard by a trio of heavy hits, each of which was powerful enough to scrap a lesser vehicle outright. But the Razorback Mk 2-V's armor was designed to absorb hits like these, and while meter-wide ablative panels fell away from *Warcrafter's* battered flanks, he knew he could withstand another barrage before he was toast.

As he forwarded his revised orders to the rest of the battalion, his command mech's repair team worked efficiently to patch the damage sustained in the opening salvo. Recent transfers from the TAC HQ on New Britain, Chiefs Stratton and

Carlyle, were proving worthy of their new assignment aboard the command vehicle.

Unfortunately, two more of Clover's Razorbacks were knocked out of the fight in the latest salvo, and Jenkins knew he needed to turn the tide or simple attrition would end them in the next few minutes.

"Colonel, this is Lieutenant Briggs," the Marine officer declared over the priority channel normally reserved for maydays or other emergencies. "We're moving to intercept the enemy."

"Roger, Lieutenant," Jenkins acknowledged, noting as he did so that the Marine dropship had broken formation with Clover a full ten seconds before Briggs' transmission. "Be advised, Clover will maintain continuous fire into their position."

"Don't let up on our account, sir," Briggs replied as his ten power-armored Marines leapt out of the dropship and began to plummet to the ground below, their ride moving to intercept the approaching aircraft. Even as they fell, their railgun rifles sent tungsten slivers stabbing into the enemy swarm, scratching five more Interceptors in the first three seconds of the Marines' freefall.

There were no two ways about it; watching Terran Marines do their thing was impressive. Awe-inspiring, even. They managed to maintain focus to such a degree that, while plummeting toward the Martian soil three thousand feet below, they were able to hit targets that were still eight kilometers downrange.

Erratically *flying* targets, at that.

As the armored warriors descended, their rocket packs lit and slowed them down. Their armored forms were clustered in a formation no larger than twenty meters across, which would have been impressive even without the fact that they were doing so in the middle of a firefight. But what was even more impressive was their dropship pilot's ability to interpose their armored transport between them and the enemy Interceptors. The Marines were literally being shielded by their pilot, who found himself staring down the rails of twenty-two Solar aerospace fighters.

Those rails soon spat tungsten, sending a wave of bolts at the Marine dropship. The fearless Marine executed an extreme corkscrew dive before pulling up so hard Jenkins doubted the pilot could remain conscious throughout the maneuver. But conscious or not, the maneuver spared the dropship from all but three railgun strikes. Impressively, those strikes failed to knock the dropship off-course, and it deftly resumed its shielding posture.

Meanwhile, the Clover mechs continued pouring tungsten and artillery into the approaching swarm of aircraft. Jenkins noted that the enemy never moved farther than sixty meters from one to another, which suggested they were controlled by some kind of distributed relay system rather than each craft being independently controlled. This hypothesis enabled him to refine the airburst pattern significantly, and when his people sent up another concerted volley, they were rewarded with six scratches instead of the two they had scored earlier.

The Marines, now grounded after controlling their descent with rockets built into their peerless power suits, fired their railguns into the approaching Interceptors. Another four of the aircraft were destroyed, leaving twelve of the original thirty-four aerospace fighters.

Jenkins realized something wasn't quite right. The enemy aircraft had initially seemed intent on destroying Clover, but the Marines had turned the tide, and it was now clear who would be victorious. So why weren't they breaking off?

"They're covering something," he muttered, linking up with

the *Red Hare's* sensors and using a command override to initiate a high-powered active sensor sweep of the area. Active sweeps took time, which he suspected he lacked in abundance, so if his theory were right, he would need to get lucky with his target zones.

Fortunately, and for perhaps the first time in his professional career, he made a proverbial hole in one as a stealth missile was revealed on an intercept course with the beanstalk code-named Hansel.

And it would impact in less than thirty seconds!

"Briggs," Jenkins barked while painting the missile and issuing virtual orders to all Clover mechs to immediately launch defensive rockets, "break off and engage that missile. I say again, engage that missile."

"Acknowledged," Briggs replied, and the wounded dropship adopted an intercept course with the missile at its maximum rated speed for the Martian atmosphere of eight hundred kph.

The rebel Interceptors immediately adjusted posture as well, redlining their engines as they sought to interdict the Marine dropship. The grounded Marines and Metalheads sent Terran fury into the pursuing ships, knocking one after another out of the twilight sky as they launched railgun bolts at the evading dropship.

"Come on..." Jenkins hissed, as *Warcrafter's* fifteens sent airburst shells into the enemy, scoring another kill with a near-miss. "Come on!" he repeated as the dropship sped toward the missile. The enemy missile was relatively slow-moving but still topped fifty-two-hundred kph as it soared across the sky.

Given their relative positions and velocities, there was no hope of the dropship physically interdicting the missile before it could strike the elevator. But every meter they shaved off the distance improved the Marine pilots' chances to hit it with railgun fire, so he redlined his Tripoli's engines and tore across the twilight blue sky.

Jenkins wanted to call for more help—to get Lieutenant Commander Knighton's Vipers to assist with the missile intercept, or even to call down orbital bombardment despite the minuscule probability of success.

But he knew that the right call was to continue providing support to the dropship, so that was precisely what he did.

Then something unexpected happened. It was minor in the grand scheme of things, but it did more to buoy his suddenly flagging confidence than he would have thought possible. The familiar sound of a song came across the P2P link with the Marine dropship, and instead of a verbal report, the pilot cranked up the volume to the chorus of Godsmack's *I Stand Alone* and rapid-fired his railgun at the rebel missile.

Bolts shot across the three-hundred-fifty kilometers faster than the blink of an eye, missing the mark high by six meters. Pursuing rebel Interceptors fired at the Marine's stern, landing two direct hits and knocking one of the craft's three engines offline. The rebel missile would reach Hansel in eighteen seconds, having climbed higher to avoid ground-based fire.

In reply to losing an engine, the pilot raised the volume of the music and fired another round at the ascendant enemy weapon. This bolt missed as well, though only by four meters.

Jenkins' Razorbacks continued pouring fire into the rebel Interceptors, scoring kills with increasing frequency, while those aircraft pursued the Marine ship as he hurtled toward his objective with single-minded purpose.

The countdown reached eight seconds to go, and Jenkins knew the pilot would only get one more shot with each of his railguns before it was over. With the eminently appropriate music blaring over the comm link and just four seconds remaining until the missile's impact with the space elevator's deceptively thin tether, the pilot fired the first of his final two shots.

This bolt missed by less than a meter and visibly distorted the missile's exhaust after the two projectiles narrowly missed a brief-but-passionate embrace. It was down to the last Marine railgun bolt, which would decide whether or not Phase Two of Operation War God was a success or failure.

When that shot came, it coincided with the climax of the song the pilot had chosen as his battle hymn. And when the sensors registered the event, Jenkins released a pent-up breath just as his people scratched the last of the rebel remote-operated Interceptors from the Marine's wake.

"Good shooting, Marine," Jenkins declared as the previously-invisible missile exploded just outside the beanstalk's danger zone. "You earned yourself a prime rib on me."

"Copy that, Clover Actual," the pilot acknowledged stoically, turning the music down as he pulled back from his climb. He soon cut one of his two remaining engines, signaling he had taken worse damage than expected as he controlled his descent back to the Martian surface. "Make it well done."

"Burning things is what we do best." Jenkins chuckled dryly. "What's your status for return to formation?"

"I can limp back to Echo, but that's about it," the pilot replied. "I've got a major fuel leak here and a bit of a scratch on my leg. I could use some alone time with the school nurse if she's handy?"

"She's doing her hair for you right now," Jenkins acknowledged while reviewing the pilot's vital signs over the data link. His heart rate and blood pressure were consistent with significant blood loss, but he was still lucid, and his reflexes were tight. He'd make it long enough for a med-flight to reach him. He alerted Echo's corpsmen to the pilot's condition and received confirmation of their status. "Rumor has it she's been hiding her best leathers. Maintain P2P linkage with Echo and return to base to get that booboo looked at."

"Oorah." The Marine chuckled before cutting the line.

"Clover," the colonel broadcast to the rest of the battalion, "advance to the objective, flank speed. Let's lock this area down."

The mechs of Clover Battalion resumed their sprint toward the base of the space elevator, anchored by metal shafts sunk deep into Mars' crust. The loading and unloading platform was well below ground, protecting it from falling debris and even most land-based attacks. But the tether itself, made of carbon nanotubes, necessarily protruded from its anchor point beneath the Martian surface.

The carbon tether, originally manufactured on Earth a hundred and sixty years earlier before being brought and deployed by a slow-drive construction vessel, stretched five thousand kilometers above the planet. This placed it and its fellows beneath the orbital paths of Phobos and Deimos, but within their gravitational influence and required them to oscillate in space to maintain their position. These oscillations, carefully orchestrated by using a combination of the moons' gravity and chemical thrusters, swayed the tethers back and forth to keep them stable. For a century and a half, no Martian beanstalk had suffered serious tether damage.

Until Operation Antivenom.

Pushing that particularly harrowing thought from his mind, Jenkins initiated P2P with the *William Wallace*'s Ground Control Officer. "GC, this is Clover Actual."

"Go ahead, Clover," Chief Styles acknowledged.

"Give me a point of origin for that missile," Jenkins commanded.

"Forwarding now," Styles replied, sending a stream of data and orbital images to Jenkins' console while *Warcrafter* sped across the smooth Martian terrain toward Hansel. He saw a high-res image of the missile's launch platform in the files sent by Styles and grimaced at what that meant.

The platform was essentially a large, cargo-hauling truck retrofitted to drag a self-contained LRM launcher. The top speed of the truck was just thirty kph, and it didn't take Sherlock Holmes to trace its path across the dusty Martian surface. He cycled back to the truck's point of origin, which was a defunct industrial compound originally on the mission's list of priority targets but had been destroyed by rebel efforts before the Terrans arrived.

Some back-of-the-napkin math confirmed Jenkins' unsettling theory: the truck had moved out of its former position two-and-a-half hours earlier. How it had remained hidden in plain sight was neither surprising nor concerning to Jenkins. He had fought the Jemmin enough to know they could play havoc with even the best Terran sensors. The enemy would maintain an advantage in that regard for the foreseeable future, so worrying about it would be pointless.

What concerned him was that if he had followed Major Xi's advice and proceeded with Phase Two as soon as he'd seized Echo Base five hours earlier, that missile truck would have been incapable of gaining a favorable firing position before his people reached and secured the elevator.

"Bad process, good result?" he muttered. It was just another way to say "I think you just got lucky, Lee," but for some reason, it sounded less damning the way he actually voiced it.

He checked in on Major Xi's progress, finding that Dragon had already secured their location with orbital drops of pop-up defenses. If things went according to plan from here on out, the second beanstalk would be secured within the hour.

Strokes of luck notwithstanding, Operation War God had gone off about as well as could have been hoped for. They'd taken serious damage, lost a lot of good men and women, and encountered Jemmin resistance intermingled with the rebels.

But considering this was the first planetary-scale invasion the Legion had conducted in the better part of a century, things could have been a whole lot worse.

10

SECONDARY OBJECTIVES

"Report, Captain?" Jenkins asked after receiving Captain Winters' P2P link, relayed via flying comm drone.

"We've secured the Southern Hub, Colonel," Winters replied. "All five emergence points are under our control, and we've sent drones four kilometers down the tunnels. No enemy activity detected."

"Good work, Captain. How's the fresh meat?"

Winters snorted. "*Green*. We underperformed Legion averages across the board: accuracy, response times, ammo conservation, the works. Without Commander Knighton's aerial support, we might not have secured the LZ before taking serious fire from the rebel contingent we overcame here. If this is the best I can do with our best Nuggets and Flakes, you might need to put me on latrine duty, sir. Still, we've got nine combat-ready mechs ready to roll on Phase Three."

Jenkins laughed. "I'm sure you'll find some way to make amends, Captain."

"Yes, sir. We lost one can during the drop, but the crew bailed before splashdown."

"Cause?" Jenkins asked. Dropping from orbit in a can was

always dangerous, but to hear that they'd actually lost a mech during drop caught him off-guard.

"Preliminary reports are it was a faulty fuel line to the main control thrusters," Winters replied grimly. "I'll ensure Chief Rimmer and his people have everything they need to conduct an internal investigation, sir."

"Very good, Captain," Jenkins agreed. "Hold your position and await further orders."

"Yes, sir."

Jenkins cut the line and linked up with Xi on the P2P. "Major, what's your status?"

"Gretel is secured, Colonel. Dragon 1st has seven combat-ready mechs ready to advance on your command. *Cam Frog* lost a leg and will need to hunker down here, and *Ebola May* had a cabin fire just a few minutes ago that fried most of her virtual systems. She's salvageable, and her crew got out before they hit extra-crispy, but she's offline for now. I've assigned *Sargon* to command the defense of Gretel, and the rest of our down-checks are back at Echo."

"Copy that," Jenkins acknowledged. "We've got eleven Razorbacks ready to roll, with our walking wounded hunkered down at Hansel during Phase Three. Between Clover and Dragon, we're at twenty-seven, make that two-seven, combat-worthy mechs capable of taking the plunge."

"Fuckin' Blinky..." Xi swore. "How'd he win the betting pool on that, too? His picking the drop music was bad enough, but him bullseye-ing the phase strength estimates will make him unbearable."

Jenkins laughed. "Feeling the heat from a fellow rising star, Major?"

"Me? Jealous?" She feigned indignation. "Of Blinky?! Stand by, Colonel," she said abruptly, cutting the mic for a few seconds before returning. "Sorry, sir. Lieutenant Worthington just informed me that our prisoners were transferred into custody at Echo Base. Should we return to Echo for re-arm?"

"Negative. I've got Captain Koch coming out with two full cans of ammo," he explained. "If Dragon 1st is fit to sprint, make for the Southern Hub. The sooner we get Phase Three under-way, the sooner we can get the hell out of here."

"I'm glad to hear I'm not the only one who's waiting for the other shoe to drop." Xi's lip curled with the anticipation of an ugly surprise. "It's not like the rebels haven't hit back, and the Jemmin ambushes were unexpected wrinkles, but it seems like things have been going too smoothly."

"Agreed," Jenkins replied darkly. "I'm not much for super-stition, but at this point, the faster we get this over with, the less chance we have of War God going pear-shaped. So if it doesn't jeopardize your people, head to the hub and link up with Captain Winters."

"Understood, Colonel," she acknowledged. "We're fit to sprint. ETA to Southern Hub, five hours twenty minutes."

"See you there, Major." He cut the link and opened a line to Captain Guan on the *Red Hare*. "Captain Guan, I need a sidebar."

"How can I be of service?" the ship's CO asked

"We're prepping to push into Phase Three," Jenkins explained, "but to maximize our assets, we're going to have to divide the force into smaller units. Captain Chao's people have performed admirably to this point, as has Captain Hao, to my surprise," he admitted, "but I'm not convinced their subordi-nates are ready to carry out independent operations on this scale. Once we roll on Phase Three, we'll be out of comm contact until the objectives have been secured. Discipline will be paramount, and I still have doubts about the Han Guardsmen following every order as issued."

Captain Guan paused for a moment before issuing his

trademark laugh. It was the sound of a man who was not only amused by but also openly disdainful of what he had just heard. "You are still concerned regarding Captain Chao's disciplinary actions during Watery Grave," he concluded.

"You think I shouldn't be?" Jenkins asked flatly.

"I think," Guan opined, sighing in unreserved bewilderment, "that you just said the men and women of Clover have performed admirably during this operation. I think Captain Chao's keenness of mind and shrewd judgment averted what could have been a true catastrophe for the Metal Legion by acting as he did when he did. I think Captain Hao formally requested a full transfer from the Terra Han Colonial Guard over to Armor Corps before our deployment for this operation," the captain continued, with that last bit catching Jenkins by surprise. "I think, if I may be so bold, your primary weakness as a field officer is that you are perhaps too inflexible in certain matters of delegation. Discipline in military ranks has always required subjective enforcement of objective limits, which means that some discretion must be afforded your subordinates. If I may speak freely," he continued blithely, though Jenkins noted that the other man did not pause before doing as he failed to ask, "I think Captain Chao understands the men and women of Clover Battalion better than anyone else, myself included."

Jenkins smirked. "Meaning that I called the wrong man?"

"Certainly not," Guan said dismissively. "Merely that you have not yet finished soliciting feedback, and your most important call is yet to be made in this regard." Guan's voice suddenly turned serious. "War is hell, Colonel Jenkins. The clash of metal and meat is, by design, a gruesome and traumatic affair. But sometimes it can be made less gruesome with the judicious application of what some might call 'tough love.' If Captain Chao saved even one life with the unquestionably brutal discipline of his subordinate by removing her toes in the middle of an operation, then by any objective measure, it was a worth-while act even if it constitutes an actionable offense."

"Which brings us back to the subjective enforcement of objective limits." In this verbal chess match, Jenkins had been bested.

"Something with which I am intimately familiar," Guan assented. "Earlier in my career, one of the junior officers aboard my ship was insubordinate during the transfer of ordnance. His disregard for the chain of command resulted in a pallet of plasma grenades spilling onto the flight deck. This officer seemed to understand the gravity of the situation as soon as the pallet fell from the loader, but his superior was unconvinced, and gave him a choice: request and receive a transfer to another ship in the Colonial Guard with no questions asked, or remove the first knuckles of his index fingers and remain at his post for the duration of his tour. That choice proved instrumental in establishing the young officer's respect for the chain of command, which remains strong and immutable to this day... just like his memory of willfully removing the first knuckles of his index fingers. In case you have not already surmised," Guan said, a note of bitterness creeping into his voice, "that young officer was me. Was it right? Wrong? Barbaric? I do not know. What I *do* know is that I am a better officer, and indeed a better man, for having endured that punishment. Given the chance to re-make that decision, I would not change it."

"Jesus..." Jenkins muttered. "You Han Guardsmen don't fuck around, do you?"

"Life is unbearable suffering, Colonel. Without a purpose to drive a person through that suffering, it would be all too easy to simply lie down and surrender to entropy. Captain Chao instilled in Captain Hao a measure of purpose she will carry with her as long as she lives. And at what price? As one who has paid that price, it is my opinion it is worth paying."

"I appreciate hearing your story, Captain," Jenkins said honestly, "but I'm not sure it helped clarify things."

Guan laughed again in his peculiar, borderline-insufferable way. "There are no easy decisions, Colonel. If they were easy, they would not be decisions, merely obvious courses of action."

"Thank you, Captain," Jenkins said graciously. "I'll be sure to contact you if I need to muddy the waters again."

Guan chuckled. "I am happy to be of service."

"These shipping tunnels are a nightmare," Podsy muttered as he and Styles went over the Southern Hub's labyrinthine subterranean passages. The Southern Hub consisted of three separate emergence points, each carved into the Martian surface and leading deep into the planet's crust.

Subterranean Martian industrial infrastructure existed for a variety of reasons. Solar radiation was a serious problem for the earliest virtual equipment used during Martian colonization, and the weakness of Mars' EM field, coupled with its extremely thin atmosphere, necessitated all sensitive equipment be installed underground to avoid frequent breakdowns in the cogitative equipment which drove the earliest Martian colonization efforts.

So the first foothold included digging vast subterranean tunnels and clearing caverns that could serve as habitats or industrial facilities. To facilitate the digging, tunnel-boring machines were manufactured on Earth and shipped by spacecraft. Once safely landed on Mars, they began to dig into various canyons and depressions on the Martian surface. After a few decades, boring machines were built on-location by automated factories with extremely limited human oversight.

In fact, the average population of Mars during the first

decade of active colonization was two hundred souls, with over a quarter of those living in an orbiting space station where they disseminated supplies sent by Earth to the various dig sites scattered across the surface. For all that time, the vast majority of Martian colonization was essentially automated and resulted in thousands of kilometers of interconnected tunnels sunk deep into the Martian crust.

The Southern Hub directly accessed nearly eighty percent of the subterranean industrial facilities beneath Mars' ruddy soil, making it the most trafficked transit hub on the planet. A total of sixty separate foundries, manufacturing centers, refineries, and ice mines were accessible via the Southern Hub, and that made it a top priority target for the Metalheads.

The only problem was figuring out how to secure all sixty facilities in a single go, and that was the cause of Podsy's and Styles' consternation.

"We've got twenty-seven mechs and seventeen combat-ready Marines," Styles reiterated, pulling up the Legion's roster to bolster his point. "Given the arrangement of the tunnels and the distances between objectives, it looks like we've got two choices. First, we divide the Legion up into five roughly equal groups, advance down these three main shafts, and branch out from there in a rolling sweep of the entire network. If we take this route, we can address every single facility on the board in a methodical advance."

"In theory, yes," Podsy allowed, "but that will take at least sixty hours from start to finish, assuming minimal resistance at each location. We don't have that kind of time."

"Agreed," Styles nodded sourly. "Which leaves us with a riskier path: a Prairie Fire. We break the force up into fifteen separate groups, splitting Marines off into pairs or singles and sending them ahead of the rest of the force by several hours. We then roll the armor down, get into position, and take fifteen locations simultaneously. If we can execute the first strike across those fifteen locales, we can take control of maybe fifty facilities in twelve hours."

"I don't like the idea of sending anyone, even power-armored Marines, in without support," Podsy scowled. "One of Colonel Jenkins' primary operating assumptions when pitching a combined arms sub-branch to Fleet brass was that Marines are significantly disadvantaged running down tunnels like this. Sure, they're fast and capable of moving more quietly than a hundred tons of rolling armor. But if even two of these tunnel nexuses are heavily fortified and the Marines clash with them en route to their objectives, the rest of the facilities will be alerted to our intentions, and things will go worse than if we'd taken the slow-and-steady approach."

"The Prairie Fire looks like the right call to me, Lieutenant," Chief Styles said in frustration. "We can consolidate a few of the teams to provide lateral support in the event—"

"No." Podsy shook his head firmly. "No half-measures. This debate is about risk and reward. If *we* bear that risk, the reward is more preserved Martian infrastructure. If we decide *not* to accept the risk, we're endangering all of this industrial capacity. We didn't come here to wilt at the last moment, Chief."

"No, sir," Styles agreed.

"All right." Podsy nodded with conviction. "I'll go talk to the general and make our recommendation. Have a top sheet ready in three minutes."

"Will do."

Podsednik made his way to the general's chair, where he waited until General Moon had completed making an entry into his interface. "Yes, Lieutenant?"

"We think a simultaneous assault on fifteen key locations followed by a rapid advance to adjacent targets will provide us with the best chance at securing the majority of the infrastructure linked to the Southern Hub, General," Podsy explained. "Chief Styles is working up the details now, but we're going with a modified Prairie Fire."

General Moon's lips twisted faintly. "A sprint to the beanstalks might have been the right call, but a Prairie Fire calls for the lighter, faster elements to go ahead by at least three hours. The old man made quite the career out of demonstrating that subterranean environs are one of the few places where Metalheads can outpace Marines."

"We understand that, General," Podsy agreed. "But a Prairie Fire could potentially seize over eighty percent of the infrastructure in twelve hours, whereas a tighter, branching advance will take sixty hours or more. A lot can happen in that additional forty-eight hours, sir, as an examination of War God's early results will confirm."

Moon stroked his chin contemplatively. "Have you run this by Colonel Jenkins or Major Xi?"

"Not yet, sir," Podsy replied before amending, "though I doubt anyone would be surprised to find the major supports a Prairie Fire."

"Predictability on the battlefield is a deadly sin, Lieutenant," the general remarked.

"It is, sir. But these rebels aren't familiar with us, and even if they are, we already proceeded with a more methodical transition from Phase One to Phase Two. Striking hard and fast in Phase Three couldn't be considered predictable."

"Probably not," Moon allowed, "but you're still proposing that we send Marines into dark tunnels, some of which are a hundred kilometers long, in singletons or pairs."

"I am," Podsy agreed. "We'll obviously leave the more central nexuses and facilities, or any facility likely to be fortified, for Armor to secure. But the Marines can handle the rest, and their combined speed and relative stealth will prove instrumental to outflanking any potentially responsive rebel forces awaiting us down there. Whatever seismic sensors the rebels have access to will pick up on rolling armor, but not on Terran Marines...at least not until they're within knife range."

"All right. Outflanking the enemy *would* provide a vital advantage in that maze, and we can outfit the Marines with extra grenades and demo to help offset their loss of maneuverability in those passages. Where's your top sh—"

"Here's your top sheet, Lieutenant," Chief Styles declared, proffering a data slate, which Podsy nodded for him to hand directly to the general. "I've prepared both options for your review, sir," Styles added after Moon accepted the slate.

The general eyed the pair of them for a moment before reviewing the document. He nodded before handing it back. "Relay this to Colonel Jenkins and Major Xi, then get them on the horn. We need to hammer out the details before they reach the hub, and ultimately, this is their call, not ours. Remember, *we* support *them*, we don't direct them. When that call goes live, I want you to have collected every last byte of relevant data for them to use in making their decision."

"Yes, sir," Podsy and Styles acknowledged before making their way back to the Ground Control station, where they did precisely that.

11

PROMETHEUS' LEGACY

"Those are the options as we see them, Colonel," Styles finished after presenting the two different insertion plans. "We're prepping supply cans for both variants right now, but we could shave ten or twelve minutes off the prep time if you make a choice in the next quarter hour."

Even before the GCO had finished his three-minute presentation, Jenkins knew precisely how the conversation with Major Xi would play out.

But no matter the outcome, he intended to make her earn it. Besides, they had another thirty-eight minutes before they reached the Southern Hub. It was more than enough time for a much-needed lesson on command.

"Roger, Ground Control," Jenkins replied. "We'll confer and get back to you." He cut the link to the *William Wallace* and said, "Your thoughts, Major?"

"We've already encountered Jemmin influence down here, Colonel," she promptly replied. "Those pop-ups at Scooter and the pair of warships hidden in the moon aren't going to be the last we hear from them. I recommend we proceed with the Prairie Fire approach: split the forces, send the Marines down the hole first, and once they're in position, we charge down the passageways and knock the whole network over in twelve hours."

"We can't get the whole network with this method," Jenkins said pointedly. "With Prairie Fire, we're automatically giving up on at least eight of the facilities, three of which are ice mines with a combined output of forty percent of Mars' industrial consumption."

"But with the branching effort, we slow the op down to a crawl," she countered. "Sixty hours underground? That's just begging for the rebels to cut us off with forced cave-ins and use guerilla tactics as long as they maintain a mobility advantage. There are tens of thousands of kilometers of tunnels down there, sir, and too much unaccounted-for ordnance potentially waiting for us. Trying to clear it all in a methodical sweep is asking for trouble."

"I understand you've got a preference for expedience, Major," Jenkins said neutrally, careful not to give away his real feelings as he did his best to impart a very real, very important bit of wisdom in the only way he knew how, "but not every job calls for a jackhammer."

"Copy that, sir," she replied tersely, "but what we're really talking about is mitigating risk. We didn't come here to play it safe, Colonel. We came here to secure the Martian infrastructure. We've already taken significant losses, and we'll take more before we go wheels-up, but those losses will pale in comparison to the losses humanity suffers if we spend more time covering our own asses than we do ramming our guns up the enemies'—"

"Speed kills," Jenkins interrupted, "but delivered force isn't *just* about speed. It's also about mass. Your plan would break most of us down into trios or pairs, and some of the Marines would be running solo, which greatly diminishes our ability to mass firepower against a determined defense. And if we deploy on your plan, no team will be closer than thirty minutes' sprint from its closest support. That's hardly ideal."

"Ideal?" she repeated in surprise. "Begging your pardon, sir, but 'ideal' isn't in the TAC dictionary. If things were 'ideal,' they'd have given someone else the ball, and that goes for every other op we've been on. I want to get the job done and get off this rock. Something hasn't felt right since we got here, and I don't just mean the gold sky."

"You might be right, but you need to understand something: your plan will get Metalheads and Marines killed," Jenkins said, bringing the conversation to the very point he had been driving at. "Yes, you might get the job done quicker, and even better, than a slow-and-steady branching advance, but we'll suffer losses as a result. Losses we wouldn't otherwise incur. I'm not sure you're ready to accept everything that goes with that kind of responsibility."

"With all due respect, Colonel," she said archly, "I would have fucked off home if I wasn't ready to do this job. I'm here to get this done. Full stop."

He let the silence linger between them before offering her one last out, mimicking a test an old mentor of his once administered during Jenkins' early career. "Major, this call affects your command more than it does mine. My Razorbacks are more than capable of breaking down into twos and threes and getting the job done. But your mixed assets will be significantly more vulnerable down there. I recommend we proceed with the branching advance, and if you feel strongly enough, then you file an official complaint, which we'll bring up for review as soon as the op's concluded—just as I think you should do regarding your objections to Phase Two's timetable."

"Respectfully, Colonel," she began, speaking much more calmly than he'd expected she would, "we're wasting time. We both know a Phase Three branching advance is the wrong call. We have to go with the Prairie Fire, and we only have twenty-nine minutes before we arrive at the Southern Hub. We should be working up teams and assignments, not arguing about this. And if you think I'm going to file a complaint about a coin-flip call that maybe goes against us, you haven't been paying close enough attention to your officers' tendencies."

He nodded approvingly. It wasn't exactly the response he had been hoping for, but it was closer than he'd gotten fifteen years earlier. "You're right. Prairie Fire is the correct call. But you'd also be right to raise hell about Phase Two. The truth is, I got lucky. Without heroics from our Marines, we wouldn't have been able to intercept that missile, and we'd have lost half of Mars' orbital lift capacity because I made the wrong call. It was bad process, good result, which we both know is unacceptable. You were right to advise a Phase Two sprint, and you weren't the only one to push for it."

"That's all hindsight and conjecture, Colonel," she rejected. "You made the call, and I followed your lead."

"Careful, Major," Jenkins warned grimly. "I don't need your tongue up my ass. That wasn't my first bad call, and it won't be my last. I accept that I'm going to fuck these things up from time to time, and I've learned to live with my failures. But it's your duty not only to yourself but to the men and women you command to challenge bad orders when you see them." He smirked. "I don't know if you've noticed, but there's a non-zero chance one or both of us never steps off this planet. I need you to understand I'm not looking for sympathy or support. I'm trying to teach you something it took me too long to learn. Is that understood?"

A brief pause. "Yes, sir, it is."

"Good." He nodded. "Then I'm going to give you permission for one 'I told you so' before we move on. Use it or lose it, Major."

Another pause. "That's not my role. It's to offer alternatives. How about we assign some roles and responsibilities and get ready to kick some Martian rebel ass?"

"All right." He grinned. "Not every job requires a jackhammer. Sometimes the best tool is a file. It's not often in our line of work, I'll admit, but it does happen occasionally. Thus far, you haven't been too keen to suggest the methodical approach in favor of the fast-and-furious one. Predictability will get you killed, Major, but more importantly, it will get everyone around you killed. Here." He forwarded telemetry from the orbital engagement with the Jemmin warships, juxtaposed against ship-to-ship engagements with Jemmin from previous battles the Legion had undertaken against them. "Take a look at this and tell me what you see."

With Styles' help, he had run the combat recorder data through multivariate analysis and drawn a startling conclusion: the Jemmin were learning the Legion's tactical tendencies. Their dart around behind Phobos and their speed as they emerged and achieved firing arcs on the Legion warships were indicative of subtle but significant shifts in their approach to engagement with the Legion.

It raised the premium on unpredictability.

She grunted. "Fuckers are learning our behaviors."

"Correct. And the odds are reasonably good that we haven't locked horns with them for the last time. Bear that in mind, Major, because if Jemmin can spot patterns in our behavior, so can anyone else if they've got access to the relevant intel."

"Understood, Colonel," she said, her usually cock-sure tone significantly subdued. "I can learn to throw a change-up."

"Good." He nodded. "Now, let's get ready to go down that hole."

"The last supply cans have touched down at the Southern Hub rally point, General," Chief Styles reported. "Captain Koch's detachment will rendezvous with Dragon and Clover and assist with the rearmament. Colonel Jenkins is requesting your review and approval of Phase Three's outline and timetable before commencing with the insertion."

"What's the finalized insertion strategy?" General Moon asked, Commodore Kline standing observantly at his side.

"Fifteen teams, including eight Marine squads and seven armor platoons, with the Marine insertion to commence on your order," Styles replied, putting a unit breakdown on the bridge's main viewer. "The seven armor platoons, with four mechs apiece, will insert at T-plus three hours. The first objectives will be secured at T-plus five hours, with the second set of objectives secured at T-plus six-point-five hours and the third wave secured at T-plus nine."

As he spoke, fifteen distinct objectives flashed yellow across the subterranean network of tunnels, and after a few seconds, those objectives turned green and adjacent objectives began to flash yellow. The initial fifteen objectives were followed by twenty-three, and then finally by the last twelve.

"We've prioritized the primary assembly plants and other facilities containing critical infrastructure and put the foundries and other low-tech facilities further down the priority tree. The Marines will secure key locations, ensuring lines of communication remain open during the advance while eliminating potential ambush sites with demo charges. Each of the fifteen objectives in the first package will be serviced by full armor platoons, which will then decentralize for movement to the second-tier objectives."

"Leaving a dozen far-flung facilities for the third tier," Moon said, thinking out loud. "The drawback of the Prairie Fire approach is that if we experience any interruptions in our operational tempo at these points," he gestured to three key transit nexuses which connected eighteen of the facilities, "the rebels could get behind us, wreak havoc along our lines of communication, cut off our people, and then mass their forces against the individual. It's how an inferior force creates superior odds."

Commander Kline stepped up to speak. "It is Sol's opinion that your Prairie Fire approach is the correct one. The loss of the third-tier facilities is an acceptable risk if it means bringing the rest of the system under control two full days faster. The velocity of this attack has the best chance to secure the facilities that will be the most difficult to replace ."

"Timetable on those third-tier facilities is T-plus nine hours for the first locations, extending out to T-plus twenty-nine hours for the farthest facility," Podsednik observed skeptically. "If the rebels want to spike third-tier facilities, they'll have plenty of time to do it. Especially if they've got any kind of working comm system down there to help coordinate their efforts."

"My people have already confirmed that there is no such communications capacity, Lieutenant," Commodore Kline said with surprising confidence. "The One Mind network was taken offline to inhibit the spread of Jemmin influence, which is the primary reason there is anything left on Mars to secure at this late hour."

"There's no lateral comm infrastructure outside the One Mind?" Podsy asked skeptically.

"No," Kline said, a confused note entering his voice. "What would be the purpose of such a redundant system?"

"Seriously?" Podsy drawled.

"You likely misunderstand my query, Lieutenant," Kline said after a momentary pause, "because you likely misunderstand the nature of the One Mind. I am not expressly authorized to divulge this information, but in my judgment, it is of tactical relevance to Operation War God. But I must insist that this remains classified until my government opts to declassify it.

"Of course," General Moon agreed.

The commodore nodded agreeably before casually explaining, "One Mind architecture incorporates all comm gear, or anything even remotely capable of transceiving data, into itself. And all One Mind assets were shut down after your virtual inoculation failed to cleanse the Martian system of its Jemmin corruption."

"What do you mean by 'all comm gear?'" Podsednik asked warily. "I mean...my wristwatch periodically connects to nearby comm nodes to adjust for gravitational time dilation. Are you saying that if it was Solarian and I was on Mars during Antivenom, it would have been deactivated when the Martian One Mind went down?"

"Of course." The commodore gave him a perplexed look. "Understand that Operation Antivenom triggered a failsafe system that only a few of the highest-level virtual security officers in Sol knew about. This system was secretly hard-coded into every single piece of Solar technology, and it was placed there in the event of a situation precisely like this one."

"A kill-switch built into every piece of transceiving hardware in the Solar System..." Podsy shook his head in ambivalent bewilderment and scorn. "And *nobody* knew of its existence?"

Kline shrugged indifferently. "Your predictable disdain notwithstanding, it was this particular protocol that saved half of the Venusian population, and which might yet spare Martian infrastructure from being sabotaged by Jemmin machinations. A corruption in the One Mind, if uncontained, could destroy or, worse yet, subvert the entire system. It would be irresponsible *not* to include a failsafe of this type."

"What about military hardware?" Moon pressed, fixing

Podsy with a look that ordered him to stand down. "I understand your reluctance to share this type of intel with us—"

"Military hardware is largely exempt," Kline interrupted far too easily for Podsednik's liking. "As such, the failsafe was installed, but there are possible workarounds. That we have encountered relatively light resistance to this point demonstrates that most Martian military assets are still inert due to these safeguards. Were they active and in rebel hands, we calculate this rebellion would have resulted in the destruction of Martian infrastructure in under three days."

Podsy wanted to argue, but something Jem had said echoed in his mind. Solar humanity was indeed different from Terran humanity, and this situation distinctly outlined some of those differences.

"Dragon and Clover have arrived at the rally point, General," Styles reported. "The Marines have already rearmed and are prepared to insert on your order."

"Signal the ground forces," Moon declared. "Phase Three insertion is approved." He then uttered four words Podsy never expected to hear a TAC flag officer say except in jest or to fuel the good-natured interbranch rivalry. "Send in the Marines."

12

THROUGH THE FIERY CAVERNS

"I'm showing T-plus four-four-five minutes, call it back," Xi sent over the Dragon 1st Platoon channel. Attached to First Platoon were *Elvira*, *Murasame* and *Culture Knight*. Most of the platoons consisted of four mechs, per TAC SOP, but Xi had selected all walker-type mechs since her first objective was relatively near the surface. That proximity to the surface, coupled with her three-mech platoon's particular capabilities, ultimately prompted her to go lean on the roster for this next step.

"Confirmed, T-plus four-four-five," acknowledged Giles aboard the humanoid *Culture Knight*. Ozzy Osbourne's *Bark at the Moon* shuffled into the playlist, which was designed to conclude when they arrived at their first objective.

"T-plus four-four-five," agreed Nakamura from the bipedal *Murasame*. "I've never been out of link for this long, Major. It's...unsettling."

"Imagine how the One-Minders must feel," Xi said knowingly while her three-mech platoon charged down the tunnel in perfect formation at seventy kph. "They've been cut off down here for weeks, and their integration of instant comm tech is a hell of a lot deeper than ours will ever be."

"Thank fuck for that," Giles muttered. "You'd never see me get wired into that abomination."

"How much different is it from jacking into your mech? Or interfacing with a planetary data net for a lifelike VR sim? You *really* can't see yourself taking that one extra step?" Nakamura challenged.

"No way, no how," Giles rejected. "These people let literally every other human being in Sol into their heads. How the hell can you operate like that, with everyone knowing your every detail? I get in enough trouble for the things I say in my sleep!"

"You sound like a man with secrets," Nakamura teased.

"We've *all* got secrets, Lieutenant," Giles retorted. "And honestly? What would be the point of living if you couldn't keep a secret from someone? Especially an *important* secret? Isn't the whole point of competition, or cooperation for that matter, to contribute something unique to the party? How the hell can you do that if everyone knows your every thought?"

"My understanding is that it's not *that* invasive, Corporal," Xi put in, although she shared his concerns. "The access you get to the One Mind is supposedly based on reciprocity. The more you let the system into your head, the deeper it lets you go in return."

"Pretty sure dirty talk like that's against regs, Major." Nakamura snickered triumphantly.

"And he *finally* gets on the board." Giles chuckled. "Seven hours-plus, and he broke through."

"I guess I'll allow it." Xi sighed, scratching the first hash mark next to Nakamura's name on a piece of paper she used to keep score of wisecracks and comebacks. "But only because that goose egg was an embarrassment to my outfit. And before you make a comment about my wardrobe choices," she warned, "remember you're up for annual performance review after this op."

"That's low, Major," Nakamura whined. "Pulling rank to keep me from complimenting your fashion sense? How else am I supposed to secure that promotion if not with flattery?"

"In case you haven't noticed," she quipped as their first objective appeared on her mech's radar, which showed the expansive cavern two kilometers down the tunnel, "I'm not much for brown-nosers. Enough chatter. Objective in sight. Entry looks clear. *Elvira* moves center-right, *Murasame* breaks left, and *Culture Knight* goes right. Watch those main power buses on the southern wall since they're practically irreplaceable. Double-check that we're broadcasting our acceptance of immediate surrender on all channels; I don't care if the Solarians say they're deaf and dumb down here, I want to give them every opportunity to end this peacefully."

"Copy that," both men acknowledged as *Elvira* drove down the tunnel in the platoon's lead, with *Murasame* in the middle and *Culture Knight* at the rear. The walker mechs moved down the pitch-black tunnel with the only visible light that which illuminated their armored hulls. As the distance closed to eight hundred meters, even those external illuminators went out, plunging the tunnel into darkness as the sound of armored footfalls echoed through the thin underground air. The mechs didn't need light to see where they were going.

To a casual observer, the sounds of the mechs approaching under cover of darkness would be terrifying.

The atmosphere was significantly thicker this far down than it was on the surface, but even with a handful of giant pressure doors near the surface to help keep the gases underground, the local pressure was barely a tenth that of Earth standard pressure. The extra gases were generated as a byproduct of ice mines, which extracted vast quantities of water and carbon dioxide ice from deep beneath the Martian surface. These frozen aquifers and dry-ice shelves were highly valued for Martian industrial activity, but the details of how they were used or extracted largely escaped Xi and her fellow Metalheads.

The upshot, however, was simple. Atmospheric pressure might be significantly higher down in the tunnels, but there was still so much CO_2 and so little oxygen that trying to breathe the stuff would be suicidal.

"Two hundred meters," Xi reported as the trio of dark mechs neared the primary entry point to the cavern. "Chain guns are weapons free. Hit anything that blooms, but I'll have your ass if you damage Hephaestus."

Her platoon-mates' silent acknowledgments flickered on her HUD, and the mighty war machines soon burst into the vast cavern. Measuring five kilometers across, it featured two access points effectively merged into one by a half-kilometer-long loading dock that adjoined the upper tunnel, the one Xi had just traversed, and the lower tunnel, which led deeper into the Martian underground.

The cavern was a mined-out aquifer which had been converted to a foundry that produced high-quality superalloys. It was likely the golden armor of the arrowhead-shaped mechs was originally produced in this very facility, which provided sixty percent of all similar alloys on Mars.

Great machines filled the cavern, working tirelessly in the near-blackness with only the dull glow of their smelters providing any respite. According to the Solarians, these machines were independent of the One Mind network and could theoretically operate autonomously for up to three months before requiring preventive maintenance and manual intervention.

The metalworking machinery ranged in size from five meters to fifty meters in height, and often several times that in girth. The central apparatus of the cavern was a high-pressure magnetized smelter which, through careful manipulation of not only temperature but also electromagnetic fields and internal pressure, allowed complex alloys to be formed that far outstripped those considered feasible without the aid of such advanced equipment.

Xi had learned in the pre-op briefing that this particular machine, unimaginatively named "Hephaestus," was one of the five most valuable pieces of hardware left on Mars, including the beanstalks.

So naturally, that was where the rebels had taken refuge.

"Contact!" Nakamura barked as a wave of RPGs streaked across the cavern, hammering into *Elvira* as she surged into the cavern's loading dock. The grenades set off minor alarms, which put Penny and Lu into motion.

As soon as *Murasame* breached the cavern, Nakamura detached two of his mech's four hunter-killer drones from the chassis and sending them out to flank the rebels from behind while the Jock took the vehicle left and *Culture Knight* went right.

The near-end of the cavern was sparsely appointed, allowing Xi's mechs to disperse and set up a crossfire. But with the rebels hiding behind the lower edges of the fifty-meter-tall machine, it would be difficult to dig them out without damaging the valuable equipment.

She saw an opening and took it, sending a spray of thirty slugs into a pair of RPG-wielding rebels. Although they were wearing their pressure suits, as was normal for Martians when moving outside of pressurized hab modules, the fifty-caliber slugs cut through both rebels. Their suits popped like balloons, sending a pink mist into the nearby hardware as they were torn limb from limb by Xi's savage chain guns.

She turned up her mech's external speakers, loudly declaring, "This is Major Xi Bao of the Terran Armor Corps. We're here on Solar authority to secure this facility. Disarm and surrender, and no harm will come to you. You are under the influence of a self-destructive directive and are not responsible for your actions. Sol will absolve you of your previous crimes if you lay down arms and surrender." She looped the message, ensuring it repeated ad nauseam in the hope that it might save lives.

She doubted they could hear her clearly, even though she had precisely modulated the transmission for the pressure and content of the local atmosphere, but she had to try.

In reply, another wave of RPGs slammed into her hull, the closest launched from behind an ingot-hauling transport vehicle two kilometers away and the farthest from three kilometers, at the base of Hephaestus. Her chain guns retargeted and fired, sending another short burst into the nearest rebel squad. Making a snap decision, she fired a missile-intercept rocket into the ingot-hauling truck the nearest rebels were using as cover. The rocket exploded the vehicle, sending deadly shrapnel into the rebel squad while denying them future use of the vehicle as cover.

In the fury of combat, one's mind works at hyperspeed. Clarity came in snippets of vision and insight. It seemed odd to her that the rebels wouldn't man the cavern's primary entry along the main tunnel, instead opting to hunker down deeper within the chamber, forcing a firefight where they were at a distinct disadvantage by ceding control of the lone entry point.

But Xi wasn't about to look a gift ride up the tailpipe. They weren't military, and maybe they hadn't thought preventing access was the best way to defend the cavern.

As she sent a short burst of suppressive fire, she moved *Elvira* deeper into the loading dock, a position that afforded her the ability to advance or withdraw from the chamber while controlling much of the exposed terrain between the massive pieces of equipment.

Murasame's hunter-killer drones, equipped with small-caliber slug-throwers instead of their usual demo charges, raced across the cavern at a hundred and fifty kph. With the towering Hephaestus forge near the center of the cavern, the drones would outflank that position in less than a minute.

From his right, *Culture Knight* took a sustained burst of coil gun fire to his armored legs. Giles' reflexes, rivaling Xi's, at least in this instance, proved deadly to the ambushers as he spun his mech's torso and sent a stream of eight micro-mortar rounds into the concealed gun nest, which had a firing window less than twenty centimeters square.

The coil gun, cycling at its maximum of eighty rounds per second, fired just twelve bullets before falling silent due to its operators being annihilated by the stream of tiny explosives. The micro-mortar shells were not much larger than fifty-cal slugs, but each contained enough explosive shrapnel to destroy soft targets up to three meters from the point of impact. Purely an anti-personnel system, *Culture Knight* used the micro-mortar with devastating effect against the unarmored rebels.

Even if the shrapnel did not kill them directly, they would be hard-pressed to survive the damage to their envirosuits.

Xi took no pleasure in putting these unfortunate people down, but she had convinced herself this job was important. These Martians had been infected with a thought virus and posed a serious threat to human interests. They had ignored the Terrans' attempts to resolve the situation peacefully, and while she knew this was a consequence of Jemmin interference, she also knew this infrastructure could very well prove decisive in the fight to save humanity.

It didn't make the decisions easier. The Jemmin had created willing human shields, so humans had to die to protect humanity. It was a sacrifice the Metalheads volunteered to make, filling out their wills during their initial training. The Martians hadn't volunteered, but they were dying in the proxy war against Jemmin.

She knew the job she had to do, and she knew why she had to do it. But that didn't stop a sharp, stinging sensation in her nose from threatening to make her cry.

She verified that her audio broadcast was still transmitting at maximum volume, offering the rebels an ongoing opportunity to surrender, and when another wave of light anti-materiel RPGs slammed into *Murasame's* left arm, her sorrow turned to anger. Her compassion for these unfortunate rebels had been overridden by her camaraderie and loyalty to her fellow Metalheads.

This moment of clarity had been forever burned into her mind. She could second-guess herself later.

They aren't fighting for *something,* she reasoned. *They are fighting against us, Terra and Sol both. They don't know it and refuse to listen. Like a mad dog, they have to be put down. For humanity's sake.*

Nakamura fired an SRM into a forklift behind the rebel fire team, sending a blast of metal and ceramic shards into the four-person team of retreating rebels. They were cut down instantly, and Xi noted on the tactical HUD that *Murasame's* hunter-killer drones had neared their flanking position on the rebels at the Hephaestus forge.

That was when the rebel SRM pod revealed itself by firing a pair of missiles across the cavern. One slammed into *Culture Knight*, tearing its left arm off just below the shoulder. The other struck *Elvira's* topside, taking one of her SRM launchers off and setting off another series of damage alarms.

"Engage that target," Xi snarled, sending a pair of AP shells into the missile pod. *Culture Knight* fired eight-kilo shells from his remaining right arm's paired cannons, and *Murasame* added an SRM to the barrage. The ordnance slammed into the far side of the cavern, causing a major cave-in and authoring a trio of rapid explosions as local pressure tanks were destroyed. The missile pod had been tucked behind a stack of platinum ingots approximately ten meters cubed, each ingot weighing two thousand kilos.

The combined fury of the Terran guns and the falling rock from the cavern roof scattered those pristine blocks of precious metal before burying them under thousands of tons of rock.

"HKs in position, Major," Nakamura reported as soon as his drones had outflanked the rebels.

"If these people want to die," Xi growled, "I'm not going to stand in their—"

"Stand by, Major," Nakamura interrupted. "I've got something on the drone cameras."

He forwarded the vid feed to her, and on it, she saw no fewer than forty rebels huddled behind Hephaestus' towering spherical chamber, half of which was dug into the cavern floor. The rebels were making the universal human sign of surrender: throwing their weapons down and thrusting their hands into the air.

"Giles, launch your aerial drones, then move toward Hephaestus and secure those rebels," Xi commanded. "I'll cover your approach from here. If they so much as twitch, I'll blow them *and* their precious forge to hell. I want a full visual inspection of this chamber before we interrogate these people."

"Copy that, Major," Giles acknowledged, driving the now-one-armed *Culture Knight* toward the cavern's center. "Drones away. Feeding telemetry to your system."

She saw a quad of aerial drones, each less than a meter in diameter, lift off from *Culture Knight's* shoulders like birds bursting from a tree. They sped off across the cavern, feeding their video and sensor feeds back to *Elvira*. Satisfied with the first few seconds' data, she added, "Nakamura, keep those HK weapons hot. I'm not about to fall for six-year-old schoolyard treachery."

"Locked and loaded, ma'am," Nakamura assured her.

A few minutes later, Corporal Giles' mech came to a stop at their position and the rebels complied with the directive to move away from the chamber's central apparatus. The drones had confirmed that no more heavy weapons platforms were within the chamber and that two other groups of rebels were present. Those rebels, somewhat surprisingly, came out from cover and willingly surrendered before being commanded to do so.

And when she got the first images of their visored faces, she saw a mixture of fear and resignation. But their fear was not directed at the Metalheads, and their resignation was clearly a far-from-recent development.

These people were terrified, and had been for days...or possibly *weeks*.

"Something's not right here," she muttered as an ominous feeling swept over her. She was missing something vital, and it was probably staring her in the face although she didn't know it.

"What are your orders, Major?" Corporal Giles inquired into the growing silence as Xi grappled with her sudden uncertainty.

"Stand by, Skeptic," she replied tersely, accidentally using his callsign from Watery Grave. "Something's not right here."

"Do you want me to run another sweep of the cavern?" Giles asked.

"I said 'stand by,'" she snapped.

"Yes, ma'am,' he acknowledged as she began to replay the combat recorder data from the first moments of their insertion to the cavern. She specifically focused on the initial video footage of the gun nests and SRM pod, which she had initially thought to be hidden behind makeshift barricades and camouflage.

But what she saw on those first images was something altogether different: the gun nests and SRM pod had not been hidden, they had been aimed at the lower tunnel entry and not the upper one. Some quick math confirmed that both the chain gun and the SRM pod would have required significant effort to manually reposition, and the expected timetables to do so aligned almost perfectly with the delay between the Metalheads' arrival and their coming under fire from those platforms.

"They went to all the trouble to fortify this cavern, bringing weapons down from the surface," she muttered, "but why didn't they have them ready to defend against an attack from the surf—"

She cut herself short when the obvious answer went off like a collision alert between her ears. For a moment, she was dumbfounded and unable to think clearly.

"No fucking way..." she seethed, goosebumps rising all across her body as she redoubled her efforts to examine the drone-flight data. "Skeptic," she barked, "send all your drones down the lower tunnel and feed me the images. Now."

"Yes, ma'am," he replied, prompting his drones to tear across the cavern at top speed. They moved sluggishly in the light atmosphere, and while they moved, she repositioned *Elvira* to get a better look at the lower tunnel on the far side of the loading dock.

"Penny," she snapped, her mind racing as she came to terms with the magnitude of the situation. "Suit up. You're going for a ride."

"Yes, ma'am," her mech's Monkey replied as Xi released the four-wheeled ATV from *Elvira's* stern, running a remote diagnostic series and finding the vehicle ready to ride. In four seconds flat, Penny was standing at the rear of *Elvira's* cockpit with her helmet affixed to her EVA suit's collar. Xi was impressed by the other woman's diligence and readiness, and she knew every second would count if her theory was right.

Nobody had expected this. *Nobody.* But the possibility had been staring them in the face all along, and no one in the command staff, from General Pushkin down to Major Xi Bao herself, had even considered the possibility during the pre-op briefings.

"Major," Giles said warily, "I've got something here."

Xi's eyes snapped to the video feed of *Culture Knight*'s third drone, and what she saw there confirmed her worst fears.

She forwarded the images, along with all combat recorder data from the trio of mechs, to *Elvira's* runabout ATV. She also loaded the same files onto a data chip, which she handed to Penny while making direct eye contact. "Get back to the surface as fast as that thing can take you. Link up with the *William Wallace* ASAP, forward those files for their review, and request *immediate* reinforcements from anything we've got up there that can move."

"What's going on, Major?" Penny asked, a rare note of fear entering the unflappable woman's voice.

It was so obvious. So painfully obvious that Xi couldn't help but laugh despite the situation's gravity. "I'm not going to lie." She sneered in self-condemnation as she magnified the images now being sent by all four of *Culture Knight*'s drones. "I didn't see *this* coming."

On each of those video feeds was a peculiar and distinctive patch of purplish residue on the lower tunnel's floor and walls. Xi had seen that residue before. Well, to be more accurate, she had *created* that residue before. Hundreds, possibly even *thousands* of times.

Even Penny, who had never before seen such images in anything but a classroom, knew exactly what they were when her eyes snagged on them. Those eyes went wide with horror, but they soon hardened with resolve, which filled her voice as she clutched the data chip firmly in her hand. "Understood, Major. What's your message for the general?"

"Keep it short and sweet." Xi smirked, prepping *Elvira's* airlock to permit the other woman passage as she composed a short word missive to the Metalheads above. "Tell them we've got rock-biters. The Arh'Kel have infested Mars."

13

THE BEST DEFENSE

"Tell me everything you know about the Arh'Kel on this planet," Xi commanded as soon as the self-described rebel leader doffed his suit's helmet. Penny had shot back up the tunnel six minutes earlier, during which time Xi had summoned the Martian rebel for an emergency meeting in *Elvira's* cabin.

"We had no idea they were here," the man replied, his voice taut and thin like a man who had spent a week alone in a foxhole. "We'd been down here protecting this forge for weeks when the first Arh'Kel showed up."

"What were they doing?" Xi pressed.

"Ignoring us, mostly." A haunted look fell over his features. "They seemed to be conducting recon, moving in threes and sixes. They came in here, looked around a bit, and left."

"You didn't open fire?" Chief Lu asked skeptically.

"We're not stupid," the rebel spat. "There weren't supposed to be *any* Arh'Kel on Mars. This is Sol!" he cried. "How did they even get here?!"

"You didn't fire," Xi surmised, "because you didn't know how many of them there were."

"Or what their purpose was," the rebel agreed. "Besides, we

only have six missiles in that pod. Well, four now," he amended sheepishly. "We sent a few teams surface-side to try to warn the others, but without the One Mind, we lost contact. I doubt they survived anyway."

"What's your name?" Lu asked.

"Marvin Hamlin," the rebel leader said, gesturing to rank insignia on his suit's left shoulder. "Martian Militia. Most of us down here are, which is how we got access to the weapons."

Xi dearly wanted to make a "Marvin the Martian" joke, but refrained given the significance of the moment and instead concluded, "You came down here to safeguard Martian interests."

"And we did just that," he confirmed. "There were a dozen raiding parties that came down the Upper Tunnel, most of which were Breakers looking to take advantage of the chaos. We repelled most of them with small-arms fire while we waited for things to sort out on the surface."

"Breakers?" Xi repeated uncertainly.

"Martian Separatists," he explained. "Breakers have been part of Mars since the Tharsis colony was founded. They're a minority, but a vocal and surprisingly influential one. They always talk a good game about fighting for what they believe in, but if you ask me, they're just a bunch of low-brow anarchists who don't even understand their own founding philosophy...if their 'beliefs' could even be called that. After they took down three of the beanstalks, we knew something had to be done to keep them from destroying everything else of value on our world, so the militia formed teams and went out to secure vital infrastructure like this."

"You've only got eighty-four people," Lu said skeptically. "And unless you're better at hiding munitions than our scanners are at finding them, you've barely got enough equipment to arm a quarter that many. How could you think you'd secure a facility like this with so little?"

"When we set out, we had five hundred," Hamlin replied grimly, "along with eight armored carriers, six missile pods, eight chain guns and enough small arms to outfit twice that many. Our primary objectives were to secure this facility and two of the nearby beanstalks. That was before we ran into the goldies."

"Goldies?" Xi repeated, suspecting she already knew what he meant.

He nodded. "New armored vehicles unlike anything we'd ever seen or heard about. They were squawking valid Solar military idents, so we approached...and that was when they blew us to hell."

Xi called up a series of combat recorder images featuring the arrowhead-shaped vehicles she had engaged on the surface. "Are these the vehicles you encountered?"

Hamlin nodded as soon as he saw them. "That's them, all right. Tore into us like we weren't even there. If we'd known they were hostile..." He visibly began to tremble, prompting Lu to place a steadying hand on the man's shoulder.

"Take a seat," Lu urged, and the other man grudgingly complied before gripping his hands into fists and taking several deep breaths.

His eyes met Xi's before keying in on her TAC uniform. "What in the War God's name is the Terran Republic doing here?"

"We're here at Sol's request," she said firmly, proffering a data slate containing documents that proved as much.

Hamlin hesitated before accepting the slate and clumsily working with the interface. It was obvious he was unused to dealing with a physical interface device, and Xi wondered just how badly traumatized these people had been after being forcibly cut off from the One Mind immediately after what must have been a confusing, terrifying period when Jemmin propaganda and Jem's counter-program warred for control over the virtual network.

"You... This doesn't make sense." He shook his head disbelievingly. "Why would Sol ask Terra for help?"

"Because we've helped them before," Xi answered as honestly as possible, "and Sol needed our help again. I know this is a lot to take in, but we don't have time. The Arh'Kel are here, which means they've been here for a long, long time. Have you seen any heavy weapons platforms? Railguns or missile launchers?"

Hamlin nodded distantly, his eyes lingering on the slate's contents. "We sent recon parties down the tunnels...six of them. Only one made it back." He produced a data chip and offered it to Xi. "They brought this."

Xi accepted the chip and plugged it into a secure data interface, where she quickly discovered that it was not Solar but rather Terran tech. "Isn't this contraband?" she asked in bewilderment.

"Of course," he replied with a shrug. "But despite what the One Mind purports, Mars' rebellious streak runs a lot deeper and manifests in subtler ways than just roving bands of hooligans like the Breakers."

Xi shook her head in wry approval as she accessed the chip's contents. "I think I'm starting to like you Martians." She soon saw still images, taken by a low-res video recorder, of Arh'Kel heavy weapon platforms. There were railguns, missile launchers, and a third type of system she had never seen in any Arh'Kel-related intel.

But that wasn't to say she didn't know *precisely* what she was looking at.

"Fuck me..." she muttered as she peered closer at the system. "Lu, come here." She beckoned, prompting her Wrench to lean over her shoulder and examine the images. "Tell me that's not what I think it is."

Lu sucked in a surprised breath before furrowing his brow. "If I didn't know better, I'd say that was a Jemmin vehicle-grade laser mounted on a rock-biter HWP chassis."

"Wait..." Hamlin interrupted in confusion. "Did you say, 'Jemmin?' What have they got to do with the Arh'Kel invading Sol?"

Xi grimaced. "The Arh'Kel didn't invade Sol. At least, they didn't do it alone. Jemmin is primarily responsible for the One Mind's collapse and ensuing chaos." She pointedly did not elaborate on the Metal Legion's role, which she knew would unnecessarily muddy the waters at a time when she needed every available hand she could get. "The Arh'Kel are being used as mindless bioweapons. Somehow Jemmin brought them down here, probably decades ago, and hid their activities from Martian view while they built up enough infrastructure to overcome Mars' defenses from within."

Hamlin's eyes narrowed incredulously. "That's impossible."

"Is it?" Lu challenged, inclining his chin toward the Terran-made data chip Hamlin had given Xi. "Because unless you also smuggled in high-precision Terran-built seismic sensors or conducted physical inspections of every single subterranean chamber large enough to house an Arh'Kel colony, there's no way you'd be able to detect their presence. Jemmin interference in your One Mind network would have hidden them from any Solar tech that might otherwise have uncovered their presence."

"This isn't our first time finding Arh'Kel infesting a planet they weren't supposed to be on," Xi said confidently. "We know how to deal with it. But to do that, I need your people to refortify your position here and await reinforcements."

Hamlin's skepticism had morphed into horror and finally rounded back into the same resignation she had initially seen in his visage. "We've all known we would die down here. We can't fight against an Arh'Kel invasion. Our coil gun only has eight thousand bullets."

"We've got plenty of firepower, most of which is already underground and working to secure facilities like this one," she assured him, although the truth was they couldn't deal with a planetary-scale Arh'Kel invasion with just the assets assigned to War God. She didn't yet know how they *could* deal with such a large-scale infestation, but if Penny was successful in contacting General Moon, Xi was confident he could figure something out. "But our priorities have obviously changed. Our new first order of business is to link up with the other Metalheads and Marines down here before deciding how to proceed." She opened a link to Giles. "What's the status of those seismics, Skeptic?"

"Running through their final bootups now, ma'am," he replied promptly. "We should have the first readings in five seconds."

"If I'm right," she said tightly, making pointed eye contact with Lu and Hamlin, "the rock-biters are already on the move, and have probably engaged with our advance teams and the platoons that are deeper underground."

"Getting readings now, Major," Giles reported before confirming, "I'm seeing vibrations consistent with Arh'Kel HWPs in a tunnel adjacent to the main one ten kilometers farther down, ma'am."

"How many platforms?" she pressed.

"At least four," he replied. "I'm still fine-tuning the sensors for this strata, but it looks like there are at least two hundred infantry with them."

"There'll be a whole lot more than that." She grunted. "Any indication where they're going?"

"Not yet. I need to place a few more sensors to triangulate."

"How far do they need to be?" Xi asked.

"At least five kilometers."

"All right." She nodded decisively, turning to Hamlin. "We need to get your people reset here, and then we're heading down."

"What?" Hamlin double-blinked in surprise. "You're not actually *looking* for an Arh'Kel horde to fight, are you?"

Seeing her opening, she flashed a shark-like smile. "It's what we do, Marvin the Martian. We fight so you don't have to. Now, let's see about beefing up these defenses, just in case these bastards get past us."

"These HKs only have enough ammo for twelve seconds' sustained fire," Lieutenant Nakamura advised Marvin Hamlin after helping set two of his four remote-controlled mech-killers in a blind near the lower tunnel. "But small-arms slugs are too weak to ward off rock-biters anyway. So I'm killing their machine guns and setting the drones to automatically home in on the nearest Arh'Kel vehicle they see. Wait for the HWPs to breach the cavern before switching these things on. When they activate, they'll head straight at a target, and their onboard explosives will detonate when they come within three meters of an enemy vehicle."

"These are suicide drones," Hamlin clarified. The trio of mechs was undergoing field repairs, with their Wrenches and Monkeys working tirelessly to patch their hulls in preparation for the next advance. While they worked, Xi had decided it would be a show of good faith to have a physical conference with the Martian Militiamen out in the cavern.

"They are," Xi agreed, gesturing to the pair of low-profile, wedge-shaped drones with the small-caliber machine guns bolted to their topsides. "And they're purpose-built to scrap vehicles, even ones as heavily armored as ours."

"But Arh'Kel HWPs aren't that well-protected," Nakamura continued, "so if it looks like you've got two or more platforms closer than ten meters apart, it's worth trying to get a twofer."

"You'll need to reorient your RPGs back onto the lower tunnel," Xi advised, gesturing to the fifteen-meter-diameter tunnel that led into the bowels of the Martian underworld. "How much ammo do you have for them?"

"We've got six launchers and twenty-two grenades," Hamlin replied, causing Xi to scowl. "Along with the four remaining SRMs," he belatedly added.

"Each of our mechs has a small-arms locker that includes one or two anti-materiel rifles apiece. You'll take those," she declared, gesturing to ideal placements for solo snipers. "Assign them to your best marksmen and put them there, there, there, and there. With any luck, they'll be able to hold the rock-biters off at the tunnel mouth long enough for the HWPs to come to the fore, at which point the HKs can engage and maybe even turn them back. We've also got two dozen hand grenades, and we'll give you half of those," she decided after considering whether she should give the Martians all of the grenades. "But without our large-bores, we'll need to keep the rest for ourselves."

Nakamura nodded approvingly. "No matter what, you need to hold those SRMs in reserve as your last line of defense. If the HKs, large-bores, and RPGs don't turn the rock-biters back, a few missiles won't make a difference."

"What do you mean?" Hamlin asked.

"You need to be ready to blow this tunnel," Xi explained gravely. "And those four missiles have just enough kick to do the job. The rock-biters will break through the collapse, probably in minutes rather than hours, but it will buy you enough time to set an overload of this facility's local fusion generator."

Hamlin's mouth fell open in shock. "You're suggesting we destroy this forge after everything we've done to protect it?"

"This is about a lot more than just this forge now, Mr. Hamlin," Xi said sharply. "If this planet is as infested with Arh'Kel as others we've seen, the rock-biters will control it in a matter of *days* if left unopposed in their march to the surface."

"At that point," Nakamura assented, "they'll tear down everything of value before returning underground and resuming their buildup of weapons and infantry. The beanstalks, the manufactories on the surface...*everything* will be gone, and a lot of the damage will probably be caused by our people bombarding them from orbit."

"I thought Arh'Kel required significant quantities of rare minerals to procreate." Hamlin cocked his head dubiously. "Solar engineers and mineralogists have spent *decades* exploring the Martian crust in search of those very compounds. We've already mined everything like that in this strata, so what are they using to fuel their growth?"

Xi grimaced. "It's likely that Jemmin provided them with enough rare earth to get them built up to this point, either with a large deposit early on or with a steady trickle of supplies delivered right under your noses."

He shook his head flatly. "That's insane. Our sensors would have picked up that kind of activity. Jemmin ships seldom come to Sol; we've have known if they were in Martian orbit."

Xi and Nakamura shared a knowing look before, in perfect unison, shaking their heads and declaring, "No, you wouldn't."

He seemed skeptical but decided to drop the matter as Corporal Giles came over to make his report. "*Culture Knight*'s ready to ride, ma'am. We obviously can't do anything about the missing arm, but the rest of her scrapes and dents are patched up. *Murasame's* got a gap in its left flank armor that we can't do much about," he added in disappointment. "It would take at least two hours to try welding something up there. The metal's too fatigued and brittle to slap something on any quicker than that. And *Elvira* will be good to go once we've sealed off the lost missile launcher's mount. That should be finished in less than ten minutes."

"Good work, Corporal." She twirled her finger in the air. "We roll in ten."

"Yes, ma'am," Giles acknowledged, turning and making his way toward the repair crews still working on patching Xi's mech.

"I need you to go over these tunnels with us," Xi urged, turning to Hamlin and proffering a data slate. "We've got almost a hundred people deployed down here, working to secure the infrastructure. We need to know if there's been any damage to these tunnels so we can chart an optimal rendezvous with the rest of our people."

Hamlin examined the three-dimensional map and gestured to a pair of cross-tunnels. "These were collapsed early on when Breakers blew one of the reactors there."

"How long ago?" Nakamura inquired.

"It's been at least two weeks," Hamlin said confidently before adding, "but I'm honestly not sure. Sometimes it feels like we've been down here for a year. How long has it been, anyway?"

"Since Antivenom?" Xi asked, mentally cursing herself for letting the op's name slip.

"What?" Hamlin asked suspiciously.

Nakamura gave her a hard look, silently reminding her that Sol still considered Antivenom to be a classified operation when it came to the Martians. The Solarians weren't certain that the Martians were trustworthy, given the depths of Jemmin influence throughout the Solar System, and didn't want to tip their hand regarding how Sol had avoided total self-destruction.

But Xi was asking these people to watch her back and cover their line of retreat. Most of the time, that was among the most dangerous tasks a warrior could be assigned, and she would be thrice-damned if she asked someone to risk their life for her without her making clear who she was.

"Your government asked us to help here on Mars because we did something similar on Luna," she explained. "We were responsible for injecting the One Mind with an antivirus that caused all the chaos down here." His eyebrows rose in alarm, but when he opened his mouth to inquire, she shut him down and pressed on. "Solar intelligence suspects, and Terran intelligence concurs, that without our antivirus, which we delivered to the One Mind network in an op we named 'Antivenom,' ninety-five percent of Solar human life would have already been extinguished, and the vast majority of Solar infrastructure would be in ruins. I'm here because Sol asked Terra to help with a crisis, and Terrans don't turn their backs on family. Now, can you hold this cavern or, if the rock-biters come in too great a force, can you blow it and buy our people on the surface enough time to protect everything we've already secured up there? There are fifty million human beings on your world who will be annihilated by the Arh'Kel if we don't stop them right here, right now. Those lives are more important than the Martian infrastructure we came here to secure," she finished with conviction. "So right now, safeguarding *them* is my priority. If you can't or won't do that, I need to know."

For a long, tense moment, Hamlin's dark visage suggested he would be anything but cooperative. Thankfully, and in a surprising display of clearheaded thinking, he nodded affirmatively. "We'll hold the cavern, Major. But if we make it out of this, you and I are taking a full bottle into a locked room, and we're not coming out again until you tell me more about this 'Operation Antivenom.'"

"Done." She nodded in agreement. "Now let's get your people armed up so they can channel their inner Jackson Pollack with the color purple."

" 1st Platoon," she called over the link after confirming all three mechs were ready to roll, "form up on me and proceed at forty-five kph. I say again, four-five kph. Any faster than that, and we'll wake 'em up before we get close enough for third base."

"We wouldn't want that, would we?" Nakamura snickered.

"I feel like I'd be remiss if I didn't ask," Giles said hesitantly. "Are we sure this is the right call?"

"Of course not," Xi replied as the trio of mechs marched down the tunnel. "We could wait a few hours for Captain Koch to come down with Joker Company and reinforce a full advance. But we're one of the shallowest teams in the op, which means most of our people are deeper, possibly cut off and surrounded by Arh'Kel as we speak. I don't know about you, but I don't want to live in a world where every minute of my life is filled with doubt about whether or not I could have done something to help them. If that means I die down here, so be it. If either of you has even the slightest hesitation, fall back and hold the cavern with the Martian Militia."

"With all due respect, piss off, Major," Nakamura quipped.

"That goes for me, too," Giles assented.

"Good," Xi drawled. "Then I've got both of you for verbal insubordination. So much for that glowing review you were hoping for, Lieutenant."

"They don't review the dead, Major. That's what our posthumous hero awards are for," Nakamura retorted.

"No, they don't," she allowed before channeling the old man's style of speech to the best of her ability. "But you know what they say..."

In perfect unison, and without any more prompting than that, all three Jocks enthusiastically declared, "Metal never dies!"

"Contact! I've got railgun fire ahead," Giles declared as they neared the first of four locations that had been on the Marines' itineraries. She checked the flying drones' video feeds, forwarded by Giles' *Culture Knight*, and confirmed what looked like railgun flashes in the cavern ahead.

This cavern, fifteen kilometers down from the one held by Hamlin's people, was an active ice mine that fed much-needed gas and water to the foundries to facilitate various metalworking processes. It was a tactically valuable position given that it intersected six different tunnels, each of which led to adjacent manufactories and foundries situated between ten and fifty kilometers from the ice mine.

"Weapons hot and increase speed to flank," she barked when she got a glimpse of what looked like a Terran Marine flipping head over feet and firing his railgun rifle mid-air. "Burn anything that isn't human, and don't worry about the machinery. The Solarians say this stuff's easily replaced."

"'Want to get paid to hurt people and break things?'" mocked Corporal Giles as they increased speed. "'Join the Terran Armor Corps. With us, it's a fulltime job!'"

"Sounds like the opening monologue of our next recruiting ad," Xi murmured as *Elvira* surged into the three-kilometer-wide, bowl-shaped cavern. "And here's the visual money shot..."

she declared, sighting in on two Arh'Kel railguns on the far side of the cavern. "AP up, on the way!"

Elvira's mains thundered, sending bolts of steel into the leftmost HWP. The enemy platform exploded, its capacitors discharging in a brilliant display of arcing electricity as its companion vehicle fired in reply. *Elvira's* bow was hammered by a direct hit, but the enemy bolt struck a fresh segment of her armor and was stopped.

Culture Knight unleashed his right arm's dual eight-kilo guns, launching a pair of HE shells into a cluster of Arh'Kel infantry that were swarming toward the cornered Marine. The shells splashed danger-close to the Marine, but judging from his continued evasions, did little or no damage to him or his power armor while laying waste to the rock-biters. Eight Arh'Kel infantry fell to those shells and another four were seriously injured, slowing their cartwheeling pursuit to a crawl as the Marine bounded away with a series of power-assisted leaps.

Murasame fired a pair of SRMs at the remaining HWP, scattering the vehicle's minimalist frame in a shower of explosive debris. And when all three mechs had emerged into the cavern, which held no fewer than two hundred Arh'Kel infantry, their chain guns went live, and the roar of fifty-caliber slugs was like the battle cry of the war god himself.

Purple gore spattered left and right as the weapons sawed through the rock-biters' unarmored stony hides. Limbs were amputated in showers of vital fluids, and the enemy infantry fired their peculiar pistols in impotent reply while beating a hasty retreat to a pair of distant tunnels.

The Metalheads walked their enemy down, pouring thousands of rounds of ammunition into the fleeing Arh'Kel before it became clear the enemy wanted no part of them just then.

"Hold on the chains and target with HE shells," Xi commanded before loading a pair of HE shells into *Elvira's* mains. "HE up...on the way!" she declared, sending two jumbo servings of steel-wrapped death into the fleeing rock-biters.

Culture Knight added his own pair of HE shells to the mix, and the quartet of explosive projectiles wrought bloody carnage among the horde of cartwheeling six-limbed enemies. No more than forty Arh'Kel infantry escaped the bloodbath, roughly half of which went down each of the southern and southeastern tunnels.

"Report, Corporal," she commanded after receiving a live-feed of the lone Marine's battle-suit data.

"They appeared eight minutes ago, Major," Corporal Hendricks replied promptly. "They seemed surprised to see me, which bought me enough time to take cover before engaging."

Xi threw her head back and laughed as deeply as she had done in months. "You actually opened fire on hundreds of Arh'Kel escorting two of their HWPs? You guys *are* crazy, you know that?"

"Must be the steady diet of crayons," he quipped, drawing another snicker from Xi.

"Are you fit to march, Marine?" she finally asked.

"Ready to bring the pain, ma'am," he replied confidently.

"Then let's do it," she declared.

"What's the plan, Major?" he inquired. "Do we continue with the tier-two objectives as indicated?"

"Negative." She shook her head. "There are four more solo Marines between us and the next high-value facility, which is the designated rally point for this sector. We hook up with them, reach that facility and whatever elements fell back there, and then fight our way back to the surface. Or we die trying," she added casually, as though it was an afterthought. Which, to her mind, it was. "What do you say, Corporal?"

"Ooh-fucking-rah, ma'am."

14

BITE THIS

"Come on, stone-fuckers!" Hammer bellowed, sending a tungsten bolt into an Arh'Kel railgun while charging *Warcrafter* deeper into the largest cavern in the subterranean network. It had been almost nine hours since Phase Three's commencement, and Jenkins' team had succeeded in overtaking their first objective before stumbling onto the largest group of Arh'Kel encountered since Durgan's Folly.

This cavern measured eleven kilometers by nine kilometers and was nearly a full kilometer from floor to ceiling at its deepest point. The ambient temperature was over forty degrees centigrade, owing to the presence of eight nearby fusion reactors that used the crust of Mars as a heat sink. These reactors fueled fifty percent of the underground infrastructure they had come down to secure and represented one of the most central and vulnerable points in the subterranean tunnel network.

Warcrafter's mains roared, sending AP shells across the cavern, where they narrowly missed an Arh'Kel HWP. The shower of stony shards skittered harmlessly off the nearby rockbiter infantry but seemed to temporarily knock the railgun offline.

Warcrafter suddenly juked left, narrowly avoiding a missile that screamed past and tore into the wall behind. The missile's author was struck by return fire from the Razorback to *Warcrafter's* immediate right, and the enemy launch pod was obliterated in a deafening crack as its unspent ordnance sympathetically detonated.

Jenkins worked furiously at his tactical plotter, forwarding priority targets to each of his platoon's jocks including Hammer. As soon as Jenkins forwarded a target to *Warcrafter's* Jock, Hammer put a pair of SRMs into it. Flake or no, he proved his mettle time and again. He wasn't the most creative Jock Jenkins had ever seen, but he was fearless and single-minded when the shit hit the fan.

Which was exactly what had happened.

The enormous cavern connected nine different tunnels, and the Arh'Kel appeared to be arriving through at least five of them. At first count, Jenkins had tallied twenty-three rock-biter HWPs, including two which appeared to have Jemmin lasers mounted on them. After the furious opening exchange, the enemy was down to just eleven HWPs, but the weight of fire was starting to take its toll on Jenkins' people.

As though the gods of war were reading his mind, the mech to *Warcrafter's* right, *Gray Cicada*, was bracketed by two Arh'Kel HWPs. The first was a railgun, which skewered the damaged mech's forward armor, sending a spray of ablative composites out in a gray plume. The other, which landed a quarter-second after the first, was one of the Jemmin beams.

That beam was on-target for less than a tenth of a second, but that was more than enough time to penetrate the mech's battered armor and dig catastrophically into its fusion power core. The mech's death throes were so violent that huge pieces of flying debris slammed into *Warcrafter's* hull with a deafening clang, sending the mighty war machine skittering a full five meters to port.

"Focus fire!" Jenkins commanded, forwarding targets to the two well-concealed Jemmin beam weapons. "Missile salvo, full spread. Fire! Fire! Fire!"

The missiles leapt from their launchers, slamming into the enemy position and blowing three of the HWPs apart. Two of the missiles hammered into the far wall, destroying metal support buttresses stretching eighty meters from floor to ceiling. The weak patch of the cavern's roof, shattered by nearby explosions and no longer held in place by the vertical supports, collapsed on the enemy position, taking another two platforms with it, including the second Jemmin beam emitter.

But the HWPs were merely the tip of the lance, as the oncoming horde of two thousand Arh'Kel made abundantly clear with their cartwheeling advance.

"Keep the coil guns to thirty-round bursts," Jenkins ordered. "Conserve ammo, and make every bullet count. Pour it on!"

The trio of mechs' coil guns whined to life, spewing deadly metal into the onrushing tide of rock-biter infantry. Hundreds fell in those first seconds, but the press of Arh'Kel soldiers drove forward with mindless disregard for their own safety. Sweeping left and right, Jenkins' mechs overlapped their coil guns' fields of fire and carved bloody ruin across the rock-biter line.

True to form, the rock-biters never faltered in their advance, driving steadily closer to the Razorbacks. If they pushed much closer, he would be forced to withdraw, which could be disastrous given that the tunnel joined the cavern at a perfect ninety-degree angle, affording the Arh'Kel HWPs a direct line of sight as they withdrew.

"Weapons free," Jenkins snarled. "Max cycle on the coils, and fire artillery for effect! Put them *down*!"

The Razorbacks' fifteens belched righteous fury, punching

explosive shells through the line of cartwheeling Arh'Kel and sending silica-based gore flying a hundred meters in all directions. Each of the six shells claimed at least fifty rock-biters, while the max-cycling coil guns spat hot death and cut down another hundred per second with their combined ferocity.

But the rock-biters kept coming, with fresh reinforcements flooding into the cavern faster than they could be sanctioned. The rock-biters wanted this cavern, and they looked like they had the strength to take it. It was like something out of a nightmare or, in Jenkins' case, the particularly vivid memory of his last sojourn into the underworld of Durgan's Folly.

"Prepare to withdraw," Jenkins growled before a flicker of motion across the cavern caught his eye. The steady stream of Arh'Kel infantry from one of the tunnels had suddenly ceased, and a brilliant explosion illuminated the far end of the chamber as an Arh'Kel HWP exploded in a blue-white conflagration.

Charging into the fray with railguns and wrist-mounted fifty caliber slug-throwers spitting hot death were four power-armored Terrans, including Major Tim Trapper Jr. The newly-arrived warriors hammered into the Arh'Kel flank, hurling grenades and firing their railguns into the enemy's midst.

"Full missile salvo and countercharge!" Jenkins roared as the tide of Arh'Kel briefly faltered. "Push!"

The three Razorbacks surged forward, their missile launchers hurling explosive ordnance at the enemy. Four hundred Arh'Kel were annihilated in an instant as the missiles carved the beginning of a swath between Jenkins' and Trapper's units. The timely arrival of reinforcements had turned the tide of battle.

Hope—the most powerful of all combat emotions. Jenkins gritted his teeth and redoubled his efforts. Now was the time to win.

Warcrafter's railgun sent a hypervelocity sliver into a newly-arrived Arh'Kel railgun, scrapping the mount a heartbeat after it emerged from its tunnel. Two more artillery shells blew a gaping hole in the enemy line and were followed by Jenkins' flanking Razorbacks, which dug the gap deeper through the sea of enemy soldiers.

The coil guns continued pouring into the enemy. They were nearing their heat tolerances, but Jenkins knew this was his only chance to link up with Trapper and the Marines. Terran bullets tore into Arh'Kel flesh, crippling, dismembering, and outright killing the suddenly resurgent aliens as they finally seemed to adapt to the appearance of the power-armored Terrans.

Trapper and the Marines charged through the Arh'Kel, firing their slug-throwers at infantry from point-blank range while conserving their railguns for the higher-value HWPs. Like superheroes who disdained everyone and everything around them, including the laws of physics, the power-armored warriors carved a bloody path to the rendezvous point at the cavern's center, where Jenkins' mechs finally linked up with them.

"You can figure out how to thank me later, Leeroy," Trapper quipped.

"*Me* thank *you?*" Jenkins grinned tightly as he forwarded another formation to the newly joined units. "Sometimes it seems like my whole career is spent bailing you and Johnny out of trouble."

"Fuck you." The major grunted, firing his railgun into one of the HWPs less than a second before it was ready to fire. "*And* the pig you rode in on."

"Don't talk about her like that, Tim," Jenkins chided as the group reformed, with the Marines huddled in the center of the formation and the Razorbacks forming a triangle with the point aimed at the tunnel through which Jenkins had arrived just a few minutes earlier. "At least not until she's out of earshot."

"Fair enough," Trapper allowed, firing his slug-thrower into a trio of too-close-for-comfort rock-biters, putting two down outright and slowing the third enough that it fell away from the formation, melting back into the horde of oncoming enemy. "I don't suppose any of you geniuses have anything resembling a plan?"

"Plan?" Jenkins repeated before a nearby comm signal connected with Warcrafter's system. He grinned when he saw who the connection's author was. "Who needs a plan when you've got a Charles Bronson complex and overwhelming firepower?"

Before Trapper could retort, six more Razorbacks burst into the cavern with guns blazing. Artillery thundered, railguns flashed, and coil guns whined as the Arh'Kel line was mercilessly hammered on the left flank by the newcomers.

"No fair," Trapper objected. "You knew they'd do that."

"Privilege of rank, Major." Jenkins smiled wolfishly as the trio of mechs and quad of power-armored Terrans adjusted course to rendezvous with the new arrivals.

"I hope we didn't miss the good stuff, Colonel," Captain Chao greeted him as his team's fresh delivery of max sustained firepower dealt utter annihilation to the enemy line. For the first time since Jenkins had arrived in this hellish chamber, they were killing more rock-biters than were arriving, and despite that particular situation's unsustainability, it felt damned good to turn the tide in their favor.

"There are more than enough party favors to go around," Jenkins assured his Battalion XO. "Help yourselves. Don't be shy."

"Shy? Me?" Chao chuckled as he forwarded his updated roster, which painted a less-than-pretty picture. "I'll be sure to tell my old man I've finally been accused of being something more than a wannabe."

"Glad to help you get that monkey off your back," Jenkins muttered as he read through the six mechs statuses, including that of Captain Chao. Although the colonel had assumed the captain's 4th Platoon had linked up with one or the other of 2nd or 3rd Platoon, it seemed he had already reunited with *both* of them. The twelve mechs of 2nd, 3rd, and 4th Platoons had been reduced to six, and Jenkins' four mechs of 1st Company were now down to three.

Which meant he'd almost lost half the metal Clover had sent down this hole, and it looked like the fight was just beginning.

Attached to Captain Chao's unit was Captain Hao, the woman whose big toes he had removed before, at Jenkins' urging, Chao had removed his own big toes as an exemplar. As usual, Captain Guan had hit the bullseye in predicting that the barbaric disciplinary measure would bear fruit. Hao had renewed her commission following the punitive action, pushing a lucrative career playing professional soccer down the road several years. She had recommitted herself to military service and, more pointedly, to the Metal Legion.

And she demonstrated that commitment by charging into the Arh'Kel at Chao's side, their two mechs leaving the others behind while the two captains made a bold play to carve a path to Jenkins' position. The enemy HWPs were hunkered down behind huge stacks of crude iron ore ingots to the northwest, stacks so large they shielded the enemy railguns from Chao's firing angle.

Jenkins immediately understood Chao's intention and knew that he needed to address those shielded HWPs or Chao would be flanked by the enemy. And with fresh HWPs arriving through the tunnels, and Legion ordnance running low after the furious exchange, Jenkins understood he had just one chance to reconnect with Chao's formation.

"1st Platoon," he barked, forwarding a target package to all three of his mechs, "priority target, weapons free. Dig those fuckers out!"

His virtual orders included the explicit command to empty their missile tubes at the enemy's makeshift bunker. In reply, his Metalheads sent all fourteen of their remaining SRMs into the enemy position, supporting the barrage with fifteen-kilo AP shells and railgun bolts.

Eight of the missiles crashed into the wall of iron bricks, hurling half-ton ingots aside and causing the stacks' outer layers to collapse without functionally impacting their defensive value. The other six missiles knifed through the narrow gaps between the stacks, gaps barely wide enough for the automated forklifts to traverse while carrying one of the ingots to its destination. Three of those missiles slammed into the far wall, while the others neutralized three of the six Arh'Kel guns using the ingot stacks as cover.

The artillery shells followed, slamming into the upper margins of the ingot stacks and collapsing great walls of iron onto the enemy. Dozens of rock-biter infantry were crushed to death by the ingots, which even claimed an Arh'Kel railgun mount as an ingot took an unexpected hop after landing atop another and skittering across the stone floor to slam into the delicate HWP's frame.

The railguns did the heaviest lifting, all three sending tungsten slivers into enemy gun mounts and violating their power cells to satisfyingly brilliant effect. Dozens more Arh'Kel infantry died in the incandescent release of energy, which transformed their purple innards into modern cave art that would have given any self-respecting post-modernist multiple orgasms.

While Jenkins' mechs scratched all but one of the HWPs

from Fort Ingot, Chao and Hao sent a furious volley of ordnance into a thick concentration of HWPs surrounded by rock-biters. Missiles slammed into the ground, propelling rocky debris, both inert and recently-living, in deadly clouds of shrapnel which clattered off the Arh'Kel, their weapons, and the cavern walls behind them. Artillery shells rained down on the enemy position, scratching another two HWPs as even more enemy weapons arrived through the other tunnels.

Three of those HWPs fired, hammering tungsten bolts into Chao's and Hao's mechs. Despite suffering just one strike, Hao's mech took the worst of it, losing the use of her front-right leg as a bullseye struck its hull joint and rendered it completely useless. Demonstrating her quick wits, Hao decoupled that leg and left it behind, adjusting her mech's balance to compensate as she fell in behind Chao's mech.

Chao's Razorback suffered two direct hits to his armored front, but Terran armor was designed to protect against the relatively slow-moving Arh'Kel railguns. The ablative armor panels briefly lit as the tungsten's kinetic energy was converted to thermal energy, and a trail of molten material dropped from the side-by-side wounds in Chao's bow as the railguns' destructive energies, the momentum of the accelerated projectiles was dissipated harmlessly.

But the deed was done, and the path had been cleared for the Clover Razorbacks to reconnect. Terran coil guns fired short, controlled bursts at the mindlessly advancing Arh'Kel, and the weight of fire was simply too much for the rock-biters to overcome...for now.

With all but three HWPs scraped from the cavern, and with Chao's people sending a fresh artillery barrage into the survivors, one of those quickly fell. The Terrans had turned the tide, but it had come with a cost since just four of the nine Razorbacks had SRMs left in their tubes. Coil gun ammo was under fifty percent, and the damage was beginning to accumulate.

"Clover, form on *Warcrafter*," Jenkins commanded as the Terran armor consolidated near the eastern edge of the cavern. Rock-biters continued to pour through the tunnels, escorting a slow-but-steady stream of mostly-railgun HWPs. The presence of the odd missile-launch platform among those HWPs, which became priority targets for Terran guns, was a grim indication of just how deeply-rooted this rock-biter infestation might be.

Railguns were the first heavy weapons the rock-biters always built, due to the relatively simple and cheap components used in their construction. For reasons that continued to elude Terran scientists, Arh'Kel weren't very good at working with liquid fuels, or combustibles of any kind. It was theorized that this disinclination led them to make missile launch platforms a significantly lower priority than railguns when building upon a newly-infested world.

Which meant that if these Arh'Kel were following the standard growth model, they had already gotten to the point where they could independently break orbit and spread their contagion to nearby planetary bodies. This also implied that, again assuming they followed the standard model of rock-biter behavior, there were at least three *million* Arh'Kel down here.

That many rock-biters would make short work of anything and everything of value on or beneath the Martian surface—and past evidence showed that once Arh'Kel of this developmental level reached the surface, they would be launching interplanetary transport ships within hours. Not months or weeks, or even days.

Hours.

The fight to secure Martian infrastructure had just gotten a whole lot more complicated. This was no longer as simple as overtaking rebel-held facilities and handing them over to Sol to avoid political complications for the Solar government. This was now nothing less than a full-blown battle for the Solar System, because if these rock-biters made it off Mars, and if even one of their probably thousands of transports made it to another world, they would become a recurring plague that might possibly wipe out all of Solar humanity. Could humanity cede the Martian industrial capacity to stop the Arh'Kel?

Very complicated.

Jenkins knew the Solar military could deal with them, and a more by-the-book officer would likely have ordered an immediate withdrawal from the scene. They were overwhelmed down here, with an estimated ten thousand enemy heavy-weapons platforms and three million Arh'Kel infantry inhabiting the tunnels beneath his treads. He and Chief Styles had done the math on Durgan's Folly, so they knew their numbers were right. Jenkins had been up close and personal in confirming the calculations.

Arh'Kel on Mars. And it looked identical. Three. Freaking. Million.

But without Mars and its infrastructure, humanity's ability to defend itself in the increasingly chaotic Nexus Wars would be hampered by the lack of rare minerals to build high-tech weapons. They *needed* these factories and foundries, and they needed them *now*, not six months from now after the last traces of Arh'Kel influence had been erased.

"We will hold this cavern as long as we've got shells," Jenkins declared, sending fresh fire orders. "Keep your fire clear of the tunnel mouths and do your best to limit structural cavern damage. We'll need these tunnels after we've dug these motherless fucks out of here."

The eagerness in the chorus of virtual replies told him all he needed to know about his Metalheads' resolve. They knew the stakes as well as he did, and every one of them was ready to do his job to the last.

Coil guns whined, artillery thundered, and railguns flared as the Terrans prepared their last stand. Crews within glanced at sidearms and rifles. They'd fight outside when the mech was dead. They would fight.

To the bitter end and beyond.

15

HOOK-UP CULTURE

Elvira's chain guns shredded three rock-biters, blowing their six-limbed bodies apart just as they reached the end of their murderous charge, intent on overcoming the cornered Marine. Her red-hot fifty-caliber barrels spun down as Xi pivoted the mech to the left, where a newly-arrived Arh'Kel railgun was lining up for a shot on her flank.

"Conserve missiles," she snapped, sending an AP shell into the Arh'Kel railgun a tenth of a second before the enemy would have sent a bolt into *Elvira's* hull. The railgun's twisted frame scattered when its capacitors overcharged, killing three nearby rock-biters and blowing a two-ton slab of stone from the cavern wall.

The fifty remaining Arh'Kel, having lost all three of their HWPs following Xi's arrival, fell back into the smallest of the tunnels. That tunnel was too small for armor to move into and led in the opposite direction from the rally point, so there was no point in pursuing the fleeing infantry.

"Fall into formation," she commanded after confirming the third Marine they had successfully hooked up with on their journey through the dark was alive. "Glad to see you're still with us, Lieutenant Briggs," she greeted him. "What's your status?"

"I'm dry on slugs and my railgun's shot," he replied irritably. "I could use one of your large-bores."

"Negative on the rifles," she replied, having already given all the large-bores to Hamlin at their rear. "But we did pick up Wang's railgun and ammo pack."

"That'll do," Briggs agreed, his professional tone belying the fact he knew as well as Xi did that the only way they could acquire a Marine's weapon was if he were dead.

"It's in my starboard cargo pod," she said as the battered Marine, who had been facing down a hundred fifty rock-biters and three HWPs on her arrival, made his way over to her mech, where he retrieved the railgun rifle and ammo pack. "He was bingo slugs when we found him, just like everyone else."

"Fucking rock-biters," Briggs growled in frustration. "How the hell did they get down here, right under Sol's nose?"

"Same way they did at Durgan's Folly." Xi shrugged indifferently. She knew she could get in trouble for sharing details from her first combat op, but she cared less and less the deeper they went into Mars. "They were delivered with sensor trickery and then left to multiply until they became a problem."

"But *who* snuck them in?" Briggs asked, taking her break with protocol regarding classified intel in stride.

Xi shook her head as he examined his weapon. "That's anyone's guess, but since there are currently two species vying for power in Nexus Space and both make a regular habit out of manipulating everyone and everything else while treating the other races like pawns on a chessboard, I'll give you three tries in case you're not too good with numbers."

Briggs snorted. "Did anyone ever tell you that you've got quite the mouth, Major?"

"Nobody. At least nobody who valued their reproductive

capability," she said with forced indifference, before feigning obliviousness. "Why?"

The Marine lieutenant laughed as he finished inspecting Wang's reclaimed rifle. "Major Trapper was right about you Metalheads. You're all right."

"Just make sure your tetanus shot is up to date, and you'll be safe...ish," she quipped before switching to the company channel, which now included three Marines and her trio of mechs. "There's another junction eight klicks ahead that has a breathable gas-condensing system and five intersecting tunnels. That's our best bet for linking up with more of our people before we arrive at the rally point. All units, confirm your status."

Her HUD flickered with virtual replies that showed the three mechs, with three Marines riding on them, were ready to move, so she drove *Elvira* to the head of the column and made her way down the tunnel.

"Move out!"

"These tunnels are huge," Giles remarked when they had gone four of the eight klicks to the gas-condensing facility. "I'm stunned we can move around as freely as we do down here."

"The earliest Martian mining efforts came before microfusion plants were a reality," Nakamura explained. "As a result, they had to make these tunnels large enough for the larger plants' primary core components to be brought down from the surface after being constructed there."

"But why not just build them on-site?" Giles objected. "This seems like a tremendous waste of effort. The amount of material that got displaced when they dug these tunnels was extraordinary."

"Twelve times Mt. Everest, according to the schoolbooks,"

Nakamura agreed. "It was the largest engineering effort ever undertaken by humans, and served as part of the 'One Star, One Mind' initiative, which was basically Sol's twenty-second century's version of the infrastructure projects at the center of the early twentieth's 'New Deal.' After cracking fusion power and unlocking oceanic mining tech we still use to extract deuterium and tritium from seawater, the issue of cost became one more related to a project's timetable than to the total resources involved, or even the scale of the job. While humanity has yet to experience what some theorized would be a 'post-scarcity' society, the mid-twenty-first century to the mid-twenty-second came awfully close in a lot of ways."

"But why go through all that trouble?" Giles' mind boggled. "This is an insane project. Digging minerals up from a dead world's crust doesn't make a whole lot of sense. If Mars were a viable habitat it would make more sense, but where's the practical payoff?"

"Remember, Corporal," Nakamura chided, "Sol tore Mercury apart and turned it into a partial Dyson Swarm *literally* because they *could*. They didn't need the energy produced by the so-called 'Quicksilver Cloud,' and there are solid arguments made to this day that they aren't efficiently using the energy harvested by it. But that project, along with this one, served as the most crucial tentpoles for the 'One Star, One Mind' initiative that served as the framework for colonizing the Solar System. How much is interplanetary colonization worth to a species like humanity? And how much is being able to transplant humanity, along with our accumulated knowledge, to a backup world in the event something catastrophic befalls Earth?"

"So you're both a historian *and* a philosopher, Lieutenant?" Xi smirked as they closed to three kilometers to go until their objective. "Color me surprised. I thought the deepest you'd have gone into the library was the underwear catalog. The men's section."

"If you don't know your history, you're fucked," Naka-mura said flatly. "Besides, a comfortable pair of skivvies can do more for one's spirits than a sexually-permissive morale officer."

"No arguing with that," Xi agreed. "All right, cut the chat-ter. I'm reading EM spikes ahead. There's a firefight—"

She was cut short when a powerful EM spike was accompa-nied by a visible flash of light, and her virtual systems confirmed the source of that light was a heavy plasma cannon. *Cyclops'*, to be specific.

"We've got Metalheads under fire ahead," she declared. "Let's hit this hole as hard as we can. Marines, dismount and follow us in."

She was both relieved and disappointed that no one snuck a "that's what *she* said" joke in, but that was probably her fault for ordering them to cut the chatter. For a brief moment, she wondered if she was no longer considered one of the guys by her fellow Metalheads.

Even just a few deployments ago, she would have expected someone to challenge her call for discipline. But it seemed that was no longer the case, and she had mixed feelings about the potentially widening gulf between herself and her crews. It had to happen. Her desire to build a combat effective small unit that had fun at what it did was balanced by the weight of saving humanity.

Every new deployment was for human survival. Every. Damn. One.

The six-element formation charged down the tunnel, with the Marines running three abreast behind *Elvira*. *Culture Knight* was at the center, and *Murasame* brought up the rear. As the first visuals of the cavern came across Xi's link, she couldn't help but grin like an idiot at the carnage being wrought by Terran hands.

The spider-shaped *Black Widow*, standing with *Cyclops* by her side, poured depleted uranium slugs into the tide of rock-biter infantry that pressed steadily in on them. The spider mech was badly damaged, having lost its number two and number five legs. It was also missing a two-meter chunk from its left-flank armor, but its fury was unrelenting as it dealt death to the silica-based aliens.

Cyclops' heavy plasma cannon cycled, the two-meter breach slamming shut as the Warlock-class mech's capacitors thrummed to life. A shiver went up Xi's spine as Blinky hurled an incinerating ball of blue plasma into the two-thousand-strong Arh'Kel horde's center. The raging inferno liquefied every Arh'Kel within twenty meters and killed the rest outright to a radius of fifty meters. Molten rock pooled at the impact point, illuminating the cavern with the fourth red-glowing pool left behind by the mighty weapon.

Blinky was pushing it by using his plasma cannon so frequently, especially in the two-kilometer cavern with its low roof, which was more prone to collapse than the others Xi had thus far traversed. But given the unrelenting tide of rock-biters, any plan that kept them off the hull was a good one, even if that plan featured the not-insignificant possibility of self-destruction.

"Make a hole, Lieutenant!" she barked, and like a matador, *Cyclops* stepped to his left while *Black Widow* surged ahead, clearing a line of fire for Xi into the heart of the Arh'Kel line. "HE up...on the way!"

Bursting into the cavern at a sprint, *Elvira's* dual fifteens boomed, launching explosive shells across the cavern at a tight cluster of Arh'Kel railguns. Three platforms were scrapped by those two shells, but Xi knew her guns weren't the only ones that needed to clear if they were to advance through this cavern.

Pivoting hard to her left, Xi almost lost her mech's footing on one of the molten patches of rock, but she recovered before her lead right leg splayed too far out of position. Spinning her chain guns up, she sent twenty-five-round bursts into the thinned horde in front of her, and as soon as she vacated the line of fire she had just exploited with her fifteens, *Culture Knight* fired his dual eight-kilo cannons across the cavern. He scored a kill on one Arh'Kel missile platform and put at least fifty rock-biters down with a fortuitous cave-in that crushed them under an avalanche of loose rock.

The trio of armored Marines sent railgun bolts into the fray, going three-for-three in scratching Arh'Kel HWPs before diving behind the armored mechs for cover from the incoming Arh'Kel small arms, each of which packed more destructive power than an anti-materiel rifle. And as they dove clear of the firing window, it was *Culture Knight*'s turn to take center stage.

For the first time in Operation War God, *Culture Knight*'s mortars were used to full effect, and when they fired, even Xi was humbled by the utter devastation they wrought.

Sixty-four mortars, built into *Culture Knight*'s chest and previously concealed behind protective armor panels, were now fully exposed as the humanoid walker trudged into the cavern. The mortars fired in such rapid succession that they sounded like a string of Founding Day firecrackers with the volume cranked up to eleven. The shells fell in a picture-perfect fan-shaped arrangement that completely cleared the field out to a hundred and fifty meters, annihilating all but a handful of Arh'Kel within the kill-zone and buying the Terrans precious time to form up.

Given that *Culture Knight* had been built on Earth as a top-tier urban warfare system capable of leveling city blocks in seconds, Xi felt a genuine chill at the thought that someone had invented the thing to kill *humans* rather than rock-biters. But as was so often the case in the history of Western civilization, it wasn't the hardware's intended application that mattered most. It was what it actually got used for, and securing Mars from an Arh'Kel invasion was about as noble a cause as Xi could envision.

It would take *Culture Knight* fifteen seconds to reload his mortars, so his chain guns roared, following Xi's lead by pivoting aside. But where *Elvira* had turned left, *Culture Knight* turned right, leaving *Murasame* in the window.

Unfortunately, the enemy had finally gotten their act together and sent a pair of railgun bolts across the cavern just as Nakamura's mech was about to open fire with his eight-kilo guns. The bolts skewered *Murasame's* lower torso, with one coming dangerously close to blowing through his left hip joint. Impressively, Nakamura was able to keep his mech upright while returning fire, scrapping one of the HWPs that had insulted his armor's integrity with a perfect shot from his eight-kilo cannon.

But that was the extent of his rebuke. *Murasame* was a purpose-built mech hunter, and with just two HK drones remaining after leaving the others with Hamlin's Martian Militia, Nakamura's vehicle was significantly less robust in an open-field exchange like this one.

Which was not to say Nakamura was impotent, as he aptly demonstrated by adding sniper-precise fifty-caliber rounds into the Arh'Kel ranks. Xi followed his lead, switching off full-auto and sniping targets with the ambush method, waiting for them to fall into her crosshairs before putting them down with center-mass shots. Without needing to be ordered, the rest of the mechs did the same, and the next forty seconds were easily the most efficient shot-to-kill ratio any Terran military unit had achieved against rock-biter infantry. During that time, the press of rock-biter bodies consolidated and the line seemed ready to charge headlong into Terran teeth once again.

So it was both a surprise and a disappointment to Xi when they instead opted to withdraw down the far tunnels, leaving the Terrans in full control of the blasted, smoke-filled cavern.

"Report, Blinky," Xi greeted him.

"We lost *Devil's Due* with all hands, Major," he reported grimly, "and we came across what was left of two Marines during our withdrawal. One was Lieutenant Worthington, whose remains and gear we recovered, but we couldn't even ID the other before we had to pull back. We'd been working a fighting retreat toward this point, hoping we could make the rally point, but got hemmed in by these fuckfaces after lucky hits took off Quinn's legs. We couldn't advance with *Black Widow's* armor nearly gone on her flank, so I planted my feet and started swinging."

"You did great, Blinky." Xi had known the losses would be heavy the second she had spotted the first purple splotch. It was still sobering to wade through the destruction. "You held on long enough for help to arrive. Any word from Captain Winters?"

"No, ma'am," Blinky replied. "He's probably cut off on the other side of the main Arh'Kel force. We think we've got a good idea of their position based on our encounters during the withdrawal, and Major? There's a *lot* of them."

"Why do they keep pulling back?" Lieutenant Briggs asked in annoyed confusion. "Rock-biters don't fall back in my experience."

"We've seen them do it," Xi assured him as a nagging thought gained traction in her mind and finally prompted her to divulge classified intel. Again. "Back on Durgan's Folly, these stone-fuckers had implants that made them behave atypically. We still don't know who installed them, but Chief Styles came up with a method to use those implants to basically shut them down."

"I heard something about that..." Briggs mused. "Whole armies of rock-biters standing around like statues, and Marine demo teams turned them to gravel with a few thousand tons of TNT. People in the know were tight-lipped about it, but a few tidbits slipped through the cracks as they always do. So that was you guys?" he asked with overt approval. "I probably should have guessed."

"I need you to examine some of the more intact remains," Xi urged, forwarding a rough diagram of the implants they had found on the Durgan's Folly rock-biters. "Look for something like this. It might give us another way to end this invasion, possibly before it even reaches the surface."

"On it, Major," Briggs acknowledged before leading his Marines into the carnage-filled cavern to pick through a couple of the more intact enemy bodies.

"Are we going to save *another* planet and not get credit for it?" Nakamura deadpanned as the Marines inspected the enemy corpses.

Xi snickered. "I'd rather do good and get no credit than get credit but do no good."

Nakamura sighed. "That's why you're the major. You think bigger than the rest of us."

"Found it, Major," Briggs called, and Xi tapped into his helmet's video feet, which showed an identical copy of the neural implants they'd found on the Durgan's Folly rock-biters.

"All right, that's good enough for me," she said confidently. "Dragons, fall in and move out!"

The five mechs and three Marines moved into the tunnel which, at long last, would lead them to the rally point. Moving at *Black Widow*'s current max speed, it would take them at least twenty minutes to get there, and that was if they didn't encounter any resistance along the way. So while they moved, she decided it was wise to explain precisely what they needed to do and just how hard they'd have to fight for it.

"Whoever dropped these bastards here did the same on Durgan's Folly," she explained as the column advanced deeper into the Martian underworld, "and with any luck, we've already got a roadmap for how to deal with them. Unfortunately, I don't have a copy of the program we'll need to use, and even if I did, I doubt I could make it work. Styles is a full two steps better as a virtual technician than I am, and it took both of us working in tandem to get it working the first time. But no matter what, we need to get a copy of that program, and there are two possible ways I see to do that. The first is we go topside and get Styles to send his copy down from the *William Wallace*, where I know for a fact it is. The other option is a little more my style. Anyone care to take a guess?" she asked coyly.

"A full-on Leeroy Jenkins to meet up with a man by the same name?" Briggs intoned as the group moved at fifty-two kph, which was the best *Black Widow* could manage after losing a pair of legs.

"Give that man a cookie." She grinned. "If I know my CO, my guess is he conveniently forgot the order to relinquish access to Styles' takeover program. As a result, he's probably got a copy on *Warcrafter's* databanks. If we can get him to forward it, I'll at least have a chance of putting it to use. But make no mistake: the last time we did this, we charged three mechs headlong into five thousand Arh'Kel and got beat to hell in the process."

"We've got seven mechs and three Marines, plus whatever the colonel's standing tall with," Blinky said confidently. "We can get it done."

"Re-run your tactical calculations, Lieutenant," Xi scolded. "Without our SRMs, and with the damage we've accumulated, we *barely* have as much throw weight in this formation as our three mechs had back on Durgan's Folly. Add to that the fact that we took hours to customize the program, and it still came down to the wire, with *Elvira* literally mounting the colonel's mech to shield him from fire and this is anything but certain. Still, it's our best play, so we need to keep things tight." She sent a series of battle plans to the rest of the unit as they charged down the tunnel. "Which means we have to make our appearance with at least as much substance as style. If the colonel is already at the rally point, we need to get in there, extract him, and fall back before getting cornered. This is a classic 'boom or bust' situation, so now's the time for off-the-wall suggestions if you've got them."

"I might have one or two of those," Briggs offered confidently.

"I'm all ears, Marine."

16

THEATER OF PAIN

Working in near-orchestral synchronism with the beat to Blind Guardian's *Theater of Pain,* Colonel Jenkins' seven mechs and now-seven Marines poured bullet after bullet, bolt after bolt, and shell after shell into the press of Arh'Kel bodies. Dozens of Arh'Kel fell each second, with multiple HWPs dying each minute to precision Terran fire, most before they could fire a single shot. The body count was already over ten thousand, with ninety-six HWPs already destroyed by Clover Company in this cavern alone.

But the rock-biters kept coming.

Tumbling limb-over-limb across the gore-strewn floor, the Arh'Kel gave every impression of a mindless horde rather than an assemblage of coordinated individuals. They were pitiless to their own, merciless to their foes, and utterly unconcerned with anything but pressing the attack.

In short, they were no different from drones. Self-replicating bioweapons. And that was precisely how they had been deployed on Mars.

"Single fire on the coils," Jenkins barked after sending that very order over the tight-band. His people were fighting back to back, covering each other's weaknesses where possible while forming a constantly-rotating circle that was moving too slowly toward the exit to have a chance at escape.

But escape was the farthest thing from Jenkins' mind. Every Metalhead on Mars knew this cavern was the rally point. It was the fallback position for this point on the clock, which meant that to abandon it was to abandon the rest of his people to the horde.

He would rather die than turn his back on his Metalheads, and with every round delivered into the enemy, it became increasingly probable that was precisely what would happen.

None of the Razorbacks had more than ten percent ammo remaining for their coil guns, and all were down to a dozen or fewer artillery shells and bingo missiles. Only two of his seven mechs had functioning railguns for which ammunition remained plentiful, but he knew the odds of all that unspent ordnance being used against the enemy were between slim and none...and slim had just skipped town, along with most of Clover's hope of reuniting with any other Terran elements this far down the hole.

Of the nine tunnels adjoining the rally point cavern, two had collapsed and no longer produced rock-biters. And until three minutes ago, the main tunnel down which Jenkins had come had remained open.

But now even that tunnel featured a steady stream of Arh'Kel. They were cut off, surrounded, low on ammo, and twenty kilometers below the Martian surface. Lee Jenkins had stared down the barrel a few times in his career, but this situation was unlike any other he had experienced. He hadn't given up the fight, as evidenced by the ongoing carnage, but he began to suspect that at some point in the last half hour, he *had* given up hope.

And in a very real and very disturbing way, that was a tremendous relief.

"Grenade!" Trapper barked, snapping Jenkins' focus to his left, where the power-armored Fleet Ground Forces officer hurled a plasma grenade into the tide of rock-biters. The plasma cloud boiled out from the point of impact, enveloping nine Arh'Kel infantry in deadly flame. Another dozen rock-biters were tossed aside by the concussive force of the explosion, but these resumed their cartwheeling charge, missing barely a step. That lost step was quickly proven to be a lethal one as Captain Hao snapped single coil-gun rounds into the advancing Arh'Kel, dropping the silica-based monstrosities with centimeter-precise hits. *Warcrafter* added its coil guns to the fray, sending solo rounds into the encroaching enemy line and proving just as deadly as the former Colonial Guardsman.

All told, that grenade was responsible for thirty-six rock-biter deaths after the Metalheads and Marines took full advantage of the temporary lull in the pressure, but despite the grenade's deadly effect, its primary significance was that it had been the last of its kind. With the Marines' slug-throwers having been dry for the better part of an hour, the power-armored warriors had been frugal and sniper-precise in their deployment of the limited ordnance. But now, those seven battle-suited Terrans had nothing but their slow-cycling railgun rifles to use against the enemy.

"Come get it," Hammer snarled, bucking *Warcrafter's* stern as high as it could rise while lowering the bow. Jenkins had to grip his armrests to keep from falling out of his chair as the floor tilted nearly thirty degrees, but the momentary discomfort was well worth it when *Warcrafter's* Jock sent a high-explosive shell into the ground eighty meters down-range. Pivoting hard to starboard, and once again threatening to dislodge Jenkins from his seat, Hammer unloaded a second HE shell into the incoming enemy line at the same distance.

The thunderous reports came less than a second apart when the pair of HE shells made a pasty ruin of a hundred Arh'Kel infantry. A few pieces of mixed rock and Arh'Kel body parts clattered off *Warcrafter's* hull, sounding very much like fat raindrops falling on a sheet-metal roof.

After adjusting position by sliding a few meters toward the bowed line in the enemy horde, the perimeter around the Terran war machines' wagon circle formation now stood at a sixty-meter radius. That figure had been a hundred meters just five minutes earlier, and Jenkins suspected they had less than five minutes left before the damned things were cutting into their hulls with handheld plasma torches.

A brilliant flash came from a far tunnel, signaling that an Arh'Kel railgun had fired. Jenkins saw a corresponding jet of flame erupt from the flank of Captain Hao's *Red Pearl*. The mech fell to the deck, its legs crumpled beneath it as the battlewagon lost all power. His tactical feed showed that she had suffered a catastrophic capacitor overload, and despite the Terran's best efforts to close the gap made by Hao's sudden incapacitation, the Arh'Kel surged forward.

Plasma torches flickered to life as a dozen rock-biters leapt onto the fallen mech's hull, where they went to work with their simple yet brutally effective tools.

Jenkins knew that Hao's fate would soon befall them all, and that certain knowledge tempted him to make a glorious and defiant last stand against their intractable foes. But he knew the correct move was to tighten the circle and fall back from the never-ending rush of enemy infantry.

A Marine sent a tungsten sliver down-range, scrapping *Red Pearl's* killer with a textbook shot that blew its primary generator. The resulting explosion was less dazzling than a hit on a charged capacitor, but it still took out a handful of nearby infantry with deadly shrapnel.

"Six-pointed formation," Jenkins barked as he sent the new formation's details to his Jocks. Five of his six still-standing mechs moved into their new positions—all except Captain Chao. "Captain, fall in," Jenkins barked, but Captain Chao had assumed sole responsibility for a different mission.

With his coil guns whining on full-auto, Chao charged into the inverted V of sprinting Arh'Kel. He had enough bullets for twenty-three seconds of sustained fire, and while Jenkins knew he should be upset with the young man for disobeying an order in combat, he also knew he would have done the exact same thing in his younger years.

"Five-pointed star," Jenkins snapped, pushing his remaining Razorbacks into a tighter formation as Chao sprinted at the enemy, dealing hot death to their ranks with his coil guns while the Arh'Kel returned ineffective fire with their large-bore small arms.

As Chao's *Razor Bamboo II* sliced through the enemy line, dashing straight at them at a dead sprint in a high-stakes game of chicken, he suddenly faltered, slowing to fifty kph for less than a second. During that brief window, a pair of Terrans dropped out of the mech's stern airlock, tumbling to a stop as Chao's battlewagon unleashed a pair of HE shells into the angry horde. The shells annihilated the leading edge of the line, dropping at least sixty rock-biters before Chao resumed his charge into the enemy's teeth.

"Good man." Jenkins nodded approvingly. Chao's Monkey and Wrench both got to their feet and low-gee sprinted toward Captain Hao's mech. "Snipe those fucks off *Red Pearl's* back, Hammer," Jenkins ordered.

"On it," Hammer growled, sending a quartet of bullets into the torch-wielding Arh'Kel, one of whom had already breached

Red Pearl's cabin with a hole large enough to fit one of its limbs through. One of the other rock-biters atop the dead mech leapt at the opening, gripping pistol and plasma torch in anticipation of scoring a quick kill.

But the only thing it got was a fifty-caliber slug, courtesy of the *Red Pearl*'s crew, who fired through the breach in their armor. The *Red Pearl*'s airlock was jammed after the railgun strike that had killed the mech fused the hatch to the frame. Hammer sniped another pair of rock-biters from the *Red Pearl*'s back, and after they fell lifelessly to the cavern floor, two of *Red Pearl*'s crew clambered out of the mech.

One was badly wounded and barely able to stand atop the fallen war machine, needing help from the other crewman, who Jenkins immediately identified as Captain Hao. Hao primed a pair of grenades one-handed, which was no mean feat, and tossed them toward her dead mech's nose, where three rock-biters single-mindedly worked to breach the secure cockpit from the outside. The grenades went off when their proximity triggers sensed the Arh'Kel, and two of the rock-biters were killed outright while the other was thrown to the deck.

Hao and her Monkey slid down their mech's flank, where they were met by Chao's crew. The human part of Jenkins wanted to disregard all other concerns and rush to their aid. They were a good twenty meters from his line, and it would take him mere seconds to reach and recover them.

But if he broke ranks, it was all over. It had been bad enough with seven mechs in tight formation pushing back against the rock-biters, but now that they were down to five, any misstep, no matter how minor, would prove deadly in seconds, not minutes.

And those minutes *mattered*.

Not because Jenkins cared whether he drew another few dozen breaths or if his next would be his last, but because there were still dozens of Metalheads unaccounted for down here. He wouldn't abandon them, which meant that no matter how much he wanted to run to Hao's aid, that was exactly what he would be doing if he gave in to sentimentality.

The battle for Mars wasn't over, not by a long shot. And Lee Jenkins wasn't about to surrender, no matter how difficult achieving victory might appear.

Besides, he had faith in Captain Chao. After Major Xi, Chao was the brightest young star in the Metal Legion. If anyone could pull off this suicide run, it was Chao.

"You've got to pull up," Jenkins muttered, and as he spoke, that was precisely what Chao did. With just eight seconds of ammo left in his max-cycling coil guns and bingo everything else, Chao's margin for error was nonexistent. The unrelenting tide of enemy infantry, previously broken by *Razor Bamboo's* artillery strikes, was once again an unbroken wall of cart-wheeling stony six-limbed bodies. *Razor Bamboo* banked hard as Chao came about, and the turn was so severe that his mech's front left leg bit deep into a patch of soft rock on the cavern floor.

The clang as part of the mech's lower limb snapped off was audible even over the deafening whine of Chao's coil guns, but the mech never faltered since all it lost was the armored "boot" that covered the omnidirectional rollers at the front-left limb's end.

Burning for all he was worth, Chao raked his max-cycling coil guns across the enemy line, firing his last bullet as he lined up on the four Terrans who were running back to the cover afforded by Jenkins' five-mech formation.

"Make a hole," Jenkins barked as Chao's mech hurtled toward them, leaving the Arh'Kel in his wake as he drove *Razor Bamboo* back to the formation. The power-armored Marines stepped into the hole made as *Warcrafter* and *Wine Merchant* opened the formation to permit Chao's mech to gain its center.

Without ammo, *Razor Bamboo* would be worse than useless on the rotating line. Chao's only value now would be to provide cover and, possibly, a tower-like firing position to the Marines, whose railguns still had ample ammunition.

Chao's mech slowed to a safe speed before coming to a stop at the formation's center. The formation tightened around it, and the four dismounted Terrans quickly boarded through its aft airlock.

Jenkins wanted to both castigate and congratulate the young man for his heroic act. In truth, Jenkins suspected that was the closest anyone in this cavern would come to a meaningful act, and he was more than a little proud of Chao for planting a flag on the occasion with such distinctly Terran style.

It was the kind of thing that people would sing songs about, except it was looking increasingly unlikely that anyone would ever hear about it.

Arh'Kel surged past *Red Pearl's* wreckage, with a few dozen of them stopping to continue the demo effort. Seeing those things dig their rocky digits into a piece of his armor, tearing panels off and rending internal components in search for the rare minerals needed for Arh'Kel procreation, was one of the most offensive scenes Jenkins had ever witnessed. He actually made to unstrap from his chair, go to the arms locker, grab a large-bore, and pump a few rounds into the damned things for daring to desecrate Terran hardware.

But by some combination of good sense and alarm at seeing a fresh warning indicator flicker to life on his plotter, he kept his seat and had his eyes on the *Red Pearl's* reactor data when the unit was remotely overloaded by Hao's command code.

The resulting explosion could have easily collapsed much, if not all of the cavern, but Captain Hao had done her math, and instead of blowing the whole cave, the explosion 'merely' killed every unarmored organism in a two-hundred-meter radius. A pair of twenty-meter-tall slabs formerly comprising part of the cavern's ceiling collapsed on *Red Pearl's* final resting place. Their sudden appearance created an opportunity Jenkins knew he needed to seize before it vanished.

"Reposition," he barked, sending new orders to his people to regroup at those boulders. Using the boulders as a bulwark, his people could gain cover from emerging railguns as they came through more than half the tunnels. "We hold with our backs to these boulders until we're down to fifteen hundred rounds, then we charge for the northwest tunnel," he advised. "Confirm your ammo counts, and hold the coils until they're thirty meters out. We fire on max-cycle, and when we break for the door, we grind the things under our treads if we're dry."

The unit's status reports came back, and they were just as he expected. None of them had more than twenty seconds' worth of ammo, and they had a combined three HE and four AP shells between them. *Warcrafter* boasted two of the AP shells, but she was out of explosives.

"Let's make these count, Hammer," Jenkins urged as they took up position beside the giant boulders. "Because when they're gone, we'll have to use our teeth."

"I always wanted to know what gravel tastes like, sir," Hammer drawled, gaining a snort from the colonel as he forwarded a pair of likely targets emerging from the same tunnel through which they had arrived. The Arh'Kel line was twice as dense as it had been before the *Red Pearl's* devastating demise, and they were sprinting across the cavern floor toward the Metalheads' position.

Jenkins smirked. "You've got to love a target-rich environment, eh, Hammer?"

"Fuckin' A, Colonel," Hammer agreed as the rock-biters neared the engagement line.

The Marines, kneeling on the cavern floor and sandwiched

between the Razorbacks, were first to fire on the enemy when they reached the fifty-meter line. Their railgun slivers skewered a dozen rock-biters apiece before slamming into the wreckage, either of Terran battlewagons or the Martian industrial equipment that filled the expansive chamber. Ignoring their losses as they usually did, the rock-biters continued their savage onslaught, and the sound of their small arms plinking off *Warcrafter's* hull steadily intensified.

"Come and get us." Jenkins sneered as the rock-biters crossed the thirty-meter line, where the Legion's coil guns instantly tore them apart.

Sweeping from side to side, the Metalheads' coil guns dropped hundreds of Arh'Kel per second, pushing the enemy line back and adding to the purple gore already covering the cavern floor. Thousands of rock-biters died in those first few seconds, and the semicircular kill-zone rapidly expanded until it was back at the hundred-meter mark.

Following Jenkins' orders, the Razorbacks adjusted posture, turning their guns to the edges of the boulders behind which the Metalheads had taken refuge. The occasional coil gun bullet tore through the boulders like pistol rounds through polystyrene, but the concerted fire cleared a pair of angelic wings to either side of the boulders. Nothing could survive the Metalheads' savage enfilades, which were powerful enough to destroy a battlewagon like *Warcrafter*.

A railgun bolt struck *Warcrafter's* flank, setting off alarms and spurring the mech's repair crews into action, but Jenkins wasn't worried about the damage. They had already burned half their ammo reserves, and Hammer depleted those reserves even further by sending one of his two remaining AP shells into the HWP that had dared to fire on them.

Their drive for the door would need to come in the next four seconds, and Jenkins knew those four seconds would be the longest of his life. His eyes were pinned to the tactical plotter, and so rapt was his concentration on the unit's ammo figures that he almost missed the unmistakable tolling of a bell in his earpiece.

It was a tolling bell that any self-respecting connoisseur of heavy metal would immediately recognize, and when the drums and guitars slammed into the familiar opening riff of Metallica's *For Whom the Bell Tolls,* Jenkins felt an unexpected (but hardly unwelcome) glimmer of hope.

17

FOR WHOM THE BELL TOLLS

Like a demon conjured from nightmares of the wicked, the scorpion-shaped mistress of metal surged into the cavern. Her chain guns wailed like banshees, while her fifteens announced the warrior maiden *Elvira's* arrival by scrapping a pair of nearby HWPs even before she cleared the tunnel.

"Hit it, Blinky!" Xi howled, diving *Elvira* aside and clearing a line of fire for *Cyclops'* heavy plasma cannon.

With the opening riff of Metallica's hit song blaring in her unit's cabins, Lieutenant Staubach announced the Metalheads' arrival with equal measures style and substance. She sent a raging inferno into the heart of the cavern, where a handful of battered Clover Razorbacks huddled beside a trio of enormous boulders.

The plasma projectile erupted four hundred meters from the stranded Clover mechs, bathing them in lethal heat that did little more than tickle their robust hulls. The unarmored Arh'Kel were not so fortunate, and the plasma liquefied a thousand of them outright while crippling and killing twice as many more.

But her mech's tactical scanner read that there were over

twenty thousand of the goddamned things in this cavern alone. They had put down at least five hundred over the last two kilometers of tunnel, but that was a drop in the bucket compared to what Colonel Jenkins' people were dealing with on this particularly unpleasant level of Hell.

Flickers of movement on the far side of the cavern showed that the infantry was soon to be joined by a growing number of HWPs.

"Holy fuck!" Xi screamed after a pair of railgun bolts slammed into *Elvira's* hull. One struck her transparent alloy windshield, rendering it nearly opaque, while the other tore her left fifteen clean off its moorings. "Scatter! Disperse!" she snapped, momentarily flustered as she flattened her mech as low as it could go. She then crab-walked away from the tunnel mouth, pouring fifty-caliber slugs into the nearest rock-biter infantry in the northwest quadrant of the cavern.

Blinky took a direct hit to the torso and his mech sagged, looking like it was about to crash to the deck. She worried that *Cyclops'* power system had been knocked offline, but he resumed his march and cleared the entryway in time for the Marines to unleash their railguns against the HWPs that had targeted them from the far side of the cavern.

Three shots notched three kills as the Marines demonstrated their uncanny abilities yet again. Xi didn't have to like it, and in point of fact, she *didn't* like it, but it looked like the Terran Marines *might* have legitimately *earned* the praise they received.

But whether the Marines earned their laurels or not was irrelevant, because Xi was determined to establish the Metal Legion as Terra's most feared fighting force.

"Let 'em have it, Skeptic!" she barked as *Culture Knight* followed Blinky into the cavern, raining micro-mortar shells down on the foul horde infesting the cavern. The Arh'Kel were so tightly-packed near the cavern's edge that every single one of his sixty-four shells killed at least ten rock-biters, with the total kill count for that particular barrage nearing the one thousand mark. For a moment, Xi was envious.

But only for a moment.

A quick glance at the distances and numbers confirmed there was no way they could clear the cavern out. They'd just fired their best shot, and while *Black Widow* and *Murasame* had yet to enter the cavern, neither one had as potent an arsenal as *Elvira*, let alone *Culture Knight* and *Cyclops*.

Seeming to read her mind, Colonel Jenkins' Razorbacks refocused their own fire, which had previously laid down a semicircular kill-zone stretching nearly two hundred meters before them. But now the Clover mechs were on the move and focusing their fire on a relatively narrow corridor, making clear their intentions.

"We're bingo ammo, Major," Jenkins declared as soon as the comm link went live. "Gonna need your cover sooner than later."

"Roger, Colonel," she confirmed. "We're inbound. Dragons!" she barked, forwarding a rendezvous point with the colonel's mechs nearly a kilometer from their current position. "Cover Clover and advance at top speed. Nakamura, keep the ticks off our backs. Charge!"

The mechs surged forward at fifty kph, spewing chain-gun rounds and plunging into the throng of Arh'Kel as they descended the gently-sloped cavern floor. They passed all manner of trashed industrial equipment, most of which looked like it had been scrapped in the last hour. Some of the cavern's equipment was still operable, but the facility as a whole was no longer a strategic asset.

Which meant Xi was free to do what she did best.

"HE on the way!" she declared, launching a high-explosive

shell at an HWP on the western side of the cavern. Her shell struck true, scrapping the platform outright. But an enemy system to the east returned fire, landing a glancing hit to her roof that came dangerously close to robbing her of her lone remaining cannon. "Fuck you!" she snarled, but before she could reload and target the bastard, *Culture Knight* fired his eight-kilo cannons and put it down. "Nobody likes a vulture, Skeptic," she quipped. "That was *my* hash."

"You're insane, ma'am," he deadpanned, "and I mean that in a good way."

She laughed maniacally. "Smartass." But her laughter was cut short when a handful of rock-biters got inside her guard during a brief lull in her starboard chain guns' cycle. "Come on, clear!" she snapped as she recycled the ammo feed system, clearing the jammed cartridge and enabling the gun to resume its stream of fire.

But the damage had been done, as four rock-biters took advantage of the brief lull and latched onto her hull. They immediately began to cut into her joints and exposed sections with plasma torches, and Xi knew the damned things could cripple her in seconds if left unaddressed.

"Level off, Major," Nakamura urged, and Xi adjusted her mech's walk cycle to minimize the usual up-down oscillations that accompanied high-speed movements. "Perfect," he acknowledged before sniping one, then two, then three of the rock-biters with center-mass shots from his chain guns. "One more..." He grunted, missing thrice before finally scrubbing the last Arh'Kel from her roof. "There. You're clean."

"Just like an ape with lice," Xi quipped. "You can do my hair any time, Nakamura."

Xi sent a fifteen-kilo shell down-range, scratching an Arh'Kel railgun just as it emerged into the cavern. Enemy railguns had reoriented following Dragon's arrival, and she knew they would soon fall under the very fire Colonel Jenkins had sought to avoid by backing up against those massive boulders. But they were committed; they had to link up with Clover before they made a run for the exit.

Their only hope for victory lay in *Warcrafter's* databanks, but she needed to hook up with the colonel's unit before she could try to use Styles' takeover program.

The barrels of her chain guns were an angry orange as they spat depleted uranium slugs into the enemy horde. Bodies fell and rocky limbs were amputated by her indiscriminate fire, which raked to both sides of her mech and carved a gory path through the mindless mob of enemy infantry.

Then something happened to the Arh'Kel horde. For a moment, it seemed as though they collectively stopped to consider something significant. It lasted just a quarter-second, but that was more than enough for her to notice it had occurred.

And when it ended, the intensity of their mindless charge somehow went up another notch, and the wall of six-limbed bodies surrounding *Elvira* surged toward her like waves driving to the shore.

"That's not good," she muttered irritably, modifying her Scorpion-class mech's sprint cycle ever so slightly by lifting her front legs an extra half-meter during their steps. This gave her mech a slight bounding motion to its gait, but the reason for her making the change was almost immediately demonstrated when *Elvira's* forelegs slammed down on a trio of Arh'Kel infantry in rapid succession. Her flank-mounted chain guns were incapable of aiming directly ahead, instead serving to clear a wide path for the mechs at her back to follow her as they moved single-file into the cavern.

After a few seconds, Xi realized the nature of the angry mob's peculiar change. The entire horde had previously been hell-bent on reaching the Clover mechs, with most of them essentially ignoring Xi and her Dragons. That was no longer the case.

They were now coming after *her*. If she could keep up the charge for another few seconds, they'd rendezvous with the colonel and be able to make their way out of this infernal pit.

"Break left and clear my path, Quinn!" Xi snapped, swerving her mech hard left at precisely the same moment *Black Widow* took two steps left of the single-file Terran column. The battered spider-mech sent a stream of chain-gun fire raking ahead of *Elvira*'s new leftward course, and the effect of their coordination was devastating.

Rock-biters fell in droves as Quinn's chain guns tore them limb from limb, paying no mind to the tide of enemy soldiers surging toward her now that she had fallen out of formation. Surprisingly, and without breaking stride, *Culture Knight* turned his torso one-eighty to deliver a pair of explosive eight-kilo shells into the tide of Arh'Kel surrounding *Black Widow*.

The shells gouged meter-deep craters in the stony floor, sending deadly shrapnel flying into the enemy horde. Dozens died and dozens more faltered, which bought Quinn just enough time to get back into formation and resume the charge with the rest of the unit.

Giles had just demonstrated himself worth every bit of the frustration and annoyance Xi had suffered after putting him in a cockpit without any formal training. If he had been even a second later in delivering those eight-kilo shells, Quinn would have been mobbed by a deadly swarm of Arh'Kel. And since *Black Widow* was bringing up the formation's rear, Nakamura's sniper fire would be unable to scrape her hull clear of torch-wielding rock-biters, as he had done for *Elvira*.

"Blinky, fire at these coordinates," Xi commanded with a grimace. She had been hoping to save Blinky's plasma cannon for later since it would have made their exit that much more straightforward, but she was out of options. If they didn't reach the colonel, it was all over but the crying.

"Firing," he acknowledged as the familiar whine of his cannon's capacitors filled the link. *Cyclops'* plasma cannon belched a slow-moving ball of superheated plasma, which touched down three hundred meters in front of Clover Company's remnants.

The field was burned clean of enemy infantry, and the path to rendezvous with Clover was finally cleared. The two formations of Terran war machines met up, with Xi's people immediately spreading out to adopt a wedge-shaped formation with *Elvira* at its center.

"Good work, Major," Colonel Jenkins congratulated her. "Now, let's get the hell out of here."

Before she could make any pithy reply, *Cyclops* was hit by four railguns in rapid succession, while another six bolts stabbed into the Clover Razorbacks. She almost shrieked in surprise at seeing Blinky's Warlock-class mech hit so hard. Without that plasma cannon, there was next to zero chance they could get out of the cavern.

The towering humanoid *Cyclops* swayed to the left, then to the right, and for a moment Xi was certain that was the end. When Blinky's mech fell, it wouldn't matter if he could get back up again. They'd have lost tempo, and that loss would be fatal.

"Come on, Blinky!" she urged, her chain guns never faltering as they carved into the approaching Arh'Kel, driving them back even as her ammo fell below the twenty-percent-capacity mark. *Cyclops* was their lifeline in this Godforsaken place. If he went, they all went.

She loaded an HE shell, raised her mech's stern, and fired that shell into the deck fifty meters to Blinky's side. *Culture Knight* and *Black Widow* followed her lead, clearing their guns into the cavern floor. Their fire, while inefficient, did the job of sweeping the area around *Cyclops* clear of rock-biters. But spread out as they were to protect the Clover mechs as well as the Dragons, they had no more high-powered ordnance with which to ward the tide of rock-biters off.

Thankfully, the Metalheads weren't the only Terrans in the cavern.

The Marines leapt forward, surrounding Blinky's still-swaying mech and laying down covering fire with their railguns. Amazingly, and against anything approaching common sense, the power-armored Terrans moved *toward* the rock-biters rather than holding position at *Cyclops'* feet. Each Marine fired his railgun, dropping twenty or more rock-biters with each shot as their tungsten slivers passed through Arh'Kel anatomy like it wasn't even there.

And then the crazy bastards shouldered their railguns, snapping them into mounts built behind their right shoulders, and went *hand to hand* with the enemy.

Power-armored fists smashed through two-centimeter-thick stony hides, splattering the cavern floor with streams of thick purple goo. Major Trapper in particular demonstrated the armor's capabilities by dropping one Arh'Kel with a punch to it center-mass before pivoting and sending a metal boot into another, and finishing the sequence with a brutal flying knee to a third rock-biter. All three were reduced to quivering masses on the cavern floor, and each of the other power-armored Marines was every bit as devastating as Major Trapper.

A rock-biter got in a lucky shot with its pistol, briefly staggering one of the Marines, who took a 'wheel-kick' from a charging Arh'Kel. The blow would have crushed every bone in an unarmored human's body, but it was barely enough to break the Marine's stride as he planted his feet. Then, using a short burst of his suit's rockets, he leapt up and back to deliver an improbable bicycle kick to the alien's stony mouth, situated between three of its legs on the thing's axis (which was apparently the universally accepted term for an Arh'Kel's center-mass section).

Another Marine was less fortunate, having suffered a similar blow that had cost him a full step of movement. Instead of leaping, he sank his armored fingers into his foe's stony limbs and then, with a heaving effort that would have made a Greek demigod jealous, he tore two of the Arh'Kel's limbs clean off before front-kicking the rest of the thing's ruined body a full three meters away.

The melee was chaos, and Xi gathered every bit of it with *Elvira's* combat recorders as she did her best to buy Blinky as much time as he needed to right his mech. The Marines, matchless warriors that they were, couldn't hope to hold out hand to hand for more than a few more heartbeats. Xi had seen heroic images like this one in recruiting films, where power-armored Marines stood toe-to-toe with rock-biters and dealt death to them like something out of a holovid.

And then she had seen those scenes' often bloody, tragic conclusions after joining the military. These Marines were spending their lives to buy them precious seconds, and if those seconds weren't enough for Blinky to get *Cyclops* back online, then even the recruiters wouldn't have the benefit of displaying these Marines' heroism to the folks back home.

Seconds ticked by as the Marines fought hand-to-hand against those rock-biters who pierced the broken perimeter. One Marine fell as a trio of Arh'Kel hammered him with their pistols while two of their fellows overbore him, dragged him to the deck, and ignited their torches.

Major Trapper hurled himself at the embroiled trio, shoulder-charging one of the rock-biters off and soccer-kicking the other so hard that something on his armored shin shattered, sending a few pieces of glittering shrapnel flying before he followed the kick with a brutal overhand punch.

And then *Cyclops'* plasma cannon capacitors emitted their familiar whine and Xi couldn't help but shriek, "Fuck, yeah!"

Blinky slowly turned his mech, raised its plasma-cannon arm just as slowly, and fired five hundred meters toward the tunnel mouth they had come through. The plasma fire was weak by comparison, less than half the strength of its predecessor, but as Blinky's feet began to move, Xi knew they needed to get moving.

"Cover the Marines and move out!" she barked, turning her remaining fifteen-kilo gun toward the cavern floor and firing the last of her explosive shells danger-close to a quartet of embattled Marines. "Fall back!" she ordered as one Marine took a fifteen-centimeter hunk of shrapnel from her shell through his hip. With two Marines each grabbing an arm, they raced back to the formation.

With Blinky's latest plasma bolt having cleared a third of their escape path, Xi's remaining mechs were able to refocus their fire to push the rock-biters away from the rest of the Marines. Unfortunately, two of the ten valiant warriors fell to Arh'Kel fire, but the other eight rejoined the charging Terran formation and were able to take refuge from the endless hail of small-arms fire.

Another volley of enemy railguns slammed into the column's rear, where the heavier-armored Razorbacks soaked up most of the damage as eleven bolts tore into Terran armor. One of the Razorbacks fell out of formation before exploding, and in a macabrely poetic turn of events, that explosion did more to harm the pursuing Arh'Kel than it did the fleeing Terrans.

Elvira's chain guns were down below ten percent ammo, and too many rock-biters stood between her mech and the escape tunnel. They needed yet another miracle.

So that was exactly what Xi decided to conjure.

"Colonel, these rock-biters are equipped with the same link implants that the ones of Durgan's Folly had," she said urgently. "Is Alice still aboard *Warcrafter*?"

"She is," Jenkins replied after a brief delay.

"She's our best bet to get it working," Xi explained. "I don't expect us to shut them down completely, but if we can disrupt this horde for just a few seconds, it could buy us enough time to get out of the cavern."

"Copy that," he acknowledged. "Link up with us over here. She'll need your help."

Tense seconds passed before the link was live, during which time Xi had to split her attention between fighting her mech and preparing for the life-saving transmission.

"I'm here, Major," Alice declared. "If I'm not mistaken, this is a self-replicating three-phase virus?"

"Close enough," Xi said, impressed by the other woman's immediate grasp of what she was looking at. "We don't need to get too specific. Tune *Warcrafter*'s comm grid to the frequencies Styles and I discovered were vulnerable and broadcast that thing as fast as you can. Last time it took us at least three million attempts before we got our first hit, so we're going to have to get luckier than that."

"I can trim that down," Alice mused, and Xi's eyes widened at the speed of the other woman's work. Xi was fast when it came to virtual engineering, but she wasn't as fast as Styles even with the aid of her neural link. But Alice was a full step better than Styles, and that was ignoring the fact that she had never seen this particular program before.

The Marines sniped at targets like children trying to hold back the ocean's tide. Chain gun bursts of twenty and then ten rounds were interspersed by growing dead space. The Arh'Kel continued to come.

Xi watched as Alice rearranged bits and pieces of code, fundamentally altering minor aspects of the program. "I wouldn't do..." she began before Alice broadcast the program on the indicated bands.

And a sudden shudder swept across the cavern, stopping all the rock-biters in their tracks.

"Push!" Xi bellowed, prompting her Metalheads to drive forward at fifty kph toward the tunnel through which they had arrived. The rock-biters began to twitch a few seconds after the signal went out, and Xi knew that this particular miracle would be a short-lived one.

But, like mediocre sex, even short was better than nothing at all.

Rock-biters began firing their small arms into the mechs' sterns, and a pair of railgun bolts struck the cavern wall beside the tunnel as Xi entered, followed by the Razorbacks, and then by the rest of her people. Her glowing chain guns cycled down, with just five percent ammo left, and *Elvira's* metal legs trampled motionless rock-biters to death as she led the Terran column toward their fallback point.

18

REGROUPING

"That was a hell of an entrance, Major," Colonel Jenkins declared, coming down *Warcrafter's* gangplank wearing his EVA suit. He reached the bottom and gripped her hand tightly before looking around the cavern she had chosen as their fall-back point. It had three tunnels adjoining it including the one they had just come up, along with a smaller tunnel that their armor could never fit down, and the main tunnel that led back to the surface.

"I'm always told 'it's not how you start.'" She grinned, returning his grip.

"You did well on that front, too," he said knowingly as Alice came down *Warcrafter's* gangplank to join them. "As did you," he said sincerely, still having difficulty with the fact that she had so quickly executed Styles' program.

He thought he saw the glimmer of a smirk on Xi's lips, but he decided to act like he hadn't caught it before she smoothed her features out.

"All people of Sol learn the fundamentals of virtual security at a young age," Alice said dismissively. "The subject interested me, so I studied it extensively as something of a hobby."

"A hobby?" Xi shook her head in bewilderment. "It took Styles *years* to develop that thing, Alice, and you made improvements to it after looking at it for seconds."

As they spoke, the power-armored Marines moved heavy ordnance cases from one mech to another. Without forklifts or overhead cranes, they were the only ones who could lug around the quarter- or half-ton magazines, which they did with the same measure of purpose that filled every other movement they made.

Alice shrugged indifferently. "As I said, it was something of a personal passion, but I am hardly an expert in the field."

"Can Styles' program work for real, like it did on Durgan's Folly?" Jenkins asked, knowing no question was more important than that one, given their current predicament.

"That's hard to say, Colonel." Xi cocked her head skeptically. "The implants we found *looked* the same as the ones we saw in Spider Hole, and we got a major reaction out of the horde back there using a largely unmodified variant of the program, so in theory, it should be possible. But honestly, I think we might have already played that card."

"Any decent virtual architecture would adapt to a system-wide attack like that," Alice agreed. "It is unlikely this version of the program will work again. It will require significant modification."

"How long will it take you?" Jenkins asked, drawing identical somber looks from both Xi and Alice. "What is it?"

"When she says 'significant modification,'" Xi explained, "she's not talking about a couple of people monkeying around with it for a few hours, or even for a few weeks. She's talking about using at least a tier-two data core to automatically refine it, incorporating whatever feedback we've just gathered. That process should only take ten or twenty minutes, but—"

"The closest tier-two data core is in orbit," Jenkins correctly concluded. "Are you saying there's no point in trying without it?"

Alice sighed. "Statistically speaking, we would be better served by throwing ourselves on Arh'Kel mercy than 'monkeying with,'" she nodded deferentially to Xi, "this program. The only other alternative I see is to slave-rig all these vehicles' cogitative devices together, in which case we could possibly perform the task in two or three days' time."

Xi nodded gravely before chewing her lip in irritation. "I'm sorry, Colonel. I didn't want to play the virus card until after we'd gotten back here, but it didn't look like that was going to happen—"

"You made the right call, Major," Jenkins interrupted firmly before casually amending, "At least, you made the right call in the cavern."

"I sent my Monkey, Penny, to the surface on our ATV, Colonel." Xi gestured to the vacant cradle near *Elvira's* badly-damaged stern. "With any luck, she's already told them there are rock-biters down here."

Jenkins nodded approvingly. "Then it looks like you made *every* call correctly, Major. Pushing down here was worth the risk, even though it looks like we're past the potential payoff point for that particular play."

Alice sighed. "Coarse alliteration of that type is considered an insult to one's intelligence among my people."

Jenkins flashed a lopsided grin. "I'm no poet, Alice, and I never claimed to be."

Major Xi interjected, pointing to the narrow side tunnel, "It looks to me like the rock-biters have already filled those passages. I've got Giles sending his last recon drone up the main shaft," she jerked her thumb toward the larger passage leading back to the surface, "but I'd bet my last vestiges of virginity that they've already filled it six klicks up from here. We didn't see any HWPs up that way, but they're obviously boiling up to the surface as fast as we've ever seen them move. I doubt we've even put a dent in their timetable."

"Looks like we were in the right place at the right time." Jenkins shook his head wryly before turning to Alice. "Am I correct in assuming that your people had no idea there were Arh'Kel on this world?"

"You are correct." She nodded gravely. "We had no reason to think they would be here."

"They did the same thing on Durgan's Folly," Jenkins mused. "It's looking more and more like this is the work of Jemmin."

"Why do you say that, Colonel?" Xi asked, a clear challenge in her voice.

"Who else could have smuggled a rock-biter colony in here?" Jenkins asked. "Jemmin is the only known faction with the ability to fool our sensors. But why would they leave them dormant? War has been raging in the Nexus for weeks now. Why wait until we arrived to activate them?"

Xi scoffed. "Frankly, Colonel, I'd rather not climb into a Jemmin's head. I've got enough trouble between my own ears."

Alice cocked her head contemplatively. "It is possible that these Arh'Kel were considered a failsafe system of some sort. Perhaps they were only activated as a last resort."

"That tracks," Jenkins agreed, "but it doesn't explain why our arrival here signaled the need to trigger a failsafe of *this* magnitude. I'm not sure how much your people know about the rock-biters, Alice, but when these things get to the surface, they'll spread to every other world in the Solar System. If we don't contain them here, it could be the end of Sol."

"Killing them before they get off Mars will not be difficult," Alice said dismissively. "But preserving Martian infrastructure is still our primary objective, is it not?"

"Infrastructure?" Xi blurted. "There's a plague of silica set to boil out of every pore on this rock, and you're still talking about *infrastructure?!*"

"Protecting Sol is a higher priority for me than it will likely ever be for you, Major," Alice said simply, without a trace of rancor or derision. "But preserving *humanity* is a priority I think you and I consider of equal merit, is it not?"

"There's none higher." Xi wasn't sure where Alice was headed.

"Then preserving infrastructure is still key to that agenda." Alice shrugged. "If your crewman indeed reached the surface, Commodore Kline will take appropriate action to contain this threat. You have *already* saved Sol, Major, and I thank you and your people for your many sacrifices in doing so," she said. The solemnity she exuded as she spoke was humbling. "Since that is likely the case, our priorities are now to save Martian infrastructure and, if possible, ourselves. Humanity's outlook is brighter with people like you than it is without."

Xi scowled. "That sounds like an appeal to my vanity."

Alice laughed. "Vanity? Perhaps. But certainly preserving an industrial base is an appeal to the fundamental principles that drive you. Indeed, that drive *us*," she added emphatically while slicing a meaningful look Jenkins' way.

It was a look he knew warranted exploration, assuming they survived long enough.

"All right." Xi returned her focus to Jenkins. "We think the tunnels above are flooded with Arh'Kel infantry and a few HWPs, maybe one for every two thousand infantry. But the HWPs are five to ten times that dense in the tunnels below, with the orbital launch equipment probably five or ten kilometers beneath that shithole we just clawed out of. Our best guess puts the rock-biters at around three million infantry."

"That would be my guess, based on cocktail napkin math,"

Jenkins agreed. "Which means there's no choice which way we go from here. If you two thought we could even *possibly* use Styles' program to shut this infestation down, it would change the calculus," he said leadingly, drawing definitive headshakes in reply from both women. "Since that option's out, so are we," he declared. "When we're finished redistributing the ammo, we'll hope we've got enough to get through these damned things and regain the surface. How's your mech, Major?" he asked, eyeing the badly-battered *Elvira*, which was missing most of the armor from its forward legs and one of her fifteen-kilo mains.

"She can take point, sir," Xi said confidently. "Since the Razorbacks' coil guns are dry, there's no point putting them front and center."

"I disagree," Jenkins said, surprised by her desire to lead the charge and its effect on full allocation of assets based on best capabilities. *"Murasame's* got the most accurate chain guns due to his platform's stability, and Elvira's guns are only good to the flanks. Charging up a tunnel with little better than rocks to throw at the enemy calls for...let's call this an audible to a running play."

Xi seemed ready to argue, but her eyes lit up when she took his meaning. "And any good running play needs a lead blocker."

"Captain Chao seems an obvious fit for that role. We'll let his volunteering for the post cancel out a disciplinary hearing for breaking ranks back in the cavern," he said with a chuckle. *"Elvira* will cover our rear, where your chains can do the most good. If they manage to climb up our asses, you'll burn and drop 'em like yesterday's salsa. We'll keep *Cyclops* central to the formation, because if it gets too thick ahead, he's the only one who can make a big enough hole."

"He's got major issues with his HPC, Colonel," Xi said grimly. "The capacitors are nearly fried, and the magnetics are out of alignment. About the only thing that works properly is the loading assembly."

"Then let's hope we don't need it," Jenkins replied with an indifferent shrug. "But if we do, we can't be afraid to call for the shot just because it might blow up in our faces. After all, what's the worst that can happen?"

"You've got a singular gift for boosting morale, sir. I've seen some enemy plasma launchers blow, and they leave a most impressive crater."

He returned the smile with a fierce one of his own. "Saddle up, Major. This ride's just gotten to the fun part. Big craters for the adults."

"Metal never dies." She snapped a salute before turning on her heel and making her way to *Elvira*.

Two minutes later, all crews had returned to their vehicles, the Marines had received the rest of the grenades and other small arms they could make effective use of, and the column was on the move toward the surface.

Razor Bamboo took the lead, followed by *Murasame*, then *Cyclops*, then the rest of the Razorbacks, with the rear brought up by *Black Widow* and *Elvira*. Battered Marines enjoyed the ride on the limping vehicles as they made yet another desperate charge.

"Oorah!" one of them yelled into the comm, and the others repeated his call.

19

SILVER RAIN

"We should have received at least three reports in the last hour, with the most recent thirty minutes ago," Podsy said precisely as the overdue clock ticked to thirty minutes. "Something's wrong down there, General."

For the past ten minutes, the general had worn the stiffest poker face Podsy had ever seen grace the man's features. Moon was a hard man, but he was hardly without visible moods, even in the midst of combat. Something was gnawing at the general, but Podsy had been unable to surmise what it was.

Seeming to sense Podsy's lingering gaze, Moon straightened in his chair and shook his head firmly. "We're already stretched as thin as possible. We can't pull the ground elements off protective duty or we'll lose the beanstalks and a dozen strategically-critical manufactories. Without more information, we're locked down."

"Captain Koch's Jokers are ready to roll," Podsy said before hesitating. He wanted to leap into the fray to help their friends and comrades, but the higher parts of his brain knew that would be a bad play. "But we don't know where they're having issues, so sending Koch down without a clear plan would be wasteful."

"It's becoming increasingly likely the problems are *everywhere*," Moon said grimly, and something in the way he emphasized that last word snagged Podsy's attention.

"A coordinated underground offensive? And one stiff enough to thwart Colonel Jenkins *and* Major Xi?" Podsy narrowed his eyes in thought. "There's nobody with sufficient tactical acumen or experience unaccounted for down there to lead a resistance that spread out, *especially* not without comm linkage. And there isn't enough Martian hardware unaccounted for to..."

Then he realized what the general was suggesting, and the color drained from Podsy's face as he understood the reason for the general's poker face. General Moon flitted a look Podsy's way, and when they made eye contact, Podsednik's suspicions were all but confirmed.

Podsy made the faintest gesture in Styles' direction, and Moon gave a slight nod in reply. At that, Podsednik made his way to the Ground Control Officer's station and leaned down close to the chief's ear. "Secure your mic, Chief."

Styles tapped a few commands before acknowledging, "We're secure."

"I need you to start working up new support packages for the ground teams," Podsy explained, his voice barely above a whisper.

"What kind of changes, sir?" Styles asked warily.

"The kind we use for rock-biters," Podsy muttered.

Styles' eyebrows shot up, then quickly lowered as he schooled his expression. "What are you basing that on?" he whispered.

"Call it a hunch," Podsy said dismissively. "We sent our best people, both Metalheads and Marines, into a concerted underground effort. Not a single one has shown back up, and they are all behind schedule. Who could stand up to our people like that across a massive front and deep underground? It sure as hell isn't a bunch of Martian rebels."

Chief Styles hung his head, nodding almost imperceptibly as the color drained from his face.

"Also, if there *are* rock-biters down there, there's a good chance that whoever put them there was responsible for the ones we fought on Spider Hole."

Styles sat up straight and looked Podsy in the eye. "I'd need the general's approval to unlock that file, Lieutenant."

"I'm guessing you've already got it," Podsy whispered

A few seconds later, Styles recoiled in surprise at seeing that the file was unlocked and he had access to the program he and Xi had written a year earlier. "I don't know what you need to do to prep that thing," Podsy said quietly, "but if the general's right, we might need it sooner rather than later."

"That's..." Styles shook his head vigorously. "I can do a little prep work from here, but the fine-tuning has to happen on the other end. *I* need to be with this thing to sink it into the colony's network if there really is one down there."

"General," called the comm operator, "I'm receiving a distress signal from the surface. It's using Major Xi's credentials. The message is originating from an ATV that just emerged from the Southern Hub. There's an audio broadcast attached."

"Let's hear it." Moon leaned forward as the speakers crackled to life.

"This is Private Penny." The voice cut out for a second before confirming Moon's and Podsednik's fears. "...ve got rock-biters. I say again, we've got rock-biters. Disposition unknown, strength unknown, activity unknown. I say again, to any Terran or Solar elements that receive this message, there is an active colony of Arh'Kel on Mars."

"Lieutenant," Moon barked as a pall of silence hung over

the bridge, "I understand you and Mr. Styles have developed an unorthodox approach to dealing with Arh'Kel crypto-colonies?"

"Yes General, we have," Podsy said in a raised voice, and the feeling of thirty pairs of eyes swiveling his way was wholly unexpected but not altogether unsettling. He saw something in those eyes he had never really seen in his fellow servicemen.

They were predictably unnerved at the mention of Arh'Kel being discovered where none had any right to be, but more than that, the bridge crew had a hopeful glimmer in their eyes.

More than hope, they were looking to *him* for hope. A quick look General Moon's way confirmed that he had teed Podsednik up for this very moment, and the Legion's lone flag officer present was watching him with unvarnished interest.

So Podsy did the only thing that came naturally to him: he told the truth. "We know *exactly* how to turn out the lights on the sneaky fuckers, General."

"Then do it," Moon commanded. "Ground Control, have Captain Koch prep everything that can move faster than sixty kph for insertion. If our boys and girls are locking horns with Arh'Kel down there, they'll need plenty of ammo, band-aids, and spare parts."

"Yes, General," Styles acknowledged before quickly relaying those very orders. "Captain Koch's people will be ready to roll in eight minutes, sir."

"Start the clock," Moon snapped, and an eight-minute countdown appeared on the main viewer.

Podsy huddled with Styles and asked, "Is there anything I can do to help, Chief?"

"I need exclusive access to *all* of the *William Wallace*'s computer cores, Lieutenant, and I need them *now*," Styles said as his fingers flew across the interface.

"General," Podsy called, "we need all of the *Wallace's* virtual systems repurposed to Chief Styles' project."

"They're yours," Moon replied a few seconds later, after mashing the buttons to make the authorization.

"What else can I do, Chief?" Podsy asked urgently.

"I need information. I need to know what the major knows, or the colonel. If I had any data from them, first and foremost confirmation that these Arh'Kel had their own One Mind devices installed, then the program is an option. If they don't, this software means nothing. I need data. An hour and a good link to our people?"

"How effective can you make it in eight minutes *without* the feedback?" Podsy pressed.

Styles opened his mouth to speak before thinking better of whatever reply he had been about to make. "I think I'd have a better chance of making a hole in one on a par five. But we've got *more* than eight minutes," he said urgently as he returned most of his attention to the work before him. "Have Captain Koch's people create a comm chain out of surveillance drones, ATVs...anything with a wireless repeater capable of transceiving a ten-gigabits-per-second signal farther than a couple hundred meters. We should be able to maintain linkage with them for close to an hour that way, which would make this more like trying to make a twenty-foot putt."

"That sounds better," Podsednik agreed, clapping the other man on the shoulder and taking the Ground Control headset so he could coordinate the building of the makeshift relay network.

"It's harebrained," Captain Koch replied after receiving the orders, "which makes it par for the course."

"You people and your golf references." Podsy scowled.

"Say again, GC?" Koch asked.

"Nothing, Captain." Podsednik sighed, catching sight of Commodore Kline having a sidebar with General Moon.

"Good," Koch replied as Joker Company's icons began to move toward the Southern Hub, "because we're rolling."

"Good hunting, Captain," Podsednik said before signing off. He made his way to General Moon's side, where he and the commodore were perusing the data packet Xi had sent up with her mech's Monkey.

"I agree that this *appears* to be the case, General," the Solar Commodore said patiently, "but you must understand. If there is the *slightest* chance this intel is inaccurate, let alone forged, my mandate is clear. I cannot reinforce your people with ground elements unless the evidence is incontrovertible that there is an external threat present on Mars that requires engagement by Solar forces."

"You have something to add, Lieutenant?" Moon asked, his voice tight with frustration at making little apparent headway with the Solar officer.

"Nothing incontrovertible, General." Podsy shook his head flatly. "But that would be the point, wouldn't it?"

"Excuse me?" Commodore Kline asked frostily.

"If someone hid rock-biters on Mars and Jemmin cruisers on Phobos," Podsy explained, "and if that someone viewed them as a failsafe... A backup, if you will, to the events we've already seen underway here in Sol following Operation Antivenom, it would stand to reason that such a failsafe would need to be over-whelming in power. Keeping it secret would therefore be of paramount importance to maintaining its tactical viability.

"We've seen this kind of thing before, Commodore," he said unflinchingly. "They hid one of these crypto-colonies right under Terran noses too. Fortunately for us, we had a tipoff regarding their location and were able to get in and deal with them before they became an existential threat to the Terran Republic. I don't know who gave us that intel back on Durgan's Folly, or what their motives were. But what I *do* know is who's giving *you* the heads-up here on Mars. And I know beyond the shadow of a doubt what *our* motives are."

"Every second counts, Commodore," Moon urged. "We came here to help you solve a crisis on Mars, and it turns out the problem was a lot deeper than any of us thought. I understand your hands are tied to some degree, but they don't hand out flags like candy. They expect people like us to make hard calls, and that's precisely what's in front of you at this very moment."

Kline looked back and forth between Moon and Podsednik. "You do not understand. If there are no Arh'Kel down there, landing Solar troops on Mars would cause a potentially devastating cascade effect on Solar society that would make the loss of Mars seem like a trivial thing. And I do not say that lightly, gentlemen."

"Make the call, Commodore," Podsy urged. "Because frankly? If we don't secure Mars and however much of its infrastructure remains, the human race's future is dependent on the largesse of beings we can't possibly understand. This is like Thomas Jefferson and the Louisiana Purchase," he said as the thought occurred. "Every fiber of his being told him not to do it. He knew it went against every principle he had built his entire political and philosophical legacy upon, and yet, he also knew that not making the purchase would doom America and put her at the mercy of foreign powers. He made a hard call, just like you're about to, and in both cases, it's the right one."

The commodore cocked his head skeptically for a long, silent moment before the sensor pit erupted in a series of alarms.

"General, I'm reading twenty...thirty...fifty..." the sensor officer called before finally rallying. "I've got over two hundred dropships descending to the Martian surface."

"Point of origin?" Moon asked, his eyes not wavering from Kline's.

"The Solar Fleet, sir," Sensors replied. "They're Marine dropships."

"With an average complement of a hundred and twenty

power-armored Solar Space Marines apiece," Commodore Kline explained, his pride suffused with resignation. "This is the single largest landing of armored Marines in human history, General, and it is happening on Martian soil. Words fail to describe what this means to Sol...and to me."

"It means you've given us a great backup plan, Commodore," Moon said. "Because we can't let the Arh'Kel reach the surface."

Kline continued with a certain edge to his voice. "But I must make preparations in the event that they do, which means," he turned officiously to General Moon, "I must advise you and your ships to remain in their current positions so that my ships can move into more advantageous firing positions to support our Marines."

"Of course," Moon acknowledged, but Podsy was acutely aware of just how close the commodore's 'advice' was to a threat.

As they watched, two hundred and thirty-eight Solar Marine dropships descended to the Martian surface, with over three-quarters of them making for the Southern Hub and the rest spreading out across the planet.

Like silver raindrops, those dropships fell.

Thirty ships air-dropped their Marines from fifty meters off the ground, pouring their power-armored warriors into the tunnel down which Captain Koch had gone minutes earlier.

The Marines set off at a sprint down the tunnel, which seemed like the hungry maw of some beast intent on devouring as much of humanity as possible.

I just hope they're in time, Podsy thought. He and General Moon shared a brief but pointed look that told Podsednik his CO was every bit as impressed by the scene unfolding before them as Podsy was.

"I'll help Chief Styles," Podsy said, turning to do just that when his eyes snagging on Commodore Kline's face. The Solarian's cheeks were moist with tears as he watched his Marines charge into the Martian underworld. Whether they were tears of joy or sorrow, Podsednik could not tell. But one thing was certain: Jem had been right.

For all their differences, Terrans and Solarians had more in common than not...and they were going to need each other if they wanted to survive.

Forty minutes later, after making as many revisions to Styles' takeover program as possible, they forwarded it to Captain Koch with orders to transfer it to either Major Xi or Colonel Jenkins.

When the comm link with Koch's Jokers finally went dead, Podsednik knew the rest was out of their hands—and nothing could have made him feel worse than to know his friends were down there, cut off and alone in the dark, surrounded by creatures that would have given H.P. Lovecraft nightmares.

20

THUNDERSTRUCK

"This isn't metal, and it's about as vulgar as Nakamura's porn collection!" Blinky protested as AC/DC's *Thunderstruck* began to play. With the formation driving at a constant fifty kph, *Razor Bamboo* had led the column up thirty-six kilometers of tunnel through an increasingly dense sea of rock-biters. Chao's forward armor was covered in a thick layer of purple goo as he rammed through hundreds of rock-biters each minute they traveled. Makeshift blades, spikes, and cow-catchers had been affixed to its bow during the ammo exchange, but only a few of these remained after slaughtering thousands of unarmored enemies.

"Oh look, I think I just passed Blinky's last shred of dignity!" Xi added as the six Marines perched atop *Razor Bamboo* leaned out at symmetrical angles from the mech's hull. For a moment, they looked like the many arms of the Indian goddess Shiva, splayed at fifteen-degree offsets from the plane of the floor.

Once locked into position, using their magnetic boots to secure them to the mech's hull, the Marines fired their railgun rifles in perfect unison up the tunnel. Their rifles were positioned at angles which were almost precisely parallel to the tunnel floor, maximizing their potential impact on the horde before them.

The extreme penetrative power of those railguns' slivers carved a bloody path through the press of enemy infantry, still largely unaccompanied by HWPs. Where the Marines' rifles would have claimed a couple dozen enemy per shot back in the cavern, on a straight stretch of tunnel like this and with the enemy wedged so tightly together, each sliver could possibly notch as many as a hundred kills with each hit. Possibly even more if they got lucky and hit an enemy capacitor.

Which this volley happened to do, causing a blast of light and a high-pitched *crack* to fill the tunnel as the enemy HWP went up in a shower of electric fire.

Like a freight train powering through a personal commuter car, *Razor Bamboo* collided with the HWP's wreckage and barely seemed to notice the impact. Metal shards clattered against the tunnel's stone walls, and after the column's mechs each took a turn rolling over the wreckage, it was a flattened field of unrecognizable debris.

"If there's no double-kick pedal, it's not metal!" Blinky insisted.

"That's just one of many foolish attempted marks of delineation," Giles shot back. "Besides, how the hell can anyone with half a brain *not* consider a song like this metal?" he demanded, drawing a chorus of approving noises from the rest of the unit.

"Because AC/DC is a *rock* band," Staubach retorted. "Metal is a subset of rock, not the other way around."

"I think we all know how Venn diagrams work, Blinky." Nakamura snickered as he fired a pair of chain-gun rounds into some rock-biters as they attempted to clamber up *Razor Bamboo*'s hull. But no matter how precise his fire was, some of the accursed things still managed to gain purchase on Chao's battered hull.

Unfortunately for them, all they got for their trouble was a swift kick from the Marines roving *Razor Bamboo*'s hull. Those kicks knocked the rock-biters to the tunnel floor, where they were trampled by the rest of the Terran column.

"Fuck it," Blinky snapped as he impressively drove his beleaguered mech up the tunnel at the heart of the column. "I'm filing an official protest on behalf of reason, good taste, and the proper definition of words. Can I get a second?"

"I'll second you, Blinky," Quinn agreed. "I never liked this song anyway."

"Your protest is made, seconded, and overruled, Lieutenant," Colonel Jenkins put in, drawing gleeful chuckles from both Xi and Quinn. "Though I'll be happy to reconsider the matter after we return to HQ."

"Why the hell are *you* laughing, Quinn?" Blinky demanded.

"Funny's funny, Blinky," she quipped. "And *that* was funny."

Xi had to concur. Given the growing density of enemy soldiers, it was becoming increasingly obvious that they wouldn't make it out of the tunnels. At this point, it was more a matter of dignity and honor than any genuine hope for victory that propelled the armored column up the tunnel.

Xi's attention was grabbed by a flicker of motion on her sensors. "Contacts," she reported. "I've got four HWPs... Make that six, pursuing at eighty kph. They'll be in firing range in two minutes."

"We couldn't stay ahead of them forever," Jenkins said matter-of-factly. "There's a small transloading cavern up ahead which intersects a tunnel that should give us a clearer path to the surface and a chance for a formation shift, although it adds another twelve minutes to the trip."

"Sounds like a worthwhile detour to me, sir," Xi agreed, slowly pivoting *Elvira* so that her fifteen-kilo main was pointed down the tunnel at the approaching HWPs. The Marines, using their magnetic boots, once again performed their bizarre firing maneuver, sending a half dozen tungsten slivers up the tunnel and killing nearly half the Arh'Kel in sight.

An alarm began flashing on Xi's HUD. It was a status update from *Razor Bamboo*'s reactor, and it showed that Chao's mech was starting to lose power.

"It looks like I need to catch my breath," Chao said sourly. "We've been leaking coolant for about twenty klicks, and it's starting to catch up with us."

"I'll take point," Colonel Jenkins declared. "Pull left and fall back to my slot. I'll overtake on the right. It's about time we got a demonstration of fancy Marine footwork, anyway."

"Ready when you are, Colonel," Lieutenant Briggs acknowledged as the column continued racing up the cylindrical tunnel.

Warcrafter, situated at the fifth slot in the column, pulled out to the right and accelerated to a hundred thirty kph in four seconds. The burst of speed was so energetic that shards of stone sprayed out from beneath the battlewagon's roller-feet, looking to Xi like water splashing up from a puddle as a car drove through it. The mech was moving so fast along the curved surface, and its legs were splayed so wide as it accelerated, that it nearly went perpendicular to the rest of the column as it raced ahead to the formation's front.

At the same moment Jenkins' mech pulled right, Chao's veered left and fell back while the Marines burned their battlesuits' rockets and leapt across the tunnel toward Jenkins' mech. As they made their borderline-psychotic jump, *Razor Bamboo* braked and jammed his right legs into the curved tunnel's left wall.

Without the benefit of acceleration to help steady him, he had to stick his right legs' metal spurs into the stone in order to hold position while the rest of the column sped past. If either of his battered legs gave out or lost their tenuous purchase even for a fraction of a second, it would spell disaster for the charging column of armor.

Xi held her breath as one mech went past Chao. Then another, a third, and a fourth, and finally he released his gravity-defying grip on the tunnel's wall and slid into position while accelerating far less impressively than the identical (but significantly less damaged) *Warcrafter*.

Meanwhile, all eight of the Marines had landed on *Warcrafter's* hull and taken up positions identical to their previous ones on *Razor Bamboo*. It was a jaw-dropping display of coordination on the power-armored Marines' part. Business as usual, defying the laws of nature.

"A thing of beauty is a joy forever," the colonel congratulated them. "Now, where were we?" he muttered before the Marines unleashed another salvo from their railgun rifles, dealing death to the suddenly thinned ranks of Arh'Kel before them.

"Where'd they all go?" Giles asked before proximity alarms began to ring in Xi's ears. The pursuing rock-biters were in firing position, and their EM signatures showed they would take advantage of that fact.

"Incoming!" she declared, raising *Elvira* up as high as she could stand to shield the Metalheads farther up the column from the inbound strikes.

When they hit, Xi's world spun into darkness.

"*Elvira's* down," Quinn declared, halting *Black Widow's* advance and coming about. "I say again, *Elvira's* down."

Jenkins checked his command HUD and found that the

major's mech was still powered up and responsive to commands. But the major was unconscious, and the mech's armored windshield, already damaged from previous engagements, appeared to have failed.

He input his command override code and assumed remote control of the Scorpion-class mech. The manual control sticks on the station to his left felt familiar in his hands, but he knew he couldn't fight the damaged *Elvira* effectively on manual controls.

So he hard-wired his neural link port to the terminal, drew a long breath, and activated the link at full bandwidth.

Normally, a pilot's familiarity with their mech's individual feedbacks would make such a "hot link" attempt merely uncomfortable or temporarily disorienting. But while Jenkins was rated on Scorpions, it had been a full three months since he had undergone rigorous link testing. Their schedule had been so hectic and unforgiving that they hadn't had time for essential skills maintenance like that.

And he paid for that shortcoming when *Elvira's* systems flooded his mind. Chief among those inputs were the pain signals that communicated the mech's current damage reports in a nauseating stream of precisely located agony. His shoulders burned where the mech's forward leg hull joints had suffered moderate damage, his eyes burned from the damage to the mech's windshield, his left kidney throbbed from the loss of her port fifteen-kilo main, and his feet felt like they were moving over a bed of broken glass due to the damage to her lower limbs.

But despite the nearly-overpowering wave of stimulus, he was able to get the mech's legs moving coherently. He raised the cruiser-grade vehicle to its standard height and commanded, "This is the colonel. I've assumed direct control of *Elvira*. Resume formation, *Black Widow*."

"Copy that, Colonel," Quinn acknowledged.

It took Jenkins a few seconds to get *Elvira's* walk cycle under control, but once he did, he was able to resume the upward march, albeit at a mere thirty-five kph.

"Hammer," he called as he struggled with *Elvira's* controls, "let's make that detour after all." With Xi out of commission and the enemy railguns closing in on them, it was only a matter of time before the rock-biters brought enough firepower to bear to permanently halt their advance. He would have preferred to continue the charge in the hope of keeping ahead of their pursuers, but any hope of that type was dashed by Xi's incapacitation. Even if she regained consciousness in the next minute and was immediately combat-ready, they had already lost too much ground.

With *Warcrafter* at their head, the column banked hard to the left as they came to a rare T intersection. This tunnel, at eighteen meters instead of the previous tunnel's thirty meters, was barely tall enough for the towering *Cyclops* to squeeze through. By abandoning this central artery, they had reduced their possible number of paths to safety to one, which connected with the cavern that was their new destination.

"*Culture Knight*," Jenkins called after half of the column had passed into the smaller tunnel, "focus a full mortar barrage on the lower tunnel's ceiling." With any luck, *Culture Knight's* mortars would collapse enough material in front of the rock-biters to buy the Terrans enough time to reach the cavern up ahead but not so much as to cause irreparable damage to the main transit line.

"Roger, Colonel," Giles acknowledged. "Full barrage focused on the lower tunnel's ceiling."

Black Widow and *Culture Knight* stood tall as their fellows ducked into the tunnel, with the former sending a six-second burst of her last chain-gun rounds up the tunnel and the latter unleashing yet another of his ultra-devastating mortar barrages.

The mortar shells hammered into the roof and walls of the tunnel, carving multi-meter-wide chunks of stone from the previously smooth surface. The range of Giles' barrage was limited by the height of the roof, but he still managed to collapse several hundred tons of rock across a fifty-meter stretch of cave.

Jenkins approved, pulling *Elvira* up long enough for the others to rejoin the column. The humanoid and spider mechs moved into the tunnel, and as they did so, the first signs of consciousness flickered on Major Xi's monitors.

"Were they sweet dreams, Major?" Jenkins asked as they put precious distance between them and the rock-biter horde, which *Elvira's* sensors showed had renewed their pursuit after the short-lived lull.

"I'm...not sure," she said groggily, vigorously shaking her head despite all the data indicating that was a bad idea. "Who is driving my mech?!" she demanded as her senses snapped back into focus.

"That'd be me." Jenkins grimaced as a fresh burning sensation swept across his scalp, indicating that she was trying to reassert control, "but I'd be happy to hand her back if you're ready."

"I am." Xi's vitals were returning to a more normal state.

"Handoff in three...two...one," he intoned before cutting his link. "Zero. She's yours."

As he handed off control, the sensory inputs vanished with such rapidity that for a moment, he was dumbstruck. His brain seized up like it would if he was trying to do calculus with an abacus. He tried to ride it out by slowing his thoughts and attempting not to fight the overwhelmingly vacuous sensation, but despite his best efforts, he heard himself groan something unintelligible.

"That good, eh?" Hammer quipped after Jenkins' senses returned.

"Like drinking battery acid with a tequila chaser," the colonel muttered.

"I'll have what he had." Hammer chuckled as the column drove up the nearly empty tunnel.

Against the odds, they reached that cavern without incident, squashing another two hundred mostly-lone rock-biters along the way. Jenkins' spirits were buoyed by the improbability of it all, and he even allowed himself to contemplate what his first meal would be after going wheels-up from this infernal place.

But his dreams of porterhouse steaks were dashed upon their arrival at that cavern, where an entirely unwelcome party was there to greet them.

Sixteen Arh'Kel HWPs, most of which were railguns, with a handful of missiles pods, were set up for a perfect ambush as soon as they emerged. And with *Warcrafter* at the column's head, it took the brunt of the onslaught, although Hammer proved his mettle by immediately flattening the mech, crashing its chassis to the cavern floor.

Three railgun bolts slammed into *Warcrafter's* lead left leg, blowing the limb completely off its hull joint. Another pair of bolts struck the battlewagon's roof, shearing fully half the mech's armor off with the near-misses that would have otherwise been kill-shots had Hammer not ducked as he did. Major Trapper and the Marines leapt off the mech's hull, firing their railguns across the cavern and scoring a trio of kills against enemy HWPs before they landed in the thick of the enemy infantry and engaged in a fight for their lives.

As *Warcrafter* fell forward into the cavern, another two bolts slammed into the mech's forward armor. One unexpectedly broke completely through the vehicle's armor and sent a spray of deadly shrapnel into the cabin, as the concussive force robbed the crew of their senses for several precious seconds.

Fortunately for the column, Hammer managed to lurch his

crippled mech aside, allowing the rest of the Metalheads to penetrate the cavern and engage the enemy.

"Weapons free!" Xi barked after seeing *Warcrafter*'s battered hulk come to a halt just inside the tunnel mouth. "Blow those fuckers to hell!"

Murasame, in the formation's two-slot, did his best to dive his mech to the side opposite *Warcrafter* and clear a line of fire for the mechs at his back, but the enemy fire was too severe, and a trio of railgun bolts slammed into his humanoid torso at the waist. In a shower of sparks and debris, *Murasame's* upper torso keeled over to the right, landing with a deafening crash on the stone floor and leaving its upright and motionless legs directly in *Culture Knight*'s path.

Once again demonstrating his quick thinking, Giles aimed his arm-mounted eight-kilo guns at *Murasame's* dismembered legs, which were connected by a slender beam at the groin. The shells separated the legs, causing them to tilt ponderously before *Culture Knight* slammed into them and sent them flying to either side as Giles unleashed his final barrage of mortar shells. With his torso's armor plates retracted, he launched sixty-two shells across the cavern, scratching five HWPs and slaughtering hundreds of rock-biters.

The enemy returned fire, launching a salvo of eight missiles at the charging mech, and with its armored panels retracted, *Culture Knight*'s fate was sealed.

Slamming into his torso, the armor-piercing missiles punched clean through the mighty *Culture Knight's* frame, erupting out the vehicle's lightly-armored back and scattering the vehicle's metal guts across the rest of the column.

Its arms fell, sundered from the ruined torso, but its legs

continued to churn for several steps before crumpling, sending the vehicle's head crashing to the ground. It was unlikely that the war machine's crew survived the hellish assault, but he had done the job of clearing a path for the Razorbacks.

And when those Razorbacks arrived in the cavern, they tore into the enemy using the last of their coil-gun rounds in a defiant display of valor before, true to form, they slammed their ammo-less mechs into the enemy.

Black Widow followed them into the cavern, spraying the last of her chain-gun rounds into the surging horde which had previously been pressed up against the cavern's walls as part of the ambush. Xi took up a position to Quinn's left to cover her from enemy fire, and the two multi-legged walkers formed a deadly albeit short-lived pair as they tore into the enemy with the last of their ammo. Xi managed to bracket an enemy missile launcher and fired an AP shell from her fifteen into the enemy platform before the distinctive clatter of rocky bodies landing on her hull filled *Elvira's* cabin.

"This is it." She grimaced, turning her mech in concert with *Black Widow* to cut down as many rock-biters as possible before their guns ran dry. She knew that when their ammo was depleted, their lifespans would be measured in seconds, not minutes, and frankly, that was all right with her.

She had come here to do her duty to Terra and to humanity, and while she had not achieved victory, she had succeeded, and could rest in the knowledge that she had done more to safeguard humanity's future during her short time with the Metal Legion than most managed in their entire lives. She was proud to have served alongside her fellow Terrans in this hellhole, and was determined to stand as tall as possible in the face of an overwhelming enemy force.

A plasma torch burst through the cabin roof, but she paid it no heed. She had to focus on taking as many rock-biters down as possible while she still had control of her mech. Suddenly, a trio of explosions went off above her, and she saw that Major Trapper and a pair of Marines had lobbed grenades onto her roof before installing themselves there and hurling more hand-held ordnance down at the approaching enemy.

With a wolfish grin, she laid into the enemy with her chain guns until one went dry. Then another, and finally, all four were bingo ammo, and all she had were the Marines on her roof and foul language to repel the enemy.

The Razorbacks had made a mosh pit out of the cavern's perimeter as they trampled and pulverized Arh'Kel bodies by the dozens with each passing second.

Just as she prepared to unleash the most inventive string of profane invective ever uttered by a human voice, an inbound radio signal came over the hailing frequencies with an audio transmission that made her question her sanity.

It was a distinctly metal version of the *Marines' Hymn*, played on a lone vintage electric guitar with moderate distortion.

Before the first bar of music had passed, the main tunnel on the far side of the cavern, which the Metalheads had hoped to use in reaching the surface, erupted in a cacophony of small arms fire, grenade explosions, and railgun rifle strikes. The breaching effort was over before the second bar of the *Marines' Hymn* had come over the speakers.

And when the third bar sounded, accompanied by savagely-shredding drumbeats, a flight of silver-skinned angels of death stormed into the cavern and transformed the place into a special kind of hell.

Slug-throwers, grenades, railgun rifles, and even crew-served miniguns, all of Solar design and wielded by Solarian Space Marines, tore into the rock-biters with reckless abandon. Dozens of the valiant warriors died in those first seconds, but their sacrifice bought their battle-brothers enough terrain to surge into the cavern en masse.

All three hundred of them.

So intense was their entry, and so fast their movements, that all three hundred Solarian Marines made it into the cavern and started mowing down rock-biters with deadly precision, filling Xi and her fellow Terrans with a wholly unexpected sense of renewed hope. They swept through the cavern like a wave cleaning debris from the shore.

21

FROM THE BURNISHED BONES OF MERCURY

From the burnished bones of Mercury,
Out to Neptune's airy sea,
We fight humanity's battles
Where and whenever they be.

First to fight for peace and order,
And to preserve unity.
Tis our honor to take up the charge
Of a Solar Space Marine

~*Solar Space Marines Hymn, Verse One*~

"Alice? Hammer?" Jenkins gasped, dragging himself from his chair and trying to focus through his one working eye. "Hammer!" he shouted, looking around *Warcrafter's* cabin and seeing nothing but dark screens illuminated by a cabin fire to the front of the vehicle.

The mech's auto-sealing foam, which automatically

deployed in the event of a breach and prevented all of the cabin's life-giving air from rushing out into the tunnel, had plugged the hole opened by the railgun direct hit. But *Warcrafter's* air was already dangerously thin, and would not remain breathable given the presence of the fire, so Jenkins needed to get his crew out of the vehicle ASAP.

He saw Alice stir at her console and was temporarily torn by who should first receive his attention. "Alice..." He fumbled for a nearby helmet and managed to latch it onto his collar. The familiar popping in his ears after the helmet sealed to his EVA suit was more than welcome, and he drank several deep breaths of air.

She turned toward him, and for a moment her eyes were blank, but the fog quickly cleared and she said, "Your eye..."

"It's fine," he said with forced stoicism before gesturing to the compartment's rear. "Open the airlock. I've got to get Hammer."

Alice obliged, and Jenkins crawled over to the pilot's chair to find that his Jock had begun to stir. "Wake up, Hammer," he growled, standing unsteadily. Hammer was already wearing his own helmet and turned with a dull look in his eyes before slowly focusing on Jenkins.

"The others?" the Jock asked groggily.

"Alice is fine. Everyone else was forward," Jenkins shook his head as he tried to help the other man stand. After a moment, they succeeded in getting upright, although it was difficult to tell who helped who. "We've got to get out," he urged, moving toward the cabin's rear, where Alice was opening the airlock.

Hammer helped her unstick the outer hatch, and when it swung open, they saw a tide of Arh'Kel being savaged by relatively slow-moving railgun bolts. The bolts were decidedly not Terran, and when Jenkins peered around *Warcrafter's* hulk to see the source, he found exactly what he had expected.

And it was an awesome, terrible thing to behold.

Wading into the sea of rock-biters were hundreds of Solar Space Marines, carving a bloody path from the far end of the cavern toward the surrounded Metalheads.

Captain Chao's *Razor Bamboo* had formed up with the other Clover survivors near the cavern's center, where they had clustered together so tightly their hulls touched every few seconds. In that tight quartet, the Razorbacks churned in a ceaseless counterclockwise rotation that crushed all Arh'Kel infantry suicidal enough to threaten their line. They formed an anchor point for the Marines to use as leverage during their charge across the cavern.

Jenkins activated his helmet's short-range comm transceiver and was immediately met with a fast-paced metal variant of the *Marines' Hymn* played on what sounded like a mid-1960s electric guitar. He couldn't help but grin like an idiot. The rock-biters were now ignoring the Terrans, having refocused their efforts exclusively on the newly-arrived Solarians. Watching the Arh'Kel cartwheel past his position en route to a rendezvous with death at the hands of the inbound Marines, Jenkins finally knew the full meaning of the word "surreal."

He quickly gathered his wits and cut the channel, silencing the raucous music as he turned to Hammer and Alice. "They'll reach us in about two minutes," he said urgently, pointing to the fallen *Murasame*. "See if you can recover anyone from Nakamura's crew. I'll go check *Culture Knight!*"

Without a word, Hammer and Alice bounced toward the dismembered *Murasame,* while Jenkins did likewise toward *Culture Knight*. It was impressive seeing a civilian like Alice conduct herself so well in the heat of combat, and he resolved to tell her as much if they made it back to civilization.

But for the moment, he had more important things to think about, like doing his duty to his fellow Metalheads.

He instinctively kept his head down as he went, and was rewarded for his adherence to discipline when a slug zipped fifteen centimeters above his helmet before dropping an oncoming rock-biter.

Just before he reached *Culture Knight*, a rock-biter rolled between him and the mech and seemed to reconsider its mindless charge toward the death-dealing Marines. Jenkins froze, acutely aware of the fact that he had nothing save a small-bore pistol on his hip, and that it would likely be useless against the stone-hided beast.

The rock-biter, towering a full three meters above the cavern floor, squared itself to him, and for a moment he was certain this was it. He instinctively drew his pistol, firing a round center-mass into the thing as it aimed its own pistol at him.

But then the rock-biter's body flew apart in a violet mist and its six limbs were flung through the air.

Jenkins stupidly looked down at his pistol for a moment before realizing what had happened. He looked over his shoulder and confirmed that a Terran Marine, or possibly Major Trapper in Marine power armor, was standing from his previous kneeling position with his railgun rifle held at the ready. Jenkins mimed the tipping of his cap before covering the rest of the ground between him and *Culture Knight*'s wreckage.

A familiar whine filled his ears, and the air around Jenkins' suit began to crackle as he dove for cover beneath *Culture Knight*'s broken form.

A moment after he reached cover, *Cyclops'* heavy plasma cannon hurled a blue-white fireball across the cavern. It splashed down well clear of the charging Marines, thinning the Arh'Kel ranks to their left flank and scratching an enemy railgun for good measure.

The battered and sluggish *Cyclops* trudged its way across

the cavern, accompanied by *Elvira* and *Black Widow* as the slow-moving trio made their way toward the Razorbacks, around whom the Marines had established a perimeter guard comprised of several dozen power-armored bodies.

Jenkins clambered up *Culture Knight*'s back, making his way to the cockpit situated between the fallen walker's broad shoulders. Once there, he tapped in an emergency override code into the cockpit's escape hatch and was rewarded by a hiss of escaping gas as the hatch popped open. There was no point looking for Giles' Monkey or Wrench; they'd been in the mech's torso when it had been hit, and he'd spotted body parts belonging to at least one of them during his climb up the fallen vehicle.

Within the cramped cockpit, the front half of which had been crushed during the fall, was Corporal Giles. His body was covered in blood, but he was still breathing since he'd had the good sense to ride with his helmet on (unlike Jenkins). The colonel was able to extricate the young man with a minimum of effort.

Jenkins dragged Giles up onto his broken mech's hull before reaching behind the young man's head, where the helmet's emergency stimulant release switch was located. Reserved for situations precisely like this one, the switch would flood the helmet with a variety of high-powered drugs that would help him regain consciousness, however temporary it might be.

Jenkins pushed the button and Giles immediately twitched, his body spasming in something like the hypnogogic jerk one experiences when almost asleep.

"We've got to move, Corporal," Jenkins urged. "Can you walk?"

"I...yes, I think so. Colonel?" he asked in confusion before looking down at what remained of his left arm. "Who the fuck took my arm?!" he demanded in apparently genuine outrage at finding himself short a limb.

"On your feet, Corporal," Jenkins barked. "We need to get to your mech's bike."

"I can't drive a bike like this, sir," Giles protested, though thankfully he stood while he did. "Hell, I can't even *whack it* without my left! What the fuck am I gonna do now when she gives me the cold shoulder?!"

Jenkins knew it was the stimulants that had elicited that last bit, but he couldn't stifle a laugh as he helped Giles down to the cavern floor, where they made their way to his mech's right leg.

Still there, although having taken at least moderate cosmetic damage, was the electric motorcycle that was standard issue for a walker like *Culture Knight*. The bike came loose with just a few sharp turns of the release clamps, and Jenkins stood the vehicle up before beckoning for Giles to climb on.

"Oh good, you're driving," Giles said blithely. "I hope you're better with two wheels than six legs."

"I'll pretend I didn't hear that," Jenkins shot back, activating the bike's motor and taking off across the cavern.

The Solarians had nearly reached their position, continuing their charge at a sprint. He tapped into the local hailing frequencies and declared, "This is Colonel Lee Jenkins of the Terran Armor Corps. I'm inbound with myself and one—" he was cut short when Hammer and Alice drove past him, riding a four-wheeled vehicle that looked suspiciously like one of *Murasame*'s suicide drones. They had Nakamura with them. "Make that four survivors."

The *Marines' Hymn* cut immediately, replaced by a hard-edged voice. "This is Marine Lieutenant Colonel Robert Cao. Confirm there are no other survivors in those wrecks, Colonel."

"Confirmed," Jenkins replied as he became acutely aware that there were no more rock-biters in his general vicinity. The

Solar Marines had unthinkably cleared this side of the cavern, though Arh'Kel reinforcements continued to pour in from all tunnels save the one the Solarians had arrived through. "It's just us four on two vehicles."

At that moment, he sped past the lead Solar Marine, who for the first time since entering the cavern halted his advance and began to beat a fighting retreat.

"Acknowledged," Lieutenant Colonel Cao said. "We'll cover your withdrawal up Charlie Tunnel. If we hurry—"

A nearby Marine, the fourth back from the arrow-shaped formation's tip, was suddenly embroiled in a hand-to-hand fight with a rock-biter who had been playing dead. The Marine, sporting silver colonel's insignia on his power-armored shoulders and chest, spun out of the rock-biter's lunging attack. Using his pirouette's momentum, he straightened his right arm and a meter-long blade sprang out of his vambrace, extending out beyond his hand like an arm-mounted sword.

That blade sliced clean through the rock-biter's stony physique, carving the foul thing into three quivering pieces with a single stroke.

"Apologies," the Marine colonel deadpanned before falling into formation with his men as they withdrew from the cavern. "As I was saying, if we hurry, we should be able to beat the enemy back to Rally Point Theta. I understand you people have a weapon you can use against these things, and my priority is helping you to use it."

"It might be more complicated than you think," Jenkins said grimly, "but we've got every intention of shutting these things down ASAP."

As they drove across the sparsely populated tunnel, Jenkins realized the scope of the Solarian losses. He counted no fewer than a hundred and twenty power-armored forms lying motionless on the cavern floor. Equally grim was the fact that he could not positively identify more than ninety Solar Space Marines still on their feet.

But in return, they had killed at least eight thousand Arh'Kel, scratched a dozen HWPs, and bought the Metalheads the chance to get back to the surface, where they could get access to Styles' program.

The mechs fell out of the cavern, preceded and followed by dozens of Solar Space Marines. Their gleaming silver armor now looked like it had been decorated by a toddler with access to entirely too much purple finger-paint, but they moved with the same pride and purpose as their Terran counterparts.

During the retreat, Jenkins learned that four of their eight Terran Marines had fallen in the cavern. But they still had *Razor Bamboo*, *Elvira*, *Black Widow*, *Cyclops*, and three more Clover Razorbacks. Along with the mechs, Major Trapper, Lieutenant Briggs, Corporal Lee, and Corporal Jia had survived, although Lee and Jia had suffered serious damage to their battle-suits' legs and could barely move under their own power.

All told, it was a far cry from what they had come down with, but Jenkins knew it was possible, however unlikely that possibility might be, that it would prove to be enough.

Their retreat took them past the sites of several running battles, with Solar Marines staving off Arh'Kel hordes at various choke-points and intersections. The fire teams were small, with some featuring as few as five power-armored Solarians and others as many as fifteen. However, they fought their gun nests, armed with RPGs and chain guns, with unbroken determination and commitment as they held back the rising tide of enemy soldiers seeking to burst onto the planet's surface.

Nobody could hold the rock-biters back forever, but the Solarians were doing as good a job as anyone could hope to do, given the circumstances.

And when the battered column finally reached the cavern

designated Rally Point Theta, it held a sight which brought smiles to the lips of every Metalhead present.

"Captain Koch," Jenkins greeted him, gripping the other man's hand tightly after dismounting the bike. "I think I speak for all of us when I say I'm glad to see you here."

"Likewise, Colonel," Koch said firmly before barking at a repair crew that was working to remove Elvira's forward armor so they could replace it with a fresh panel. His gaze snagged on Jenkins' bloody left eye, but he made no comment as an uncomfortable silence grew between them.

"Ok, how did you know you'd need to bring a full armor set for her mech?" Jenkins asked with mock skepticism after the awkward eye-related silence had passed.

Koch grinned. "A good doctor knows his patient's habits, and a good Wrench knows how his Jocks like to ride their gear. I'm actually a little concerned about the tailpipe damage she took," he muttered in disappointment. "We can slap something together to cover her stern, but it won't be much good against vehicle-grade weapons. These Razorbacks, on the other hand... There's not a lot I can do for them other than rearm and run a few beads of weld over the worst parts."

Captain Chao approached, noticeably favoring his left leg but still moving with purpose as he said, "You can cannibalize main components from these vehicles to make two nearly-repaired units."

"Could do," Koch allowed, "but that would take an hour or more—"

"Not true," Chao interrupted. "My people were not previously at liberty to share details, but these units were designed for such swaps to be made in the field without the aid of repair vehicles like yours. With your loaders and repair mechs, it will take fifteen minutes at most."

"And how are we supposed to do that?" Koch asked, curiosity warring with annoyance in his voice and expression.

Chao produced a data slate, which Koch immediately began to examine. "Key fastening hardware in modular joints and other connections is composed of mimetic alloys that were of proprietary design and can be released with precisely attuned electrical impulses. By providing you with the contents of that slate, which clearly implicate the people of Terra Han in conspiring with Vorr agents to produce hybrid tech of this type, I am breaking at least five sworn oaths and subjecting myself to the death penalty when I return home."

"Not all oaths are equal," Jenkins said approvingly as Koch slowly began to nod while perusing the slate's contents.

Chao nodded. "I concur."

"All right," Koch agreed. "Assuming this checks out, we can salvage two full Razorbacks for you two to ride. We can probably patch up *Black Widow*'s flank and make her combat-worthy, and *Elvira's* going to be good to go except for the missing main and an exposed ass."

"You brought spare missile pods?" Jenkins asked in borderline disbelief.

Koch smirked. "I'm good, but not *quite* that good. We've got bolt-on units that pack six tubes apiece, and they'll plug right into her fire control system. There'll be no reloads, but I don't imagine that will be an issue." He produced a data chip and handed it to Jenkins. "That's got Styles' most recent update of the program we used on Durgan's Folly. He said it's the best he could do given the constraints, but that it should give us a fighting chance."

"Perfect," Jenkins agreed. "This will either work or it won't. We won't need a mulligan, so go ahead and lash as much single-shot ordnance as you can to our hulls. It doesn't have to look pretty, it just needs to hold up long enough to clear on-target."

The towering Lieutenant Colonel Cao, in his three-meter-tall power armor, approached and made the customary hand-over-the-heart Solar salute. "My people report the enemy has accelerated their advance and will overwhelm our defenses in thirty-two minutes. The up-tunnels are filling up with rock-biters too. Anyone you want to send surface-side needs to leave immediately."

"We can get these field repairs done in that window," Koch said earnestly before saluting Jenkins and adding, "but my people will be standing with you this time, sir."

Jenkins wanted to rebuke the other man in the interests of efficiency. It was possible that Koch's people could still return to the surface, where they could continue to serve the Legion and, by extension, the human race with their efforts.

But whether it was the mild concussion, the general stress of the situation, or a rare moment of narcissism, Jenkins nodded in agreement. "I wouldn't have it any other way, Captain."

Koch turned on his heel and began to bark orders to his six busily-working crews.

"That was a hell of an entrance down there, Colonel Cao," Jenkins said, looking up at the towering Marine as Major Xi came their way. "I'm sorry I missed the first bit. If it was anything like the last, it belongs in the history books."

"We arrived with three hundred and thirty-one Marines," Cao said matter-of-factly, turning to look at his troops as they made field repairs to each other's armor and checked their weapons. "I returned to Theta with eighty-four, six of whom will never armor up again."

"We'll make them count," Jenkins assured the Marine.

Cao hesitated for a moment before chuckling as Xi arrived

and keyed into the conversation. "You're different than I expected. Less...aboriginal than we were led to believe."

"We get that a lot around here," Jenkins deadpanned as Major Xi gave him a salute. "How's the head, Major?" he asked, gesturing to her helmet's cracked visor and dented topside.

"If another corpsman tries to give me a concussion exam, he'll need one a hell of a lot more than I do, sir," she said stiffly, "along with a skilled proctological surgeon."

Cao laughed. "I may have spoken too soon."

Jenkins gave the Marine colonel a withering look before nodding deferentially. "If you think you're fit to ride, that's good enough for me."

"Thank you, Colonel," she said with a curt nod before turning to Colonel Cao. "And thank *you*, Colonel, for saving our asses back there."

"We live to serve, Major," Cao said measuredly. "So, you two were the Terrans who stormed Luna One?"

"That's right." Jenkins nodded, feeling a knot form in his throat as he became acutely aware of the power disparity between the unarmored Terrans and the battle-suited Marine.

"And we'd do it again." Xi jutted her chin out defiantly. "Just like we'd come back down to this shithole if needed."

"We 'Solarians,'" he said the word with equal measures of disdain and amusement, "refer to Mars as the War God's Tomb. It is a dead world that we regard with reverence for its role in spreading life throughout the Solar System before turning red from its own death. It is an enduring monument to the transience of life, and one we hold in the highest regard. It is far from a 'shithole,' Major."

"War god?" Xi repeated sardonically. "You mean you people actually believe in Ares?"

"After a fashion, yes," Cao agreed. "Gods are projections of ourselves and our needs. They represent our disembodied ideals, our unseen enemies, and the forces we do not yet understand. It would be foolish not to believe in the relevance and importance of one's own needs, so yes...we 'believe' in the war god just as surely as we 'believe' in any other manifestation of human self-awareness. But we do not believe the war god is a real person, or some conscious entity observing and guiding our actions from the underworld." He chuckled.

"More's the pity for you," Xi quipped triumphantly, "because I've *seen* the war god. I even had the privilege of sharing a field with him, and received both his rebukes and his blessings while we fought against the Finjou. His name was Benjamin Akinouye." She puffed her chest out with pride. "He was as real as any human standing in this cavern, and he was *definitely* the latest incarnation of the war god. And if this is indeed his tomb, I say we clear out its pest problem with *his* name on our lips."

Jenkins couldn't help but grin as the young woman poured her considerable passion into the unexpected speech. When Colonel Cao turned to him expectantly, all Jenkins could do was shrug. "What she said."

Colonel Cao audibly sighed before turning and marching back to his Marines. He muttered in bemused exasperation, "Terrans..."

Jenkins turned to Xi after the Marine had gone. "How's Alice coming with the program's final prep?"

"She's ready to go when we are, sir," Xi said confidently. "Which of the Razorbacks will you be riding?"

"I'll be with Captain Chao in *Razor Bamboo*," Jenkins replied. "His vehicle's got all the command gear I'll need to coordinate the charge."

Xi nodded. "I'll tell Alice to transfer to Chao's mech."

"Belay that," Jenkins said before she could do as she had said. "*Razor Bamboo* won't be broadcasting the transmission."

Xi cocked her head in confusion. "What do you mean, sir?"

"We'll blame the bump on the head for that," Jenkins said, placing a hand on her shoulder and giving it a firm squeeze while making eye contact with her. "This one's yours, Major. Alice will be doing her virtual wizardry from *Elvira*. The rest of these mechs will be down there to protect you while you buy her as much time as she needs. Captain Koch assures me that after his people are done with her, *Elvira* will be the best-armored mech in the column."

He could see in her eyes that she was ready. There wasn't a moment's hesitation in her expression. Not a millisecond of doubt as he handed her the most important assignment left in Operation War God. Her rise through the ranks had been meteoric and unprecedented, and she had earned every single hash that decorated her mech's hull, along with all the interstellar fame that went with being the youngest field officer in the history of the Terran Armed Forces.

"Understood, Colonel," she said eagerly. "We'll get it done."

"If you want an extra pair of hands, Hammer's available." He gestured to *Warcrafter's* displaced Jock, who was busy helping the work crews remove entire legs from Razorbacks in preparation for consolidating the best components onto two of the vehicles.

"Thank you, sir," she agreed. "Turns out I'm short a Monkey. Speaking of which, what happened to the rest of the Jokers?"

"They split up in two groups," Jenkins explained, having received Koch's report just before speaking with the man. "Half of them came down here, and the others went down Bravo tunnel at the Southern Hub. Each group started with five hundred Solar Marines as escort and aimed to link up with us."

They both knew it was possible that the other half of Joker Company would never return to the Martian surface. With the surging Arh'Kel breaking for the surface, intent on spreading their vile influence across Mars and throughout the Solar System, every second counted.

"Metal never dies, Major," Jenkins was surprised to hear himself say.

"Amen," she agreed somberly before just as unexpectedly declaring, "Cry Havoc, and let slip the God of War."

Jenkins nodded approvingly at her riff on one of the Bard's most quoted lines. "Looks like Dragon's very own Iron Maiden just picked our walk-up music," he said when the only track that could possibly fit the situation sprang to the fore of his mind.

Judging by her fiercely enthusiastic grin, she had already guessed what song they would play during the final battle for the War God's Tomb.

22

HALLOWED BE THY NAME

Nine Metal Legion mechs rode down the tunnel. Although incorporating *Kochtopus* and the other three Joker mechs had nearly doubled their number, it had done little more than add a quarter to their tactical value, given the circumstances. But Xi wasn't complaining; she'd take every gun she could get, even those wielded by nearly-immobilized Marines who had mag-locked themselves to the hulls of mechs like *Kochtopus*, *Black Widow*, and the Razorbacks.

They had to drive back down the tunnel and make for the nearest Arh'Kel-occupied cavern for Styles' program to have a chance. If they waited for the rock-biters to invade Rally Point Theta, it was unlikely the density of enemy infantry would get high enough for the virus to infect the entire colony. As with every other time they had put tracks down on some Godforsaken world, the only way out for the Metalheads was to charge straight into the enemy's teeth.

Xi wouldn't have had it any other way.

Razor Bamboo and *Grass Mud Horse*, the last functioning Razorback Mk. II-Vs, led the column while *Cyclops* took up the next slot in the formation. They trampled hapless rock-biters under their roller-feet while spewing coil gun bullets on max-cycle, easily clearing a full three kilometers of tunnel well ahead of the column.

Behind *Cyclops* was Quinn's *Black Widow*, and at the formation's center was Xi's re-armed *Elvira*. The only mechs capable of firing on the enemy at this point were the Razorbacks at the column's head, but Xi knew that would change soon enough.

At the formation's rear, Koch's Joker 1st Platoon, led by *Kochtopus*, rumbled down the tunnel. Their relatively light armaments made them suited only to covering the unit's rear from swarming Arh'Kel, but the look in Koch's eye told Xi all she needed to know about their resolve.

"All right, kiddies," Xi quipped as the first EM signature pinged on *Elvira's* sensors. "This one's for the old man, so I want to hear it loud, and I want to hear it *proud*." She began to play Iron Maiden's *Hallowed Be Thy Name* as Colonel Jenkins had coyly suggested, and its low, somber opening notes provided the perfect backdrop for the Metalheads as they began to chant in time with the track.

Like the growing rumble of thunder, the rhythmic one-word battle cry arose from the Metalheads on the comm link. Broadcast on their mechs' external speakers, the comparatively thicker air in this part of the tunnel network carried their vow to whatever passed for ears in Arh'Kel physiology.

Hearing that word spoken with such savagery filled her with pride as the number of enemy HWPs blossomed from one to four, then to twelve before shooting up to forty. With each meter they drew nearer to the enemy-held cavern ahead, which measured six kilometers across and nearly two kilometers tall at its center, the number of confirmed enemy targets increased.

And with each one that flickered to life on her tactical

HUD, the intensity of the Terran battle cry increased until it was a deafening, full-throated roar.

"Havoc!"

"Havoc!"

"Havoc!"

"Havoc!"

With the old man's most powerful name on their lips and Iron Maiden filling the cavern's airwaves, the Metalheads burst into the space intent on cleansing the War God's Tomb of hostiles. The re-armed Razorbacks' fifteens thundered, sending HE ordnance soaring across the expansive cavern. Missiles erupted from the bolt-on launchers affixed to *Razor Bamboo's* and *Grass Mud Horse's* hulls, and the Marines riding them into battle added railgun bolts to the improbably precise volley.

Twelve HWPs were scratched before *Elvira* arrived in the cavern, and those that survived the initial barrage rallied to return fire, hammering bolt after bolt into the Razorbacks' bows. Even after Koch's best efforts for a half-hour, the mechs' armor was still badly compromised, but Xi was ecstatic to see that despite taking massive damage from the volley, neither *Razor Bamboo* nor *Grass Mud Horse* was knocked out of the fight.

Following the Razorbacks was Blinky's *Cyclops*, and despite moving with a noticeable limp, the Warlock-class mech's stride didn't falter as its plasma cannon lobbed a blue-white fireball across the cavern. The plasma burst, precisely-calibrated to maximize damage while minimizing the risk of a cave-in, seemed to splash on impact with the cavern wall rather than explode as did most of Blinky's discharges. Four HWPs were destroyed outright, another two were knocked over by the force of the fiery blast-wave, and hundreds of Arh'Kel were incinerated.

Next into the fray was *Black Widow*, whose upper abdomen bristled with bolt-on missile launchers that sent thirty-six SRMs streaking across the cavern. Arh'Kel small-arms fire improbably intercepted half of these in-flight, but the rest struck with thunderous force, erasing another thirteen enemy platforms.

"Don't stop 'til we reach the backs of their teeth!" Xi yelled over the cries of *"Havoc"* as *Elvira* sprinted into the cavern. She immediately fired her lone remaining fifteen and sending an HE shell across the cavern, scratching a rock-biter missile pod to spectacular effect. The platform's ordnance exploded, magnifying the impact of her strike ten times over and eradicating everything within fifty meters as a shower of boulders collapsed from the cavern wall and crushed dozens of rock-biters while effectively sealing off one of the five tunnels leading into this cavern.

The Solar Marines sprinted alongside the Terran mechs, firing their railguns at enemy HWPs while largely conserving ammo. The line of Arh'Kel infantry surged toward them, but for Styles' program to work, they would need as many rock-biters in knife range as possible.

Suddenly, *Grass Mud Horse* was struck by a half-second-duration beam from the far side of the cavern. The beam slashed through the cleverly-named Razorback's forward armor like it wasn't there, carving a meter-wide gash across the mech's roof and vaporizing a Solar Marine before cutting out.

Razor Bamboo's mains thundered in reply, blowing the enemy platform apart with bullseyed AP shells. A staggered volley of railgun bolts slammed into the charging Razorbacks, causing *Razor Bamboo*'s charge to falter as its forward left leg was blown apart at the second joint.

The enemy volley also landed a pair of strikes on *Cyclops* as the mighty mech's plasma cannon slowly recharged in preparation for a second shot. One bolt skewered the mech's right knee while the other slammed into its heavy plasma cannon, and the combined force of the impacts spun *Cyclops* dangerously off-axis, the mech's forward momentum causing it to tilt to the right.

Even Blinky's superior piloting skills were unable to overcome the perfectly-executed one-two punch, and the Warlock-class mech crashed to the cavern floor with ground-shaking force. During the fall, *Cyclops'* leg came apart at the damaged knee. His chain guns continued to fire for a full second before going silent, and Xi confirmed that Blinky's vital signs were still showing as stable as she charged past his fallen mech.

"Stay loose, Alice," Xi called over her shoulder as the throng of Arh'Kel soldiers pressed inexorably in on the charging column, which swept across the cavern floor, carving a path of bloody ruin through the mindless horde of rock-biters. "We're almost in position," she declared, seeing that there were already a thousand Arh'Kel within range.

But she knew that this time, unlike on Durgan's Folly, they needed to make their first effort work. Their previous use of the takeover to stun the horde had increased the risk of failure this time around, so they could ill afford to waste time on low-percentage attempts.

"The program is ready," Alice assured her as the tide of enemy bodies came within twenty meters of the mechs. "What is your target density in the local broadcast zone?" the Solarian asked with enviable poise.

"Five thousand," Xi replied.

"An efficient figure," Alice agreed as the Marines perched atop and running alongside *Elvira* began sporadically firing their slug-throwers at the rock-biters. "Let us hope they do not surmise our intention and withdraw."

"Don't jinx it," Xi quipped as she bracketed a handful of Arh'Kel HWPs and unleashed twelve of *Elvira's* twenty-four missiles.

The bolt-on launchers fired in unison, their recoil at the

moment of launch temporarily knocking Xi's stride off-rhythm and making her miss a step during her sprint. Her mech dipped hard to starboard, jolting Alice, Hammer, and Lu against their harnesses and even giving Xi minor whiplash, which temporarily robbed her of her vision.

"Everybody hang on," she belatedly yelled over her shoulder as five of her missiles struck their targets, with two more swerving off-target by two hundred meters and the other five being intercepted by enemy counterfire.

"We've got a fire in the aft compartment," Lu called as a series of alarms went off. "Locking it down before it melts the wiring," he declared as he moved to the cabin's rear with a fire extinguisher in hand.

"Substandard bolt-ons," Xi muttered irritably, suspecting they were the cause of the fire when their exhaust vented through weak points in her mech's rear armor. A check of her HUD showed that twenty-five hundred Arh'Kel were in the immediate vicinity, and the Marines' fire had only grown in intensity in the past few seconds as the Arh'Kel hurled themselves at the column with cutters in hand. "That's right, sand-fuckers. Come to Mama," she snarled as the urge to unleash her chain guns in such a target-rich environment steadily increased to the point she was uncertain she could resist.

And then, as had happened in the lower cavern, the entire horde shuddered. It was barely noticeable, doing little more than causing one in ten of the rock-biters to visibly break stride, but Xi was convinced that Alice had correctly identified the failure point in their plan. The horde was going to adjust its posture, and with so many tunnels leading into the cavern, it was possible they could retreat faster than the Metalheads could pursue.

"Hit it, Alice!" she barked, looking down and seeing just under three thousand Arh'Kel in the immediate vicinity of the signal. Even as she spoke, the rock-biters began cartwheeling away at a sprint, sapping the number of in-range enemy soldiers.

Alice's reflexes, while not quite as good as a Jock's or a Marine's, were exceptional compared to the human norm. As such, she initiated the takeover a half-second after Xi gave the order, and the nearby Arh'Kel immediately broke away from the rest of the horde. While the Arh'Kel outside of the immediate broadcast range collectively fell back, those near *Elvira* began behaving erratically.

"Flank speed!" Xi ordered over the command channel, and the column increased speed until they were moving at just over ninety kph. The rate at which the number of nearby Arh'Kel fled fell in those first few seconds, and Xi directed the column toward the most population-dense area of the cavern in the hope of buying Alice the longest transmission window possible. "Marines, hold fire on enemy infantry," she added, knowing the order would cost lives but also knowing that every single live Arh'Kel in the broadcast zone increased their chance of over-taking the horde.

"Holding fire," Lieutenant Colonel Cao and Lieutenant Briggs simultaneously acknowledged. "Hand to hand only."

"Boot 'em off but don't kill them," she agreed as the first Arh'Kel slammed into *Elvira's* hull, where it received a curb-stomp from a Solarian Marine's armored boot. "At least not yet," she amended with a borderline-insane cackle.

"You people are unhinged," Colonel Cao growled, delivering a soccer kick to a rock-biter as it clambered up *Elvira's* hull. "You would all be in retraining camps if you were of Sol."

"Save the sweet talk for later, Colonel," Xi retorted, taking the Solar Marine's comments as unvarnished praise. "We're still on the clock here!"

The column continued sprinting through the rock-biters, who flowed away from them like the seas before Moses. The number of in-range Arh'Kel was now down to fifteen hundred, and at this rate, it would fall below a thousand in another ten seconds.

"It's now or never, Alice," Xi called. "If you've got any tricks up your skirt—"

Before she could finish that thought, the local rock-biters collectively stopped. Then, like a rippled across a pond with *Elvira* at the center, the horde of fleeing enemy infantry halted their retreat. The previously raging sea of enemy soldiers was rapidly transformed into a placid summer lake, and for a moment Xi was unable to process what had just transpired. It was so anticlimactic that she forcibly blinked several times before finally accepting that her eyes had not deceived her.

They had done it!

"Hold position," Xi called, causing the column to slow its advance until finally coming to a stop. "Nobody move," she added, perhaps unnecessarily since nary a sound broke the eerie silence that now hung over the cavern.

"Is this what you expected, Colonel Jenkins?" Colonel Cao asked.

"Essentially," Jenkins agreed, his voice tight and pained. "We've only done this once before, but it had a similar effect then as what we're seeing here."

"How long did they remain in this state?" Cao pressed.

"Honestly, we're not sure," Jenkins admitted. "Several days at least, but that was after we reprogrammed them into smaller groups that went and infected the rest of the crypto-colony with the same program."

"But that reaction?" Xi said grimly. "The one right before we triggered the attempt. We haven't seen that before. It's like they knew what was coming and tried to disperse before the program could take hold."

"Elaborate, Major," Cao demanded.

"I'm talking about when they began running from us immediately before our initiating the broadcast," she explained. "Not only is that atypical for Arh'Kel in general, but when we previously used this method, they came at us in unrelenting waves."

"Is that correct, Colonel Jenkins?" the Solar Marine CO asked tightly.

"It is," Jenkins agreed.

"Alice," Xi called over her shoulder while still live on the comm link, "are you ready to break them into smaller groups and send them out?"

"I do not believe that will be necessary," Alice said skeptically. "The density of Arh'Kel in these tunnels appears to be sufficient to propagate the signal throughout the tunnel network. I am already receiving feedback through this program," she gestured to her workstation, "showing that it has affected a hundred and fifty thousand enemy soldiers. The rate of expansion is inconsistent, but it is clear that a significant portion of the expected three million Arh'Kel have already been exposed to the program. There, it just passed two hundred and fifty thousand and appears to be accelerating."

Xi's brow rose in surprise. "Jesus, they really *were* packed in like sardines." She sent a silent order to Captain Koch to execute a rescue and recovery of *Cyclops'* crew.

"Then on behalf of Sol, I convey our gratitude," Marine Colonel Cao said officiously, "although I do so while making an official request on behalf of Mars, Sol, and, if you will pardon my presumption, all of humanity."

"What is it, Colonel?" Jenkins asked.

"I am under orders to eradicate this threat as soon as humanly possible," Cao explained, "which includes clearing the tunnels leading back to the surface and securing all infrastructure. I'm afraid my people are insufficiently armed to eliminate the estimated forty-six thousand rock-biters that stand between the Southern Hub and us. Since I was charged with escorting your unit, I find myself in the peculiar position of asking for your assistance to remove those impediments to Solar security."

"You're asking Metalheads if they'd like to shoot at Arh'Kel?" Captain Chao said in a well-practiced monotone.

"Essentially, yes," the Solar colonel agreed.

Xi grinned. "Colonel, you've got a lot to learn about us." She spun *Elvira's* chain guns up in preparation for the task ahead. "Give the order, and we'll provide a free lesson."

Four hours later, after clearing the upper tunnels between them and the Southern Hub and putting an end to thirty-nine thousand Arh'Kel along the way, the Metalheads emerged and prepared to go wheels-up from the War God's Tomb.

And for as long as she lived, Xi would think of Mars as the final resting place of General Benjamin Akinouye's spirit.

23

PARTING GIFTS

"I'm not going to lie, Colonel," General Moon said, standing at the base of *Grass Mud Horse*'s gangplank as Jenkins made his way onto the *William Wallace*'s drop deck. "I didn't see this one coming."

"None of us did, General," Jenkins said, careful not to shake his head for fear of dislodging the blood-soaked bandage he had wrapped across his ruined eye. He was surprised at just how little pain he felt following the near-total loss of the organ, but he suspected his neural implants were largely responsible for the diminished pain.

Moon gestured at his eye. "Is it gone?"

"Looks like it." Jenkins shrugged indifferently, drawing an approving snort from the general.

"We'll get you a temporary implant," Moon assured him, but Jenkins shook his head dismissively.

"I was thinking of a black leather patch," he said without an ounce of irony. "Depth perception's not an issue for my current duties, or even when riding Jock, especially with the neural linkage. And if recent history's any indication, the Legion can't afford to have me on rehab leave for six months while I break in a new eyeball."

The general nodded deferentially. "If you feel the same way when we return to HQ, I'll support your decision. And frankly, I tend to think you're right." He inclined his chin toward the battered remnants of Captain Winters' mechs, which almost entirely survived the harrowing subterranean ordeal. "Winters only lost two mechs and nine personnel after he got hemmed in on the eastern front."

"I heard," Jenkins said approvingly. "He's a good officer. Leading that many Nuggets and Flakes through that particular patch of hell was a job I didn't envy him. Honestly, I didn't think they'd survive after we were cut off."

"Neither did he," Moon agreed. "Which was why he collapsed the tunnels as he worked a thirty-klick retreat topside. The Solarians might not like the damage he did to their passages, but he also managed to block at least a dozen industrial facilities from rock-biter influence."

"Which my people assure me is the course of action they would have preferred, General," Alice said, descending the gangplank and coming to stand beside Jenkins on the *Wallace's* drop deck.

"We appreciate Sol's diplomatic response, ma'am," Moon said, clearly uneasy about her interjecting herself into the conversation.

"I would like to communicate with my people via a secured link if that is possible?" Alice asked, seeming to sense the general's unease.

Moon nodded agreeably. "I'll have a link set up in your quarters by the time you arrive."

"Thank you, General," she said graciously before making meaningful eye contact with Jenkins and disembarking the drop deck.

After she had gone, Jenkins sighed. "If all Solarians are as resourceful as she is, Terra needs to do everything in its power to reunite in some capacity."

Moon nodded, gesturing to the corridor. "I've read your preliminary reports. Let's take this debriefing to the conference room."

Two hours later, Jenkins had finished with his verbal report, and the general was visibly impressed by what he heard.

"Cry 'Havoc,'" the general repeated with a wry grin. "The old man would have loved that."

"Yes, sir," Jenkins agreed, having learned enough of General Akinouye before his passing to know it was true.

"Something's still bothering me though, Lee." Moon drummed his fingers on the metal slab that served as the conference table's top. "Why weren't these rock-biters activated weeks ago?"

"Nobody's got anything more than conjecture on that front, General." Jenkins shrugged. "The best working theory we've got is that the Arh'Kel were some sort of failsafe, and that whoever put them there—which was almost certainly Jemmin," he added, drawing an approving nod from the general, "had other plans for Mars that didn't involve the wholesale slaughter of fifty million humans and the devastation of its infrastructure."

"Do you think they were planning to use Sol's manufacturing base to fuel their war effort?" Moon asked skeptically.

"It's one possibility," Jenkins allowed, "but honestly? Jemmin's operating on a whole different cognitive level from humanity. Trying to figure out its motives isn't likely to be a productive exercise. Let Fleet Intelligence sift through the data and compare notes with the Solarians after they've had a few weeks to go over it all. We did our part, sir. I'm not interested in doing intel's job too."

"Spoken like a true Metalhead." The general chuckled. "I envy you that. I never really wanted to be a general, Lee," he unexpectedly confided. "But you can't turn your back on the Corps when she needs you, ungrateful bitch that she is from time to time."

"Sounds like that's a story worth hearing," Jenkins replied before his comm link chimed. It was Alice, whom he greeted with, "What can I do for you, ma'am?"

"If you and General Moon are available, I have an urgent matter to discuss," she explained, prompting the men to exchange wary looks before the general nodded invitingly.

"We're in the Flag Conference Room," Jenkins replied.

"I'll be there shortly," she said before cutting the line.

"That doesn't sound good," Moon opined.

"I'm not so sure," Jenkins said dubiously before his mind switched gears. "Chief Styles is your new GCO?"

"Acting GCO," Moon allowed, "but yes, and he did a fine job of it. It wasn't exactly an extended tour of duty, but both he and Lieutenant Podsednik impressed me. In fact, I think we should field-promote Styles to second lieutenant ASAP and install him on the bridge. The Legion doesn't have many technicians of his ability, and if we're going to keep rolling, we'll need people like him teaching others what they know."

"We're probably past worrying about his questionable legal history," Jenkins agreed. "I think it's a long time coming, and it's absolutely the right call."

"We'll make him go through the hoops once things have calmed down," Moon continued, "but talent's talent, and unlike Podsednik, Styles doesn't have an extensive history of disregarding authority."

Jenkins cocked his head in surprise. "I thought you just said you were impressed by Lieutenant Podsednik?"

"Impressed, yes." Moon snorted. "But he's trouble with a capital T. I'm not talking about him air-holing Aquino back at Silver Savannah Six. That fucker had it coming, and then some. I had a nephew die under the coward's command, but nothing ever came of it because of his political connections."

"I'm not sure I follow," Jenkins said hesitantly.

The general sighed in frustration. "Podsednik's ready to take the reins, but I'm not sure he can be counted on to be anything but a loose cannon. Loose cannons have their place, and that's usually wheels-down, charging into the teeth of the enemy. No offense intended, Colonel," he added with a wan smile.

"None taken, sir." Jenkins chuckled. "Sun Tzu said something about knowing yourself to be essential if you want to win consistently, and like most things he wrote about, he was right."

"If we were dropping Podsednik in a mech and giving him a company," Moon continued, "I'd have already pushed him up to captain and hoped he caused the enemy half as much hell as he causes us. But standing overwatch on the bridge while Armor's on the ground? It's not a place for loose cannons, Lee, and I'm speaking from experience here as much as anyone can. The Legion hasn't had the best luck these last few decades in cultivating ship commanders, and we've taken unnecessary losses as a direct consequence of that failure. If he gets a bug up his ass and goes haring off for some reason or other, people on the ground *will* die."

Jenkins had read some of the reports on the engagements Moon was likely referencing, and the truth was, he agreed with Moon's conclusions. However, he wasn't convinced Podsednik was as unreliable as the general seemed to think.

Colonel Jenkins' gaze drifted over to the wall, where a

recessed display case contained models of every single mech design every deployed under the TAC banner. From the ultra-light Grasshopper-class Recon mech, up to the mighty Bahamut line of Siege mechs, of which only the prototype *Zero* had ever been built, eighty-nine distinctive models were neatly arranged according to mass and class. As varied in appearance as they were in functionality, those mechs represented everything the Terran Armor Corps was and would ever be, both literally and metaphorically.

"Permission to speak freely, General?"

"Of course."

"The only times Lieutenant Podsednik has disregarded the chain of command has been when his personal loyalties conflicted with his duty."

"I'm not sure how that's supposed to change my opinion, Lee."

"When he killed his CO at Silver Savannah, he was doing it in part because he knew the cost of cowardice in that situation," Jenkins explained. "New Ozzies aren't like the rest of us Terrans. The ones who pulled through that nightmare are made of sterner stuff, and are intolerant of hesitation. Podsednik's far from the only Oz survivor who's behaved like this. It's part of who he is, and it's part of who we'd be if we'd gone through what he's been through."

"I understand the nature versus nurture phenomenon, Lee," the general said, the hint of a warning threaded through his voice.

"When he violated the *Bonhoeffer's* computer core," Jenkins continued, "he was doing it because he placed greater value on his loyalty to the men and women down on the ice than his loyalty to his then-unknown CO Colonel Li. He was willing to risk angering Li if it meant buying us a chance to turn the tide of the Jemmin forces there."

"If there's a point in here, I'd like to hear it, Colonel."

"If we want men and women like Lieutenant Podsednik to armor up and toe the line, it seems to me that our first priority is to ensure they're operating in an environment that's conducive to maximizing their contributions," Jenkins explained, meeting and holding the general's unrelenting gaze. "The Metal Legion is unlike any other branch of the Terran Armed Forces, General, and from where I'm sitting, that's a categorical advantage. We've taken on other branches' cast-offs and rejects and wet-behind-the-ears greenhorns, and even gone through every prison in the Colonies to recruit criminals into our ranks. And, often with minimal training, we've succeeded in converting an unprecedented number of them into Metalheads either one of us would not hesitate to have at our backs during a high-stakes charge. We haven't succeeded *despite* our roster's atypical makeup, General. We've succeeded *because* of it. We've put people in situations where they can succeed, and we've bent as far as we reasonably can in finding where they can best serve the Legion. If Lieutenant Podsednik's personal loyalty to a handful of Metalheads is going to override his obligation to the chain of command..."

"You're saying we should limit his ability to disrupt the unit by adjusting the terrain, specifically by giving him assignments where he has no real choice but to follow the chain of command. Especially if his personal loyalties come into play," the general mused. "That's a slippery slope, Lee. If we start modifying assignments based on individual preferences and personal relationships, maintaining discipline can turn into a high-wire act."

"We may not have the throw weight of Fleet or even the Colonial Guards, but the Terran Armor Corps is an *exceptional* branch of TAF, General," Jenkins said with conviction. "And if you're worried about Metalheads chafing over officers like Podsednik receiving what might be viewed as preferential treatment, all I can say on that front is that Podsy's poll numbers are probably higher than either of ours throughout the Legion right now. He's popular with everyone precisely because they know he's a straight shooter and a bit of a maverick. And begging the general's pardon, but who in this Legion *isn't* something of a maverick?"

Moon's expression remained passive for a long moment before he broke into a grin. "Well done, Colonel. I'm not sure you convinced me, but I *am* sure you've given me food for thought."

The chime at the conference room's door sounded shortly thereafter, and in came Alice with an eager look on her face. "I'm sorry for the delay," she apologized. "I was in sickbay when Captain Winters regained consciousness, and I wanted to convey Sol's appreciation to him." She moved to the chair opposite Jenkins and to the right of General Moon, who sat at the head of the long table. "First, you will be interested to learn that all inhabitants of the Inner Solar System are now fully aware of the events on Mars. My people are understandably impressed by your efforts here and understand the severity of the price you paid."

"We agreed to help secure Mars," General Moon said measuredly. "Killing the rock-biters was just an added bonus."

Alice rolled her eyes as the hint of a smile played across her lips. "Your bravado notwithstanding, I have also been instructed to relay to you that when we arrived, there were seventy-eight functioning industrial complexes on or beneath Mars' surface."

Jenkins instinctively sucked in a breath in anticipation of what was essentially their report card. His worst-case estimates placed the damage at nearly half of all Martian infrastructure, which would be nothing short of disastrous for the war effort.

Judging from the general's expression, he was similarly bracing for the bad news.

"After your efforts, however," she continued blithely, "there are now sixty-three facilities capable of being brought back online within the month."

Despite being braced for bad news, Jenkins was unable to keep his jaw from falling open.

"That sounds...optimistic," General Moon murmured into the growing silence.

"Very," Jenkins agreed.

"The damage done to several of the facilities was considerable," Alice explained, "but only six of the caverns were complete losses, with the firefights we engaged in accounting for the majority of the damage. It seems the Arh'Kel were not interested in destroying infrastructure as they ascended to the surface. Whether that would have changed at some future point, it seems we will never know, because I have also been assured by General Yuan and Commodore Kline that the Arh'Kel presence on Mars has been eliminated."

"Already?" Jenkins asked disbelievingly. "Your Marines wiped out three million Arh'Kel in two days?"

"Three-point-one-five-six million at last count," she confirmed. "Extensive sub-surface imaging confirms that no Arh'Kel presence remains hidden on Mars, and every other planetary body of Sol capable of harboring a similar infestation is in the process of being examined. In another week, Sol should be clear of this threat, one way or another. We owe the Terran Armor Corps an effectively immeasurable debt, gentlemen, and are prepared to make a meaningful gesture of restitution for your efforts."

"That won't be necessary, ma'am," General Moon said neutrally, but Jenkins could tell the general was every bit as intrigued as he was at this particular turn in the conversation.

Alice held up her hands deferentially. "Forgive my forwardness, but subtlety is not something which we of Sol often employ, so I will not insult either of you with a clumsy attempt to do so now. I have discussed TAC's current fiscal status with General Pushkin at some length, and I have studied the Terran Armed Forces' regulations governing materiel asset acquisition. I am prepared to make...what is the term?" She furrowed her brow for a moment before triumphantly snapping her fingers in what was easily one of her most endearing affectations, from Jenkins' perspective. "An off-the-books contribution to the Terran Armor Corps' arsenal."

Jenkins leaned forward and shook his head. "That's not really how it works. Any materiel donations you make have to be registered and received through the Republic's official channels. You can designate that those donations go to the Metal Legion in an effort to get them to us."

"It's true," Moon agreed before surprisingly adding, "but too often, such designations do nothing more than prevent other branches—let's be honest, we're talking about Fleet here—from intercepting those supplies for themselves."

"I am familiar with the governing statutes," she said dismissively. "But this is wartime, so the standard acquisition limitations are somewhat ameliorated...or perhaps it would be better to say that they can be ignored, or, at worst, delayed for a significant interval."

Jenkins was legitimately uncertain if this was some kind of trap, but judging from the general's expression, Moon didn't seem to think so. "That's true," General Moon allowed, "but we're still only allowed a six-month window, and even then the window is only valid if we deem the donated assets to be mission-critical to ongoing operations."

"Which is why it is fortunate that Operation War God is not yet concluded, and that Sol is prepared to make a formal request for ongoing TAC assistance to help us secure Martian interests until we have had the opportunity to repair the damage caused in the aftermath of Operation Antivenom. The Metal Legion was solely responsible for Antivenom, having unilaterally conducted the operation which directly resulted in extensive damage to Sol. Some might argue this unilateral decision-making obligates its leadership to assist with the post-operation 'mop-up duty,' if my understanding of military lingo is accurate," Alice said knowingly before looking at each of them in turn. "Do you not agree?"

Moon and Jenkins exchanged surprised looks. The general's brows lowered fractionally as he turned to Alice. "How do we know you're not asking us to put our heads in a guillotine?"

"Because Sol will only make this formal request for ongoing assistance if you wish to receive our materiel support," Alice said, as though that much was self-evident. Which, in hindsight, it probably should have been, given the way she'd initially said it.

"Forgive us, Alice," Jenkins said earnestly. "We Terrans aren't used to cutting backroom deals with Solarians. We pretty much all grew up thinking you people were the mutant lovechildren of ivory tower elites and twentieth-century Maoists."

"And we largely considered Colonials to be, as I have previously alluded, aboriginals consumed by a fascination with what we considered to be vestigial, undesirable facets of primitive humanity." She shrugged indifferently. "I suppose there is something eloquent to be said here regarding the dangers of preconceptions, but I cannot formulate it at this time."

General Moon leaned forward, lacing his fingers and propping his forearms on the metal tabletop. "Before we accept or decline any offer, we'd have to have some rough idea of its parameters."

Alice threw her head back and laughed before stifling the outburst and holding up a hand apologetically. "I'm sorry, I shouldn't have done that. This is all just so bizarre to me. We of

Sol do not conduct conversations in this way. It is like something from bad fiction. I sincerely apologize if I offended either of you."

"It's all right." Moon gestured invitingly.

"We managed to secure approximately seventy-three percent of the total Martian industrial capacity that remained upon our arrival, which was nearly triple our earliest estimates prior to enlisting your assistance," she explained, casually suggesting that they had expected to lose three quarters of all Martian infrastructure due to their peculiar political inhibitions regarding deployment on Martian soil. "In light of this overwhelmingly positive outcome, we are prepared to allocate six facilities, totaling roughly five percent of all Martian output, for a period of not less than six months, to resupplying the Terran Armor Corps with materiel assets of your choosing." She produced a data slate, which she handed to General Moon as she continued, "The capabilities of these facilities are uniquely suited to addressing the Metal Legion's needs, with five of these manufactories designed to produce ground vehicles, while the sixth is one of our five remaining Interceptor production facilities. We will field all materiel, energy, and operating expenses during this six-month period, and hope you will accept this gesture as a meaningful display of our appreciation for all you have done for us."

General Moon quirked an eyebrow incredulously, holding the expression for a long moment before clarifying, "When you say 'roughly five percent of all Martian output,' you mean the *military* output, correct?"

She cocked her head in confusion. "No, but then, Sol makes no distinction between types of industrial output."

"Ballpark estimate," Jenkins asked, "how many mechs and Interceptors are we talking about here?"

"In six months, assuming the arrangement does not extend

beyond that window?" she clarified, drawing an approving nod from the colonel. "If the vehicles are representative of the those currently on the TAC roster, three hundred mechs and one hundred Interceptors. 'Ballpark estimate,'" she reiterated with a coy grin. "We would also provide limited access to relevant Solar technologies, such as improved armor and more stable power core systems than those you employ, although the limitations would be greatly relaxed if you reciprocated to some meaningful degree, or if your government happened to sign a bilateral technology exchange program."

General Moon grunted. "You're talking about our railguns." Jenkins had come to suspect, like many other Terran military servicemen, that Terran railgun tech had been a gift from the Vorr. The more he learned of the machinations employed by races like Jemmin and the Vorr, the more he believed that was the case.

"Primarily, yes," she agreed, "along with whatever advances Terra has independently made in beam technology. But again, I would not ask you to commit treason by providing military technology to a foreign state. I am simply stating a fact. If Terra were to share some of this technology with Sol, it would be of mutual benefit, and would lead to our reciprocity on that particular front."

"I can't even begin to comment on something like that," Moon said with evident frustration as Jenkins' eyes snagged on something in the display case. He had a legitimate 'lightbulb moment' as the general added, "and the fact that you bring it up complicates things significantly."

"I am simply being forthright," Alice said solemnly as Jenkins stood from the table and made his way to the display case. "These are merely back-channel overtures, nothing more, and nothing less...except for the offer of materiel support, which is yours if you wish to take it. There are no so-called 'strings' attached on that matter."

"Even if we accept your *extremely* generous offer," General Moon allowed as Jenkins opened the display case and retrieved the rightmost model from the recessed shelf, "we don't have the crews to service three hundred additional mechs, let alone a hundred Interceptors. We've already seen our recruiting efforts hit a wall in recent weeks, and if things continue on their current trajectory, we won't even be able to replace our losses, let alone add four hundred skilled Jocks to the rolls."

"That *is* a significant obstacle," Alice agreed as Jenkins turned the model over in his hands while the other two engaged in the awkward "back-channel" negotiations. "Solar citizens cannot enlist in the Terran military without renouncing their citizenship and becoming Terrans, and there is currently no mechanism by which this might be legally achieved to the satisfaction of TAF requirements."

"We might not need three hundred crews," Jenkins said confidently.

"Colonel?" Moon asked, swiveling his chair toward the display case as Jenkins reverently turned and placed the model on the table between Moon and Alice. Moon's eyes locked on the model and realization dawned as a broad grin played out across his features. "Outstanding thought, Colonel."

Alice looked at the model in confusion. "I do not understand, nor do I recognize this vehicle from the active TAC roster."

"That's because only one was ever built," Jenkins replied, gesturing to the model of the Bahamut-class Siege-grade mech for which only the prototype, *Bahamut Zero*, was ever constructed. "And its last ride was down to the Brick, our last op before Antivenom."

"But the Bahamut line wasn't the only Siege-grade mech

our engineers *designed*," Moon said pointedly. "It's just the only one that got a working prototype built. Some of the others are huge, with designs ranging up to a thousand tons. That's ten times the armor of most battlewagons, and fifty times the average Recon mech."

Alice seemed to understand and nodded approvingly. "Which limits the impact of your personnel shortcomings." She narrowed her eyes contemplatively. "I am no engineering expert, but I suspect that two of the four facilities could be modified to produce vehicles of the scale you describe. The other two will likely be limited to more typical designs." She cocked her head expectantly. "Are you suggesting that you intend to accept our offer?"

Moon exhaled through gritted teeth. "I'm not going to lie. We'd be fools to refuse it, but we all know we're placing TAC's future in your hands by agreeing to this, even with the protection afforded by the skullduggery and legal gymnastics. When the Piper comes, he'll demand payment, and if we screw this up, it could be the end of the Metal Legion. The Senate will tie us up with so much red tape we'll look like festival gifts, and Fleet will be all too happy to consolidate whatever bits and pieces of TAC they like while tossing the rest into mothballs." He drew a breath before nodding decisively. "Yes, we're interested in accepting your support. I don't have the authority to unilaterally sponsor this, but I can assure you that General Pushkin will agree with me. As soon as we return to TAC HQ, you'll have an official agreement, but not before."

She smiled. "Then as a gesture of good faith, we will commence construction according to your guidelines—which must obviously include the technical schematics for the vehicles you wish to be produced."

"We can provide those before we debark," Moon agreed, standing from the table and proffering his outstretched hand.

"After all, *they're* wholly-owned TAC property," he added with a grin as she shook his hand.

"I understand that this is unlikely to significantly reduce trepidation for either of you," Alice said after releasing Moon's hand, "but I would be remiss if I did not state unequivocally and for the record that it would be anathema to everything fundamental in Solar social psychology for us to betray you after your efforts on our behalf. We understand that this materiel support is meaningful and represents significant wealth by any objective measure, but we also understand that it does not absolve us of our debt to you. And we fully intend to repay that debt."

"I'm having a hard time seeing how you could offer us anything more," Moon told her graciously.

It seemed like she wanted to reply to that, but instead, she said, "My people will need to begin work immediately. I should inform them of your decision."

"I feel it's prudent to stress," Jenkins said sheepishly, "that we can't risk this agreement becoming public knowledge. Not now, and certainly not any time soon. The Legion doesn't have many friends in the Republic, and I doubt our work here is going to score us many points with the folks back home."

"We will, of course, maintain secrecy," she agreed. "After all, you have already saved us from catastrophe twice. The least we can do is reciprocate."

She turned and left the conference room, and when she had gone, General Moon muttered, "This is one of those moments we will look back on every single day and wonder about."

"We made the right call," Jenkins said confidently. "General Pushkin has been pushing for this kind of thing, and he's been right to do so. If we don't line up alternative support, the Legion's days are numbered. You've seen the PR campaigns. Fleet has everyone convinced they're the only option now that the Nexus Wars are upon us. I'm not saying this won't blow up in our faces, but at least this way, we have a chance to solidify our position."

"I agree," Moon nodded, and at that, the two began pouring over the ship's data files.

Specifically, the technical documents for the abandoned Siege-grade mech designs.

24

THE FINAL PIECE

"Thank you for coming," Jem said after Styles and Xi arrived in Podsy's quarters.

Jem's disembodied voice, transmitted through a data slate connected to the ruby-red crystalline shaft that housed Jem's 'consciousness,' was no longer discomfiting to Podsy. But judging by the looks on Xi's and Styles' faces, they were still at least mildly disturbed by hearing the gestalt intelligence entity address them.

"Time is against us," Jem continued, "so I will be blunt. My calculations have led me to a theory regarding Vorr behavior that I am not yet ready to disclose, but which requires additional information. I understand this is not an ideal way to initiate what you all suspect is a pending request for aid, but I cannot overemphasize the importance of keeping this theory a secret for the time being."

"Before we get indignant, we should at least hear what you want," Styles said, forestalling Xi's retort—which probably would have been delivered before he could intervene if she weren't suffering from a concussion.

"The information I require is classified," Jem explained, "and unlikely to be easily acquired."

"Naturally," Xi replied drily.

"But your collective abilities should be equal to the task," Jem continued. "What I require is as much information as possible regarding the ship referred to as '*Gatekeeper*' by human records."

"'*Gatekeeper*?'" Podsy repeated in surprise. "You mean the Jemmin ship that brought the wormhole gate to Sol, and presumably to just about every other star system where they currently are?"

"*Gatekeeper* is *not* Jemmin," Jem chided. "It was built by the precursors, or 'Architects,' as some Jem'un referred to them. The same civilization that built the gates also built *Gatekeeper*, as well as a handful of other ships and artifacts the Jem'un discovered during our exploration of the galaxy."

"You sound like you already know more about it than we do," Styles observed, drawing approving nods from Xi and Podsednik.

"My records regarding *Gatekeeper* are extremely limited," Jem explained. "And the longer I cogitate on that fact, the more convinced I become that my lack of knowledge pertaining to Architect technology is no coincidence."

"Do you think someone wiped your memory at some point?" Xi asked, her interest visibly piqued.

"That is unlikely, at least in the sense you probably mean," Jem replied. "What is more likely is that it was purposefully left out of my formative matrix when the personalities and memories of the surviving Jem'un who comprise me were integrated into what I now am. I retain only enough information regarding *Gatekeeper* to spark curiosity regarding it, and it is my belief that this curiosity was both predicted and is possibly even a fundamental component of my purpose."

Styles' brow furrowed. "You're saying that your...progenitors left you a trail of clues to follow?"

"Substantively, yes," Jem agreed.

"For what purpose?" Podsy asked.

"That I have not yet ascertained," Jem said with seemingly genuine frustration. "It is my belief that I was designed with inherent limitations that would prevent me from becoming a threat to individual sentience."

"Meaning that you couldn't go full-on artificial super-intelligence." Podsy nodded knowingly.

"Correct. And after several thousand of your years spent in quiet contemplation, I have determined that this limitation is an extraordinarily powerful boon to my existence."

"How so?" Styles asked. "By minimizing your need for self-control?"

"It would be inaccurate to frame it in that way," Jem denied. "But that is not to say you have completely misapprehended my meaning. Without the constant fear of causing untold damage to this galaxy and everything in it, I have been relatively free to explore my capabilities and expand my consciousness in accordance with what seem to be natural impulses."

"But you have to admit," Xi said skeptically, "there's not much 'natural' about you."

"That is true," Jem allowed, "and I do not discount the possibility that I am, in effect, a 'ticking time bomb' designed to cause some future calamity for a purpose I am, and will likely remain, unaware of. But I do not believe this to be the case, primarily because I believe I was designed with these limitations in order to facilitate my cooperation with beings like yourselves."

Styles, Xi, and Podsednik exchanged uncertain looks before Podsy took point in addressing the elephant in the room. "What if, by giving you this information, we're playing into Jemmin's hands?"

"Again, to assert such a scenario is impossible would be irresponsible," Jem replied, "but I do not believe Jemmin would orchestrate such a complex plan when a much simpler and less expensive one could be executed to the same effect. If you bring me information regarding *Gatekeeper*, I will integrate it into my calculations and formulate a final theory as to the true nature of the Vorr-Jemmin conflict. However, I cannot responsibly share my incomplete theory yet, as to do so would jeopardize any potentially beneficial courses of action we might take related to that theory."

"This isn't the first time you've asked us to trust you on faith, Jem," Xi observed.

"No, it is not," Jem agreed, "and I understand the predicament this places you in. However, I must insist that I would not be asking this of you if I did not think it was of the utmost importance. And since Sol was the most recent addition to the Illumination League, any data that might be stored on Earth or elsewhere in the Solar System would be of immeasurably greater value to my calculations than that which might be possessed by the Finjou, the Arh'Kel, or even the Vorr."

"The information Jem's asking for wouldn't be in public forums," Styles mused. "Anything related to the wormhole gate's arrival would be kept under absolute control by Sol's government."

"I am capable of insinuating myself into the One Mind network," Jem offered. "I do not think it would be overly difficult for me to extract the information, but for a variety of reasons, I do not think that would be the preferred course of action."

Xi shrugged emphatically. "Why don't we just ask Alice?"

"Come again?" Styles blurted.

"No, she's right." Podsy nodded in agreement. "This will ultimately affect Sol as much as Terra. Why shouldn't they be included in some capacity? Besides, it beats getting caught with our hand in the cookie jar on our way out the door."

"This has something to do with the Vorr salvage we picked up on the *Pearl*, doesn't it, Jem?" Styles suddenly asked.

"It does," Jem affirmed. "But I cannot go into any greater detail than that at this time."

"I'll go ask Alice," Xi declared, making for the door that led out of Podsy's quarters.

"I'll come with," Podsy offered, standing from his bunk and becoming acutely aware that his prosthetic legs never went to sleep, as people termed that sensation. The clanking of his footfalls as he and Xi made their way to Alice's quarters served as a constant reminder that part of him was gone and would likely never come back to him.

But as he looked at Xi Bao, who seemed to be overflowing with both confidence and poise as she strode through the *William Wallace*'s corridors, he knew that whatever he had lost paled in comparison to what humanity had gained.

He knew greatness when he glimpsed it, and Xi Bao was that and more. Whatever small part he had played in helping her reach her current heights would likely go down as his most meaningful contribution to the human race.

As far as legacies went, one could do a lot worse.

"So instead of trying to sneak into Sol's records, steal copies for ourselves, and skip town without anyone the wiser," Xi concluded, "we thought we'd just come and ask for what we need."

"It seemed like the neighborly thing to do," Podsy added.

Alice seemed equally intrigued and amused by their request, and for a long moment, Xi wondered if the Solar woman would deny them. "Give me a moment," Alice said before picking up a data slate and tapping commands into it as fast as Xi could manage with the same interface. As Alice interacted with the device, Xi spared a look around the woman's quarters. Her belongings were simple and few, neatly arranged and accessible with little concern for privacy.

In fact, her unmentionables were folded neatly atop her silver-and-white body glove. No self-respecting Terran woman Xi knew would leave her underwear out in plain view as anything but a provocation or joke, but it seemed that the Solarian disregard for privacy manifested itself in a variety of amusing ways.

"There," Alice spun the slate around, handing it to Xi. "That is everything a deep search with seven levels of reflection turned up on *Gatekeeper*. There are approximately four petabytes of data there, half of which is classified and released on condition that only Jem or TAC field officers and higher review it. This information is not to be shared with any other Terran Armed Force branches, and not with any corporate interests. That is Sol's condition for the release of this data."

Xi blinked in surprise. "Um, thank you," she stammered, having expected a runaround of some kind before uncomfortable negotiations.

"We are all in this together, Major," Alice said matter-of-factly. "If humanity does not stand for itself, no one will. If you say Jem requires this, and that you trust Jem, I am willing to risk everything I consider to be of value to assist however I can."

"I appreciate that." Xi nodded agreeably. "We'll get this back to Jem so it can begin processing the data."

"How long did Jem think this process might take?"

"We didn't get a clear answer on that front," Podsy replied.

"But it sounded like the process would take days, or more likely weeks."

Alice nodded. "If there is anything else I can do before we depart Sol in the morning, please let me know."

"This is more than enough," Xi assured her. "Thank you, ma'am."

"It is both my pleasure and my privilege, Major."

With that, Podsy and Xi left Alice's quarters, shared a bewildered look, and made their way back to his quarters, where Jem began the laborious task of incorporating the data into its calculations.

Whatever they might be.

EPILOGUE: PUSHING ALL-IN

"Gentlemen. Major," General Mikhail Pushkin greeted the newcomers as General Moon, Colonel Jenkins, and Major Xi arrived at his office. His eyes were sunken, his skin was pale, and he generally looked like twice-warmed-over dogshit compared to his usual jovial self. "Forgive me for not rising," TAC's senior officer apologized while gesturing to his leg, which sported an external frame affixed to his bones by pins and rods.

Moon scoffed. "Another skiing accident, General?"

"Horseback riding." Pushkin grunted and shuffled a stack of flimsies and data slates off to one side of his desk before sighing. "My granddaughter would not take no for an answer, and I never could refuse her anyway. But it is not important. What *is* important is your return," he declared as the trio sat in chairs situated in front of his desk. "Sol has already re-tasked twenty-six warships, including two full Battle Carrier groups, to the as-yet-unnamed Sol-Terran joint defense force. They have also transferred two thousand Solar Marines to this task force. Whatever you did impressed them."

"What's happening in the Nexus?" Moon asked. "When we

arrived there, the fighting was down to just a few hundred ships engaged mostly in posturing and harassment."

"Fleet is not sharing its intel of late," Pushkin told them. "They cite security concerns and operational integrity issues. The flow of information has all but stopped, including from Admiral Fitzgerald's First Fleet at New Ukraine."

"Is that why Admiral Zhao is off-world?" Xi asked.

Pushkin nodded grimly. "He left without so much as a word, and has not been heard from in eight days."

Jenkins spied headings on the flimsies that indicated they were supply requisition requests. *Denied* requisition requests.

General Pushkin nodded sourly after seeing Jenkins' gaze linger on the pile of documents. "Yes, and it gets worse. The *Red Hare* has been impounded, along with all of its Razorbacks. Luckily for us, Sol requested we maintain a presence on Mars to assist with the rebuilding effort, so all they will get is a pile of scrap parts after you Frankensteined together nine working mechs to lend the Martian effort." He chuckled, his jolly demeanor peeking through for a brief moment as he mockingly wagged a finger at them. "You are going to put me into an early grave if you keep pulling stunts like that. Senate oversight committees have been pestering me nonstop for the last two days. If this keeps up, a shattered tibia will be the least of my worries."

"Sorry, sir," Jenkins told the general, his face serious. "We'll try to be more considerate of your health next time we save the Legion."

At that, the room erupted into laughter, led by the suddenly-revitalized General Pushkin. "So what's this I hear about Martian mechs?" Pushkin asked after the mirth had subsided. "'Golden Arrowheads,' you called them?"

"The official line from Sol is that they were an abandoned experimental line of fast-strike vehicles," Xi explained. "But they were more than that. If they'd had halfway-decent crews, they might have given us a real problem down there."

"We don't know why they were there." Moon shrugged. "Just like we don't know how the Arh'Kel got Jemmin beam weapons integrated into their HWPs, or why Jemmin beams were on the surface."

"Solar Intelligence has a theory there." Pushkin tapped one of the data slates to his right. "It arrived shortly before you did via courier. The short version is that they think the Vorr were behind both the Jemmin beams on the surface and their inclusion in the Arh'Kel arsenal."

"How?" Jenkins asked.

"It gets a little...technical." Pushkin snorted derisively. "But essentially, they ran extensive calculations which concluded that the most tactically-viable reason for anyone to introduce both the neural implants and the Jemmin technology into an Arh'Kel crypto-colony was to unequivocally implicate Jemmin in that colony's existence.

"But that's not the most bizarre part of this theory." Pushkin leaned forward intently. "The most bizarre part is that they think the rock-biters were originally put on both Mars *and* Durgan's Folly by Jemmin and were later modified with the neural links by the Vorr."

The trio of returned Metalheads looked at each other in confusion before Moon said, "I'm going to have to let that one sink in for a while."

"Arh'Kel colonies develop like clockwork." Jenkins steepled his fingers contemplatively. "Introducing a variable like a whole new weapons system into what is essentially their pre-programmed knowledge set? It had to have either been done at the genetic level or through the implants. My money would be on the latter, but it doesn't explain why they would interfere differently on Durgan's Folly and Mars. Why not implicate Jemmin as clearly here as in Sol?"

"Maybe the Vorr didn't *want* to implicate Jemmin at Durgan's Folly," Xi mused, "because that would have interfered with their plans. Remember, they weren't exactly looking for a firefight with Jemmin back on Shiva's Wrath. They anticipated we would discover the crypto-colony at Durgan's Folly when we did, probably because they were the ones who tipped us off to its presence," she added irritably. "They didn't introduce the weapons technology, there since doing so wouldn't serve their agenda."

Pushkin nodded in agreement. "The Solarians think something along those lines as well. They think Spider Hole was a test run to see if we could overcome the Arh'Kel implants, and they think it was to prepare us for War God."

"You seriously believe the Vorr have been playing us that precisely?" Moon asked darkly.

Pushkin shook his head. "No, that is simply what the Solarians have theorized. But like any good theory, it can cause whiplash if you're not expecting it. The Solarians think that, if their theory is accurate, the Martian crypto-colony's original purpose was to sow discord—"

"But they turned it into a potentially alliance-breaking surprise attack by implicating Jemmin," Xi interrupted eagerly, "which might have put an end to Jemmin-Sol cooperation long enough for the Nexus Wars to be decided."

"Correct, Major." General Pushkin nodded approvingly. "That is essentially their theory, but we have little time for such conjecture. As you have no doubt noticed," he waved a hand disgustedly at the stack of flimsies, "our supply lines are drying up. I have pulled every string and called in every favor, but I'm afraid my bag of tricks is nearly empty."

"What are we short?" Jenkins asked.

General Moon scoffed. "You name it. Ordnance, power trains, armor panels... We've gone through nearly everything we saved up in these last few ops. Hell, we've only got half the ammo left in reserve that we used on War God. Coupled with what we brought back, we barely have enough to field a battalion on a single op. At least, that's how things were when I left," he said, gesturing to Pushkin.

Pushkin grimaced. "It is not quite *that* bad, but it is close. By the time in-transit shipments arrive, we will have barely enough ordnance and consumables to field a single battalion for *two* ops." He emphatically held up a pair of fingers. "Fleet and their cronies in the Senate are demanding we open up TAC's books on all operations. They haven't expressly said as much, but if we don't submit to their inspections and turn in our records—*all* of them, including those pertaining to War God's end," he added grimly, "we won't see another materiel supply requisition released to us until the elections two months from now."

"How's Director Durgan doing in the race?" Jenkins asked.

"Better than feared but not as well as hoped." Pushkin rubbed his eyes in resignation. "He is trailing Vice President Fields by eight points according to the latest polls. A gap that wide has only been overcome two times in our republic's history."

Moon snorted. "Fuck the polls."

"Hear, hear," Xi agreed.

General Pushkin smirked. "Your eloquent support for the director notwithstanding, it is possible that these next few months will be the last in TAC's history where we were able to exercise the level of operational autonomy we've enjoyed since Ben joined the Joint Chiefs. I am not attempting to dampen the mood," he said apologetically, "merely to illuminate the importance of how these next few months play out. The Legion's future depends on its leaders not missing a single beat."

"That would be us," General Moon added wryly, "in case you were wondering."

"What's this about Jem and *Gatekeeper*, Major?" Pushkin asked, turning to Xi. "Calling the report you filed 'incomplete' would be an understatement."

"It contains everything we know, General," Xi explained. "Jem wanted to examine all available data regarding the Nexustech ship that transported the wormhole gate to Sol back in the twenty-first century when humanity was inducted into the Illumination League."

"But Jem didn't elaborate as to why it wanted that data?" Pushkin pressed.

"Only to say that it pertains to a theory Jem has on the Vorr's motives, and possibly their capabilities pertaining to the Nexus War," Xi replied.

"Frankly, I'm disappointed we didn't get more out of it before agreeing to supply it with classified intel," Pushkin said, his disapproval evident in his tone and visage, "but if we are going to trust a non-human, it would be Jem."

"I agree," Moon concurred. "But that trust can only go so far."

"Agreed," Jenkins affirmed. "I don't have any reason to mistrust Jem, but since Antivenom, it hasn't done a lot to contribute. Lieutenant Podsednik—"

"*Captain* Podsednik," Moon corrected. "At least, he will be as soon as we get settled here and have time to process the paperwork."

"You think he's ready to take the helm, General?" Pushkin asked Major General Moon.

"I do," Moon agreed before slicing a look Jenkins' way and adding, "with certain structurally-imposed restrictions. His heart is certainly in the right place, and he's got the chops to do the job. It's time to see if he can deliver."

"I agree." Pushkin nodded. "Shit or get off the pot. We can't afford to coddle people. Either they can contribute, or they can get out of the way for someone who will. On that front," he handed a data slate to General Moon, "the latest batch of Nuggets is ready for readiness evaluations."

"I'd like to volunteer for that, sir," Xi said eagerly.

"Negative, Major. Both you and Colonel Jenkins are to be placed on mandatory fifteen-day restricted duty. You both suffered cranial trauma on Mars, and one of you somehow lost an eye," he added, giving an approving nod to Jenkins' new black-and-brown leather eyepatch.

"But, sir—" she protested.

"Argue with me, and it becomes *thirty* days, Major," Pushkin snapped.

She sank back into her chair, her ears bright red as she wisely bit her tongue. The general stared her down for a few long, tense seconds before picking up a pair of data slates and tossing one to Jenkins and the other to Xi.

"During your convalescent interval," he explained, "you'll officially be conducting another recruiting drive."

"And unofficially?" Jenkins asked after perusing the data slate's contents, finding it contained materiel resource lists similar to those he had taken for his negotiations with Chairman Kong of Falcon Interworks. It had been those negotiations that yielded the *Red Hare* and its Clover Razorbacks, but unlike then, the items listed on the slate were only a tiny fraction of the value he had been authorized to barter with Kong.

"Unofficially, you'll be using your celebrity to scrounge up whatever ordnance and equipment you can get your hands on," Pushkin replied, his expression slowly morphing into one of triumphant condescension. "Consider this your first vacation since Durgan's Folly, Colonel. Major. I expect you both to make the most of it."

Xi looked legitimately mortified as she blurted, "Vacation?!"

"Yes. And a well-earned one, at that," Pushkin said sincerely.

But despite his superior's words of encouragement, Jenkins was suddenly filled with a sense of dread at the prospect of stepping away from the Legion, even if it was to conduct important negotiations. His Metalheads needed him, to be sure, but he was just now realizing how much *he* needed *them*.

"Your fifteen days starts now," Pushkin informed them, waving a hand toward the door. Moon mirrored the gesture. "Dismissed."

"Thank you, sir," they replied in unison, turning and making their way through the door before stopping and looking at each other in stunned confusion.

"Was he serious?" Xi asked into the growing silence.

"Seemed to be," Jenkins said in mild disbelief.

"But...but..." she stammered.

"Cheer up, Major," Jenkins said as the reality of the situation sank in and he decided to make a joke at her expense. "And look on the bright side. You're about to step into a world where your face is as recognizable as anyone this side of the President."

"How is that the bright side of *anything*?" she asked warily.

He couldn't help but grin as he replied, "Think of all the marriage proposals you're about to receive. That alone should be worth the price of admission—from my end, at least. Watching you fight off a bunch of would-be suitors is going to be more fun than gunning down a thousand rock-biters."

She rolled her eyes, slowly closing them and groaning pitifully as she began rubbing her temples. "I knew I shouldn't have given away my brass knuckles!"

They laughed together outside General Pushkin's door before surrendering to the idea of mandatory downtime.

After all, how bad could it be?

Have You read Superdreadnought 1, also from CH Gideon?

Alone and unafraid. Sometimes you prevent war by hunting down your enemies.

Integrated with a superdreadnought, the artificial intelligence known as Reynolds takes his ship across the universe in search of the elusive Kurtherians. He comes to a revelation. He's better in the company of living creatures.

He needs a crew. He needs information. And he needs to continue his search and destroy mission.

Needing a crew and getting a crew are two completely different things. Reynolds is out of his element as he tries to reach out and make friends. Through it all, he has his vessel, the superdreadnought, the most powerful warship in the galaxy.

Or so he believes.

AVAILABLE ON AMAZON RETAILERS AND IN KINDLE UNLIMITED!

AUTHOR NOTES - CRAIG MARTELLE

MAY 20, 2019

Thank you so much for your continued support for the Metal Legion! We wouldn't be here and telling these stories if it weren't for you.

It's been a while since Metal Legion 5, but I think the delay was worthwhile to recharge our mech batteries. Metal Legion 7 is already in the works and we hope to bring that one to you in a month or so. So many great stories to tell in the Solarian-Terran universe, especially with the Nexus War heating up. What to focus on? Where will the Metal Legion hammer out their greatest legacy?

They are one landing away from being pounded into non-existence, but that is what makes them so valuable. If they don't do it, no one will. Conceding territory to an enemy is almost like surrendering.

Metal never dies! Fire up the fusion generators and send these metal monsters marching into the maw of the beast. With some heavy metal blaring from the speakers. So motivating. I've been a part of a couple insertions, both helicopter and amphibious armored vehicle (AAV). Jamming on the way in, no matter how loud the ambient noise is how it's done. Even if the zone is hot, the troops are going into the heart of it, nothing to support themselves besides what they are carrying.

Oorah.

I'm a little old for that stuff now. The definition of courage is doing something you don't want to do but you know it has to be done. Run to the gunfire, not away from it. If you don't, who will? That is what we tried to bring to the Metal Legion. I think we have. Esprit de corps and the fury of driving toward a singular purpose.

Cheers and hats off to my co-author on this one, Caleb Wachter who is doing the majority of the heavy lifting in bringing these characters and this story to life. Caleb is a literary powerhouse.

In the meantime, I'll be up here, in the sub-Arctic, where we just started seventy-some days of continuous daylight. That's right, twenty-four hours a day. Light. Sun making loop-de-loops on the northern horizon. Not quite a rise in the east, set in the west geography. Alaska is different.

And we celebrate that, too.

Until next time, peace, fellow humans.

Please join my Newsletter (www.craigmartelle.com – please, please, please sign up!), or you can follow me on Facebook since you'll get the same opportunity to pick up the books for only 99 cents on the first Saturday after they get published.

If you liked this story, you might like some of my other books. You can join my mailing list by dropping by my website **www.craigmartelle.com** or if you have any comments, shoot me a note at craig@craigmartelle.com. I am always happy to hear from people who've read my work. I try to answer every email I receive.

If you liked the story, please write a short review for me on Amazon. I greatly appreciate any kind words, even one or two sentences go a long way. The number of reviews an ebook receives greatly improves how well an ebook does on Amazon.

Amazon – www.amazon.com/author/craigmartelle

BookBub – https://www.bookbub.com/authors/craig-martelle

Facebook – www.facebook.com/authorcraigmartelle

My web page – www.craigmartelle.com

That's it—break's over, back to writing the next book.

BOOKS BY CRAIG MARTELLE

Craig Martelle's other books (listed by series)

Terry Henry Walton Chronicles (co-written with Michael Anderle) – a post-apocalyptic paranormal adventure

Gateway to the Universe (co-written with Justin Sloan & Michael Anderle) – this book transitions the characters from the Terry Henry Walton Chronicles to The Bad Company

The Bad Company (co-written with Michael Anderle) – a military science fiction space opera

End Times Alaska (also available in audio) – a Permuted Press publication – a post-apocalyptic survivalist adventure

The Free Trader – a Young Adult Science Fiction Action Adventure

Cygnus Space Opera – A Young Adult Space Opera (set in the Free Trader universe)

Darklanding (co-written with Scott Moon) – a Space Western

Rick Banik – Spy & Terrorism Action Adventure

Become a Successful Indie Author – a non-fiction work

Enemy of my Enemy (co-written with Tim Marquitz) – a galactic alien military space opera

Superdreadnought (co-written with Tim Marquitz) – a military space opera

Metal Legion (co-written with Caleb Wachter) - a military space opera

End Days (co-written with E.E. Isherwood) – a post-apocalyptic adventure

Mystically Engineered (co-written with Valerie Emerson) – dragons in space

Monster Case Files (co-written with Kathryn Hearst) – a young-adult cozy mystery series

For a complete list of books from Craig, please see www. craigmartelle.com

OTHER BOOKS FROM LMBPN PUBLISHING

For a complete list of books by LMBPN Publishing, please visit:

https://lmbpn.com/books-by-lmbpn-publishing/

All LMBPN Audiobooks are Available at Audible.com and iTunes

To see all LMBPN audiobooks, including those written by Michael Anderle please visit:

www.lmbpn.com/audible

Made in the USA
Middletown, DE
14 October 2022

12723606R00187